MEAN STREETS

MEAN STREETS

THE SECOND PRIVATE EYE WRITERS OF AMERICA ANTHOLOGY

EDITED BY
ROBERT J. RANDISI

THE MYSTERIOUS PRESS • New York

Printed in the United States of America
First Printing: October 1986
10 9 8 7 6 5 4 3 2 1

Library of Congress Cataloging-in-Publication Data

Mean streets.

Contents: Introduction / by Robert J. Randisi —
House call / by Max Allan Collins — Body count /
by Wayne D. Dundee — [etc.]
1. Detective and mystery stories, American.
I. Randisi, Robert J. II. Private Eye Writers of
America.
PS648.D4M44   1986   813'.0872'08   86-16303
ISBN 0-89296-169-4

ACKNOWLEDGMENTS

CONTENTS

MEAN STREETS

ROBERT J. RANDISI

INTRODUCTION

"Down these mean streets a man must go who is not himself mean, who is neither tarnished nor afraid."

RAYMOND CHANDLER,
"The Simple Art of Murder"

Living up to *The Eyes Have It: The First PWA Anthology* may be a near impossible task. Stories from *Eyes* garnered five award nominations and won two.

The MWA Short Story Edgar committee honored "By the Dawn's Early Light" by Lawrence Block and "The Reluctant Detective" by Michael Z. Lewin with Edgar nominations, and the Block story won. (Block's story appeared in *Playboy* prior to its appearance in *Eyes*, but *was* written *for Eyes* at my request and Otto Penzler's insistence.)

The PWA Short Story committee named the Block story, "Iris" by Stephen Greenleaf, and "The Rat Line" by Rob Kantner as nominees, and again "By the Dawn's Early Light" was the winner.

This marked the first time since the creation of PWA and the Shamus award that one man had swept both awards with the same work. An enviable daily double. (In 1984

1

Warren Murphy won the Edgar and Shamus Best Paperback awards, but he did it with two different books.) In addition, it should be mentioned that Larry Block's story is, in part, the basis for his latest Matt Scudder novel, *When the Sacred Ginmill Closes*.

Is the second PWA anthology as good as the first? That's an unfair question, so it's probably just as well that I pose it to myself.

The Eyes Have It was, for me, the culmination of a five-year dream. For that reason, I'd have to say that *Mean Streets* is simply gravy, and not quite the personal thrill that the first one was. It is, however, in my opinion, no less good. I will not go so far as to predict five award nominations and two winners, but I think that when the returns are in, *Mean Streets* will have stood its ground quite nicely.

Back from *Eyes* are the following teams of author and P.I.: Max Collins and Nate Heller; Loren D. Estleman and Amos Walker; Stuart Kaminsky and Toby Peters; Rob Kantner and Ben Perkins; John Lutz and Alo Nudger; Sara Paretsky and V. I. Warshawski; and Bill Pronzini and "Nameless."

New to the anthology are William Campbell Gault, with Brock Callahan *and* Joe Puma; Sue Grafton and Kinsey Millhone; Arthur Lyons and Jacob Asch.

New to the anthology scene in general are Dick Stodghill, who introduces Henry Paige; and Wayne Dundee and Joe Hannibal.

Dick Stodghill has had numerous stories in *Alfred Hitch-cock's Mystery Magazine* and *Mike Shayne Mystery Magazine;* Wayne Dundee and Hannibal first appeared in the defunct *Skullduggery/Spiderweb* magazine. When we bought "Body Count," it was his third sale. (The second was to *The Saint Mystery Magazine,* which folded before the story could appear.) Since that time Wayne has founded a magazine called *Hardboiled,* and he and Hannibal have appeared within its pages twice more.

With the appearances of *New Black Mask Quarterly, Hard-boiled,* and this anthology, plus the continued contribution of *Alfred Hitchcock's Mystery Magazine,* 1986 should be a banner year for P.I. short stories.

I started this introduction with a quote, and I'd like to close with another one. This one is from a novel titled *Taste of Ashes* by PWA's 1984 Life Achievement award winner, Howard Browne. His protagonist, Paul Pine, very neatly explains what a P.I. should be:

> Private dicks had no business being married. Private dicks should live with nothing except a few books and a bottle or two on the pantry shelf and a small but select list of phone numbers for ready reference when the glands start acting up. Private dicks should be proud and lonely men who can say no when the hour is late and their feet hurt.

Walk the mean streets now with twelve of today's finest P.I. writers and their "private dicks," who may or may not be tarnished or afraid, and whose feet may or may not hurt.

BOB RANDISI
Longwood, Florida
January 1986

MAX ALLAN COLLINS

HOUSE CALL

Nineteen thirty-six began for me with a missing persons case. It didn't stay a missing persons case long, but on that bitterly cold Chicago morning of January 3rd, all Mrs. Peacock knew was that her doctor husband had failed to come home after making a house call the night before.

It was Saturday, just a little past ten, and I was filling out an insurance adjustment form when she knocked. I said come in, and she did, an attractive woman of about thirty-five in an expensive fur coat. She didn't look high-hat, though: she'd gone out today without any makeup on, which, added to her generally haggard look, told me she was at wit's end.

"Mr. Heller? Nathan Heller?"

I said I was, standing, gesturing to a chair across from my desk. My office at the time was a large single room on the fourth floor of a less-than-fashionable building on the corner of Van Buren and Plymouth, in the shadow of the El. She seemed a little posh to be coming to my little one-man agency for help.

"Your name was given to me by Tom Courtney," she said. "He's a friend of the family."

State's Attorney Thomas J. Courtney and I had crossed

paths several times, without any particular mishap; this explained why she'd chosen the A-1 Detective Agency, but not why she needed a detective in the first place.

"My husband is missing," she said.

"I assume you've filed a missing persons report."

"Yes I have. But I've been told until twenty-four hours elapse, my husband will not be considered missing. Tom suggested if my concern was such that I felt immediate action warranted, I might contact you. Which I have."

She was doing an admirable job of maintaining her composure; but there was a quaver in her voice, and her eyes were moist.

"If you have any reason to suspect a kidnapping or foul play," I said, keeping my voice calm and soft, to lessen the impact of such menacing words, "I think you're doing the right thing. Trails can go cold in twenty-four hours."

She nodded, found a brave smile.

"My husband, Silber, is a doctor, a pediatrician. We live in the Edgewater Beach Apartments."

That meant money; no wonder she hadn't questioned me about my rates.

"Last evening Betty Lou, our eight-year-old, and I returned home from visiting my parents in Bowen. Silber met us at Union Station, and we dined at a little restaurant on the North Side—the name escapes me, but I could probably come up with it if it proves vital—and then came home. Silber went to bed; I was sitting up reading. The phone rang. The voice was male. I asked for a name, an address, the nature of the business, doing my best to screen the call. But the caller insisted on talking to the doctor. I was reluctant, but I called Silber to the phone, and I heard him say, 'What is it? . . . Oh, a child is ill? Give me the address and I'll be there straight away.'"

"Did your husband write the address down?"

She nodded. "Yes, and I have the sheet right here." She dug in her purse and handed it to me.

In the standard barely readable prescription-pad scrawl of any doctor, the note said: "G. Smale. 6438 North Whipple Street."

"Didn't the police want this?"

She shook her head no. "Not until it's officially a missing persons case they don't."

"No phone number?"

"My husband asked for one and was told that the caller had no phone."

"Presumably he was calling on one."

She shrugged, with sad frustration. "I didn't hear the other end of the conversation. All I can say for certain is that my husband hung up, sighed, smiled and said, 'No rest for the wicked,' and dressed. I jotted the information from the pad onto the top of the little Chicago street guide he carries, when he's doing house calls."

"So he never took the original note with him?"

"No. What you have there is what he wrote. Then Silber kissed me, picked up his black instrument bag and left. I remember glancing at the clock in the hall. It was 10:05."

"Did you hear from him after that?"

"No I did not. I slept, but fitfully, and woke around 1:30 A.M. Silber wasn't home yet. I remember being irritated with him for taking a call from someone who wasn't a regular patient; he has an excellent practice, now—there's no need for it. I called the building manager and asked if Silber's car had returned to the garage. It hadn't. I didn't sleep a wink after that. When dawn broke, so, I'm afraid, did I. I called Tom Courtney; he came around at once, phoned the police for me, then advised me to see you, should I feel the need for immediate action."

"I'm going to need some further information," I said.

"Certainly."

Questioning her, I came up with a working description and other pertinent data: Peacock was forty years old, a member of the staff of Children's Memorial. He'd been driving a 1931 black Cadillac sedan, 1936 license 25-682. Wearing a gray suit, gray topcoat, gray felt hat. 5' 7", 150 pounds, wire-frame glasses.

I walked her down to the street and helped her hail a cab. I told her I'd get right on the case, and that in the future she needn't call on me; I'd come to her at her Edgewater Beach apartment. She smiled, rather bravely I thought, as she slipped into the backseat of the cab, squeezed my arm, and looked at me like I was something noble.

Well, I didn't feel very noble. Because as her cab turned down Plymouth Court, I was thinking that her husband the good doctor had probably simply had himself a big evening. He'd show up when his head stopped throbbing, or when something below the belt stopped throbbing, anyway. In the future he'd need to warn his babe to stop calling him at home, even if she did have a brother or a knack for doing a convincing vocal imitation of a male.

Back in my office I got out the private detective's most valuable weapon—the telephone book—and looked up G. Smale. There was a listing with the same street number— 6438—but the street was wrong, South Washtenaw. The names and house numbers tallied, yes, but the streets in question were on opposite sides of the city. The reverse directory, listing street numbers followed by names and numbers, told me that no G. Smale was listed at 6438 North Whipple.

What the hell; I called the Smale on South Washtenaw.

"I don't know any Dr. Peacock," he said. "I never saw the man in my life."

"Who do you take your kids to when they're sick?"

"Nobody."

"Nobody?"

"I don't have any kids. I'm not a father."

I talked to him for fifteen minutes, and he seemed forthright enough; my instincts—and I do a lot of phone work—told me to leave him to the cops, or at least till later that afternoon. I wanted to check out the doctor's working quarters.

So I tooled my sporty '32 Auburn over to 4753 Broadway, where Dr. Peacock shared sumptuous digs with three other doctors, highly reputable medical specialists all. His secretary was a stunning brunette in her late twenties, a Miss Kathryn Mulrooney. I like a good-looking woman in white; the illusion of virginity does something for me.

"I know what you're going to ask," she said, quickly, before I'd asked anything. All I'd done was show her my investigator's ID and say I was in Mrs. Peacock's employ. "Dr. Peacock had no patient named Smale; I've been digging through our files ever since Mrs. Peacock called this morning, just in case my memory is faulty."

She didn't look like she had a faulty anything.

"What's even stranger," she said, with a tragic expression, "he almost never answered night calls. Oh, he once upon a time did—he hated to turn away any sick child. His regular patients seldom asked him to do so, however, and this practice has become so large that he wasn't accepting any new cases. It's unbelievable that . . ."

She paused; I'd been doing my job, asking questions, listening, but a certain part of me had been undressing the attractive nurse in my mind's eye—everybody needs a hobby—and she misread my good-natured lechery toward her for something else.

"Please!" she said. "You mustn't leap to horrid conclusions. Dr. Peacock was a man of *impeccable* character. He loved his family and his home, passionately. He was no playboy; he loathed night clubs and all they stand for. He didn't even drink!"

"I see," I said.

"I hope you do," she said curtly. "That he might have been involved with a woman other than his wife is unthinkable. Please believe me."

"Perhaps I do. But could you answer one question?"

"What's that?"

"Why are you referring to the doctor in the past tense?"

She began to cry; she'd been standing behind a counter—now she leaned against it.

"I . . . I wish I believed him capable of running around on Ruth, his wife. Then I wouldn't be so convinced that something . . . something *terrible* has happened."

I felt bad; I'd been suspicious of her, been looking to find her between the doctor's sheets, and had made her cry. She was a sincere young woman, that was obvious.

"I'm very sorry," I said, meaning it, and turned to go.

But before I went out, another question occurred to me, and I asked it: "Miss Mulrooney—had the parents of any patient ever blamed Dr. Peacock for some unfortunate results of some medical treatment he administered? Any threats of reprisal?"

"Absolutely not," she said, chin trembling.

On this point I didn't believe her; her indignation rang shrill. And, anyway, most doctors make enemies. I only wished she had pointed to one of those enemies.

But I'd pushed this kid enough.

I dropped by the Edgewater Beach Apartments, but not to talk to Mrs. Peacock. I went up to the attendant in the lobby, a distinguished-looking blue-uniformed man in his late fifties; like so many doormen and lobby attendants, he looked like a soldier from some foreign country in a light opera.

Unlike a good soldier, he was willing to give forth with much more than his name and rank. I had hoped to get from him the name of the night man, who I hoped to call and get some information from; but it turned out *he* was the night man.

"George was sick," he said. "So I'm doing double duty. I can use the extra cash more than the sleep."

"Speaking of cash," I said, and handed him a buck.

"Thank you, sir!"

"Now, earn it: what can you tell me about Dr. Peacock? Does he duck out at night very often?"

The attendant shook his head no. "Can't remember the last time, before the other night. Funny thing, though."

"Yeah?"

"He was rushing out of here, then all of a sudden stopped and turned and stood five minutes blabbing in the phone booth over there."

Back in the Auburn, my mind was abuzz. Why else would Dr. Peacock use the lobby phone, unless it was to make a call he didn't want his wife to hear? The "poor sick child" call had been a ruse. The baby specialist obviously had a babe.

I didn't have a missing persons case at all. I had a stray husband who had either taken off for parts unknown with his lady love or, more likely considering the high-hat practice the doc would have to leave behind, would simply show up with some cock-and-bull story for the missus after a torrid twenty-four-hour shack-up with whoever-she-was.

I drove to 6438 North Whipple Street. What my reverse phone book hadn't told me was that this was an apartment building, a six-flat. Suddenly the case warmed up again; I found a place for the Auburn along the curb and walked up the steps into the brownstone.

No "G. Smale" was a resident, at least not a resident who had a name on any of the vestibule mailboxes.

I walked out into the cold air, my breath smoking, my mind smoking a little, too: the "patient" hadn't had a phone, but in a nice brownstone like this most likely *everybody* had a phone. Nothing added up. Except maybe two plus two equals rendezvous.

The doc had a doll, that's all there was to it. Nonetheless, I decided to scout the neighborhood for Peacock's auto. I went two blocks in all directions and saw no sign of it. I was about to call it an afternoon, and a long one at that, when I extended the canvassing to include a third block, and on the 6000 block on North Francisco Avenue, I saw it: a black Caddy sedan with the license 25-682.

I approached the car, which was parked alongside a vacant lot, across from several brownstones. I peeked in; in the backseat was a topcoat, but the topcoat was covering something. Looking in the window, you couldn't tell what. I tried the door. It was unlocked.

I pulled the rider's seat forward, and there he was, in a kneeling position, in the back, facing the rear, the top half of him bent over the seat, covered by the topcoat. Carefully, I lifted it off, resting it on the roof of the car. Blood was spattered on the floor and rear windows; the seat was crusty black with it, dried. His blood-flecked felt hat, wadded up like a discarded tissue, lay on the seat. His medical bag was on the seat next to him; it too had been sheltered from sight by the topcoat, and was open and had been disturbed. The little street map book, with the address on it in Mrs. Peacock's handwriting, was nearby, speckled with blood.

A large-caliber bullet had gone in his right temple and come out behind the left ear. His skull was crushed; his brain was showing, but scrambled. His head and shoulders bore numerous knife slashes. His right hand was gloved, but his left was bare and had been caught, crushed, in the slamming car door.

This was one savage killing.

Captain Stege himself arrived, after I called it in; if my name hadn't been attached to it, he probably wouldn't have come. The tough little cop had once been chief of detectives till, ironically, a scandal had cost him—one of Chicago's few verifiably honest cops—his job. Not long ago he'd been chief of the PD's Dillinger squad. It was on the Dillinger case that Stege and I had put our feud behind us; we were uneasily trying to get along these days.

I quickly showed him two more discoveries I'd made, before he or any of his boys in blue had arrived: a .45 revolver shell that was in the snow, near the car, on the vacant lot side; and a pinkish stain in the snow, plus deep tire tracks and numerous cigarette butts, in front of the apartment building at 6438 North Whipple. The tire tracks and cigarettes seemed to indicate that whoever had lured the doctor from his bed had indeed waited at this address; the pink stain pointed toward the violence having started there.

"What's your part in this?" he said, as we walked back to the scene of the crime. He was a small gray man in a gray topcoat and gray formless hat; tiny eyes squinted behind round, black-rimmed lenses. "How'd you happen to find the body, anyway?"

I explained that Mrs. Peacock had hired me to find her husband. Which, after all, I had.

A police photographer was taking pictures, the body not yet moved.

"How do you read this, Heller?"

"Not a simple robbery."

"Oh?"

I pointed to the corpse. "He took God knows how many brutal blows; he was slashed and slashed again. It takes hate to arouse pointless violence like that."

"Crime of passion, then."

"That's how I see it, Captain."

"The wife have an alibi?"

"Don't even bother going down that road."

"You mind if I bother, Heller? You ever seen the statistics of the number of murders committed within families?"

"She was home with her daughter. Go ahead. Waste your time. But she's a nice lady."

"I'll remember that. Give your statement to Phelan, and go home. This isn't your case, anymore."

"I know it isn't. But do you mind if I, uh . . . if I'm the one to break the news to Mrs. Peacock?"

Stege cleared his throat; shot a wad of phlegm into the nearby snow. "Not at all. Nobody envies duty like that."

So I told her. I wanted her told by somebody who didn't suspect her and, initially, I'd be the only one who qualified.

She sat in a straight-back chair at her dining room table, in the Peacocks' conservative yet expensively appointed apartment high in the Edgewater Beach, and wept into a lace hanky. I sat with her for fifteen minutes. She didn't ask me to go, so I didn't.

Finally she said, "Silber was a fine man. He truly was. A perfect husband and father. His habits regular and beyond reproach. No one hated Silber. No one. He was lured to his death by thieves."

"Yes, ma'am."

"Did you know that once before he was attacked by thieves, and that he did not hesitate to fight them off? My husband was a brave man."

"I'm sure he was."

I left her there, with her sorrow, thinking that I wished she was right, but knowing she was wrong. I did enough divorce work to know how marriages, even "perfect" ones, can go awry. I also had a good fix on just how much marital cheating was going on in this Christian society.

The next morning I called Stege. He wasn't glad to hear from me, exactly, but he did admit that the wife was no longer a suspect; her alibi was flawless.

"There *was* a robbery of sorts," Stege said.

"Oh?"

"Twenty dollars was missing from Peacock's wallet. On the

other hand, none of his jewelry—some of it pretty expensive stuff—was even touched."

"What was taken from the medical bag?" I asked.

"Some pills and such were taken, but apparently nothing narcotic. A baby specialist doesn't go toting dope around."

"An addict might not know that; an addict might've picked Dr. Peacock's name at random, not knowing he was a baby doc."

"And what, drew him to that vacant lot to steal a supposed supply of narcotics?"

"Yeah. It might explain the insanity, the savagery of the attack."

"Come on, Heller. You know as well as I do this is a personal killing. I expect romance to rear its lovely head any time, now. Peacock was rich, handsome enough, by all accounts personable. And he had, we estimate, upwards of five hundred patients. Five hundred kiddies, all of whom have mothers who visited the doctor with them."

"You know something, Captain?"

"What?"

"I'm glad this isn't my case anymore."

"Oh?"

"Yeah. I wish you and your boys all the best doing those five hundred interviews."

He grumbled and hung up.

I did send Mrs. Peacock a bill, for one day's services— twenty dollars and five dollars' expenses—and settled back to watch, with some discomfort, the papers speculate about the late doctor's love life. Various screwball aspects to the case were chased down by the cops and the press; none of it amounted to much. This included a nutty rumor that the doctor was a secret federal narcotics agent and killed by a dope ring; and the Keystone Kops affair of the mysterious key found in the doctor's pocket, the lock to which countless police hours were spent seeking, only to have the key turn out to belong to the same deputy coroner who had produced it. The hapless coroner had accidentally mixed a key of his own among the Peacock evidence.

More standard, reliable lines of inquiry provided nothing: fingerprints found in the car were too smudged to identify; witnesses who came forth regarding two people arguing in the death car varied as to the sex of the occupants; the last-minute phone call Peacock made in the lobby turned out to have been to one of his business partners; interviews of the parents of five hundred Peacock patients brought forth not a single disgruntled person, nor a likely partner for any Peacock "love nest."

Peacock had been dead for over two weeks, when I was brought back into the case again, through no effort of my own.

The afternoon of January 16th, someone knocked at my office door; in the middle of a phone credit check, I covered the receiver and called out, "Come in."

The door opened tentatively and a small, milquetoast of a man peered in.

"Mr. Heller?"

I nodded, motioned for him to be seated before me, and finished up my call; he sat patiently, a pale little man in a dark suit, his dark hat in his lap.

"What can I do for you?"

He stood, smiled in an entirely humorless, businesslike manner, extending a hand to be shook; I shook it, and the grip was surprisingly firm.

"I am a Lutheran minister," he said. "My name, for the moment, is unimportant."

"Pleased to meet you, Reverend."

"I read about the Peacock case in the papers."

"Yes?"

"I saw your name. You discovered the body. You were in Mrs. Peacock's employ."

"Yes."

"I have information. I was unsure of whom to give it to."

"If you have information regarding the Peacock case, you should give it to the police. I can place a call right now—"

"Please, no! I would prefer you hear my story and judge for yourself."

"All right."

"Last New Year's Day I had a chance meeting with my great and good friend, Dr. Silber Peacock, God rest his soul. On that occasion the doctor confided that a strange man, a fellow who claimed to be a chiropodist, had come bursting into his office, making vile accusations."

"Such as?"

"He said, 'You, sir, are having an affair with my wife!'"

I sat forward. "Go on."

"Dr. Peacock said he'd never laid eyes on this man before; that he thought him a crazy man. 'Why, I never ran around on Ruth in my life,' he said."

"How did he deal with this man?"

"He threw him bodily from his office."

"When did he have this run-in? Did he mention the man's name?"

"Last October. The man's name was Thompson, and he was, as I've said, a chiropodist."

"You should go to the police with this."

The reverend stood quickly, nervously. "I'd really rather not."

And then he was on his way out of the office. By the time I got out from behind my desk, he was out of the room, and by the time I got out into the hall, he was out of sight.

The only chiropodist named Thompson in the Chicago phone book was one Arthur St. George Thompson, whom I found at his Wilson Avenue address. He was a skinny, graying man in his early forties; he and his office were seedy.

18

He had no patients in his rather unkempt waiting room when I arrived (or when I left, for that matter).

"I knew Silber Peacock," he said, bitterly. "I remember visiting him at his office in October, too. What of it?"

"Did you accuse him of seeing your wife?"

"Sure I did! Let me tell you how I got hep to Peacock and Arlene. One evening last June she came home stinking, her and Ann—that's the no-good who's married to Arlene's brother Carl. Arlene said she'd been at the Subway Club and her escort was Doc Peacock. So I looked in the classified directory. The only Dr. Peacock was Silber C., so I knew it was him. I stewed about it for weeks, months, and then I went to his office. The son of a bitch pretended he didn't know who I was, or Arlene, either; he just kept denying it and shoving me out of there, shoved me clear out into the hall."

"I see."

"No you don't. I hated the louse, but I didn't kill him. Besides, I got an alibi. I can prove where I was the night he was murdered."

He claimed that because his practice was so poor of late, he'd taken on menial work at the Medinah Club. An alibi out of a reputable place like that would be hard to break. I'd leave that to Stege, when—or if—I turned this lead over to him.

First I wanted to talk to Arlene Thompson, whom I found at her brother's place, a North Side apartment.

Ann was a slender, giggly brunette, attractive. Arlene was even more attractive, a voluptuous redhead. Both were in their mid-twenties. Ann's husband wasn't home, so the two of them flirted with me and we had a gay old time.

"Were you really seeing Doc Peacock?"

The two girls exchanged glances and began giggling, and the giggling turned to outright laughter. "That poor guy!" Arlene said.

"Well, yeah, I'd say so. He's dead."

"Not him! Arthur! That insane streak of jealousy's got him in hot water again, has it? Look, good-lookin'—there's nothing *to* any of this, understand? Here's how it happened."

Arlene and Ann had gone alone to the Subway Club one afternoon, a rowdy honky-tonk that had since lost its liquor license, and got picked up by two men. They danced till dusk. Arlene's man said he was Doc Peacock; no other first name given.

"Arthur went off his rocker when I came in, tipsy. He demanded the truth—so I told him! It was all innocent enough, but got him goin'. He talked days on end about Doc Peacock, about how he was going to even the score."

"Do you think he did?"

The redhead laughed again, said, "Honey, that Dr. Peacock whose puss has been in the papers ain't the guy I dated. My Peacock was much better-looking—wavy hair, tall, a real dreamboat. I think my pick-up just pulled a name out of his hat."

"Your husband didn't know that. Maybe he evened the score with the wrong Peacock."

She shook her head, not believing that for a minute. "Arthur just isn't the type. He's a poor, weak sister. He never had enough pep to hurt a fly."

It was all conjecture, but I turned it over to Stege, anyway. Thompson's alibi checked out. Yet another dead end.

The next day I was reading the morning papers over breakfast in the coffee shop at the Morrison Hotel. A very small item, buried on an inside page, caught my eye: Dr. Joseph Soldinger, 1016 North Oakley Boulevard, had been robbed at gunpoint last night of thirty-seven dollars, his car stolen.

I called Stege and pointed out the similarity to the Peacock case, half expecting him to shrug it off. He didn't. He thanked me, and hung up.

A week later I got a call from Stege; he was excited. "Listen to this: Dr. A. L. Abrams, 1600 Milwaukee Avenue, fifty-six dollars lost to gunmen; Dr. L. A. Garness, 2542 Mozart Avenue, waylaid and robbed of six dollars. And there's two more like that."

"Details?"

"Each features a call to a doctor to rush to a bedside. Address is in a lonely neighborhood. It's an appointment with ambush. Take is always rather small. Occurrences between 10:00 and 11:00 P.M."

"Damn! Sounds like Mrs. Peacock had been right all along. Her husband fought off his attackers; that's what prompted their beating him."

"The poor bastard was a hero, and the papers paint him a philanderer."

"Well, we handed 'em the brush."

"Perhaps we did, Heller. Anyway, thanks."

"Any suspects?"

"No. But we got the pattern now. From eyewitness descriptions it seems to be kids. Four assailants, three tall and husky, the other shorter."

A bell was ringing, and not outside my window. "Captain, you ever hear of Rose Kasallis?"

"Can't say I have."

"I tracked a runaway girl to her place two summers ago. She's a regular female Fagin. She had a flat on North Maplewood Avenue that was a virtual 'school for crime.'"

"I *have* heard of that. The West North Avenue cops handled it. Old dame keeping a way station for fugitive kids from the reform school at St. Charles. Sent up the river for contributing to the delinquency of minors?"

"That's the one. I had quite a run-in with her charming boy Bobby. Robert Goethe is his name."

"Oh?"

"He's eighteen years old, a strapping kid with the morals of an alley cat. And there were a couple of kids he ran with, Emil Reck, who they called Emil the Terrible, and another one whose name I can't remember. . . ."

"Heller, Chicago has plenty of young street toughs. Why do you think these three might be suspects in the Peacock case?"

"I don't know that they are. In fact, last I knew Bobby and the other two were convicted of strong-arming a pedestrian and were sitting in the Bridewell. But that's been at least a year ago."

"And they might be out amongst us again, by now."

"Right. Could you check?"

"I'll do that very thing."

Ten minutes later Stege called and said, "They were released in December."

January 2nd had been Silber Peacock's last day on earth.

"I have an address for Bobby Goethe's apartment," Stege said. "Care to keep an old copper company?"

He swung by and picked me up—hardly usual procedure, pulling in a private dick on a case, but I had earned this—and soon we were pulling up in front of the weathered brownstone in which Bobby Goethe lived. And there was no doubt he lived here.

Because despite the chilly day, he and Emil the Terrible were sitting on the stoop, in light jackets, smoking cigarettes and drinking bottles of beer. Bobby had a weak, acned chin, and reminded me of photos I'd seen of Clyde Barrow; Emil had a big lumpy nose and a high forehead, atop which was piled blond curly hair—he looked thick as a plank.

We were in an unmarked car, but a uniformed man was behind the wheel, so as soon as we pulled in, the two boys reacted, beer bottles dropping to the cement and exploding like bombs.

Bobby took off in one direction, and Emil took off in the

other. Stege just watched as his plainclothes detective
assistant took off after Emil, and I took off after Bobby.

It took me a block to catch up, and I hit him with a flying
tackle, and we rolled into a vacant lot, not unlike the one by
the Caddy in which Peacock's body had been found.

Bobby was a wiry kid, and wormed his way out of my
grasp, kicking back at me as he did; I took a boot in the face,
but didn't lose any teeth, and managed to reach out and grab
that foot and yank him back hard. He went down on his face
in the weeds and rocks. One of the larger of those rocks
found its way into his hand, and he flung it at me, savage
little animal that he was, only not so little. I ducked out of
the rock's way and quickly reached a hand under my topcoat
and suitcoat and got my nine-millimeter Browning out and
pointed it down at him.

"I'm hurt," he said, looking up at me with a scraped,
bloody face.

"Shall we call a doctor?" I said.

Emil and Bobby and their crony named Nash, who was
arrested later that afternoon by West North Avenue Station
cops, were put in a show-up for the various doctors who'd
been robbed to identify. They did so, without hesitation. The
trio was separated and questioned individually and sang and
sang. A fourth boy was implicated, the shorter one who'd
been mentioned, seventeen-year-old Mickey Livingston. He
too was identified, and he too sang.

Their story was a singularly stupid one. They had been
cruising in a stolen car, stopped in a candy store, picked
Peacock's name at random from the phone book, picked
another name and address, altered it, and called and lured
the doctor to an isolated spot they'd chosen. Emil the
Terrible, a heavy club in hand, crouched in the shadows
across the street from 6438 North Whipple. Nash stood at the
entrance, and Goethe, gun in hand, hid behind a tree
nearby. Livingston was the wheel man, parked half a block
north.

Peacock drove up and got out of his car, medical bag in hand. Bobby stuck the gun in the doctor's back and told him not to move. Peacock was led a block north after Emil the Terrible had smacked him "a lick for luck." At this point Peacock fought back, wrestling with Bobby, who shot the doctor in the head. Peacock dropped to the ground, and Emil the Imbecilic hit the dead man again and again with the club. A scalpel from the medical bag in one hand, the gun held butt forward in the other, Bobby added some finishing touches. Nash pulled up in the doctor's car, Livingston following. The corpse was then tossed in the backseat of the Caddy, which was abandoned three blocks away.

Total take for the daring boys: twenty dollars. Just what I'd made on the case, only they didn't get five bucks' expenses.

What Bobby, Emil, and Nash did get was 199 years plus consecutive terms of one year to life on four robbery counts. Little Mickey was given a thirty-year sentence, and was eventually paroled. The others, to the best of my knowledge, never were.

Ruth Peacock moved to Quincy, Illinois, where she devoted the rest of her life to social service, her church, and Red Cross work, as well as to raising her two daughters, Betty Lou and Nancy. Nancy never knew her father.

Maybe that's why Ruth Peacock was so convinced of her husband's loyalty, despite the mysterious circumstances of his death.

She was pregnant with his child at the time.

AUTHOR'S NOTE: I wish to express my indebtedness to the classic true-crime article "The Peacock Case," by LeRoy F. McHugh (who was, incidentally, the basis for "McCue" in Hecht and MacArthur's *The Front Page*). Fact, speculation, and fiction are freely mixed in the preceding story; real people, composites, and fictional characters mingle therein.

WAYNE D. DUNDEE

BODY COUNT

"**I** want to warn you right up front," Myra Caine said after I'd settled into the booth across from her, "that getting involved with me may expose you to grave danger."

I grinned. "You're beautiful enough to take a man's breath away," I conceded, "but I hardly think that could prove fatal."

She gave a quick, impatient shake of her head. "It's no joking matter, Mr. Hannibal. This maniac may have me on the brink of hysteria, but I'm not overreacting. He's crazy and he's dangerous and he's already responsible for three deaths."

"You're certain of that?"

"If you mean did I actually see him do it, of course not. But he told me he did, and I believe him. Three men are dead, there's no denying that."

"But the police failed to see any connection in those deaths, and two of them remain on the books as accidents."

"Yeah, well I know better. *I'm* the connection. And the first two killings were only made to *look* like accidents."

A buxom young barmaid appeared at that point to take our drink orders. In the rather tense silence that followed her interruption, I hung a cigarette from the corner of my mouth, set fire to it, and studied my prospective client through the curling smoke.

She was a beauty all right. Early thirties, medium height, heart-shaped face highlighted by almond eyes and a sensual, full-lipped mouth above a terrific body well displayed in a pantsuit of clinging blue silk. All topped off with thick chestnut hair and wrapped in some exotic, unfamiliar, but doubtless very expensive scent.

"Let's do it this way," I said after the drinks had arrived. "I'll tell you everything the judge has already told me, and then you can fill in the holes. Fair enough?"

She reached for her highball glass. "Fair enough," she said.

"You're a call girl. Five hundred a night. Very exclusive. You've been operating here in Rockford for approximately six years, and you regularly entertain some of the most prominent men in northern Illinois. Everything was going great for you until a couple weeks ago when one of your johns—"

"I hate that term."

"—until one of your customers started getting too possessive. He claimed he loved you and even went so far as to propose marriage. When you laughed it off, he went a little crazy. Said he wouldn't allow other men to touch you and if any did he swore he'd kill them. You refused to see him anymore, naturally enough, but you failed to take his threat seriously. And then came the night one Albert Renman died shortly after spending some time with you. From all appearances, it was one of those freak accidents; he fell going up the back steps of his house, fell and broke his neck. But the next day you got a phone call from your loony admirer—"

"His name is Earl Mardix."

"—and this Mardix claimed he was the one responsible for Renman's death. You hung up on him when he tried to give you all the gory details. It shook you up plenty, but you managed to convince yourself that he was just trying to take advantage of a grisly coincidence. Only a couple nights later the same thing happened all over. A man named Edward Traver left your bed and turned up dead within the hour. This time it was what appeared to be a single-vehicle car wreck. But you knew better, even before the phone call from Mardix came just as it had the first time. You tried to threaten him with the cops, but he called your bluff because he knew the last thing a girl in your position wanted was a police investigation coming down around her. What you did instead was to contact Judge Hugh Farrow, one of your regular customers of some years' standing. You told him you had some nut harassing you without bothering to tell him that this nut had already killed two men. The judge agreed to help you by calling on the services of an ex-con who owed him some favors, an aging strongarm specialist named Max Cobb. Cobb was to track down Mardix and rough him up enough to scare him off you. But things didn't go according to that plan at all. This time there was no attempt to make it look like an accident. Max Cobb was found in an alley yesterday morning with his throat slit from ear to ear."

Myra Caine closed her eyes and exhaled a ragged breath.

I went on. "You had no choice but to tell the judge the whole story then. I'll bet he gave you a royal chewing out, but he was no more anxious to go to the cops now than you were. Because of his involvement in hiring Cobb, he was in it up to his ears. So he got in touch with me. Gave me the rundown as he knew it and set up this meeting with you."

"He filled you in very thoroughly," the Caine woman observed. "He must trust you a great deal."

"Yeah," I said. "Too bad you didn't have some of that trust when you decided to turn to him for help. You should have leveled with him right off the bat."

"You don't like me very much, do you?"

I shrugged. "I don't know you well enough to like or

dislike you. But I do have a high regard for Hugh Farrow. He's a decent man. I'd hate to see his career and reputation go down the tubes because of some . . ."

"Because of some what? Tart? Tramp? Whore? Go ahead and say it, if it will make you feel better. I've been called a lot worse by a lot better than you."

"Look, I don't have to like you to do my job. You ought to be able to relate to that."

Bright red color flared high on each cheek, and suddenly those lovely almond eyes were leaking tears.

She started to get to her feet, but I put out a hand to stop her. "Hey," I said. "Come on, no need for that."

She settled back down after a minute and began digging for a handkerchief. I stabbed out my cigarette and gave myself a mental kick in the pants. I'm no good at handling bawling females, especially when I'm the one who triggered the tears.

"Look," I said, "you've got enough troubles without me pointing an accusing finger and spouting off at the mouth. I don't usually do things like that. I'm sorry, all right?"

She was busy with the hanky and made no reply. I left her sniffling and honking, got up and walked to the bar to get our drinks refilled. When I returned, she seemed to have regained her composure.

Without looking at me she said, "I don't make a habit of wearing my emotions on my sleeve and I never *ever* cry in front of anyone."

"So we're even," I said. "We both acted out of character. Now we can get on with the business at hand."

Her gaze lifted. "Then you'll do it? You'll help me?"

"I'd pretty much decided that when I agreed to meet with you."

"You're doing it because of Hugh, right?"

"Probably."

"At least you're honest."

"Then let me be honest about something else, too. I'll do everything I can to nail Mardix and keep you and the judge out of it. But you have to understand it may not be possible to do both. I won't jeopardize my P.I. license or any more lives just to keep you two in the clear. Stopping Mardix is priority one. If I can't see any other way, I'll have to bring the cops in on it."

She studied the contents of her glass for a long moment, then nodded and said, "All right, I accept that. You have my leave to do whatever you feel is necessary."

A light rain was falling by the time we emerged from the out-of-the-way little bar. It had taken the better part of an hour to hash over the remaining details of the case. I'd scribbled notes and sipped good bourbon, and all the while her perfume and the nearness of her had been working on me. When it comes right down to it, beautiful women are a dime a dozen. But in addition to her great looks, this one had the most stunningly powerful aura of sexuality I'd ever encountered. Before I knew it, it had penetrated my shell of animosity and was stirring yearnings in my gut that were hard to ignore. I could almost understand why a man would pay five hundred dollars for a night of her favors.

Meeting Myra Caine at a public establishment—rather than at my office or her apartment—had been my idea. It had been evident from what the judge had told me that Mardix had her under some sort of surveillance, and I wasn't about to make it that easy for him to spot me and possibly mark me as his next target. This way I'd been able to stake out the bar ahead of time and make sure no one was following her.

The next move seemed obvious enough: I planned on taking advantage of the fact that Mardix, for whatever reason, had relaxed his vigil. I had to do some fast talking to dissuade Myra from returning to her place, but I won out in the end by reminding her of what she'd said about going along with whatever I felt was necessary.

The ride to the St. George Hotel was made in sullen silence on her part. I parked near the side entrance and hustled her in through the worsening rain. The St. George was on Seventh Street, not far from my Broadway office. I chose it for that reason, and also because I knew the house dick there, a crusty old retired cop named Bill Grissom. The place had seen better days and was undoubtedly a far cry from what a five-hundred-dollar-a-night call girl was used to, but it was clean and relatively free of riffraff, and a twenty in Grissom's palm got me a promise he'd keep an eye on my brand-new client until I returned.

Back outside, the March rain was being kicked into stinging sheets by a cold, gusting wind. As I threaded my old Mustang through the tail end of the lunch-hour traffic, I had to flip on the defogger as well as the wipers to keep the windshield clear enough to prevent my crawling into some-body's trunk.

Hugh Farrow was waiting for me in the study of his sprawling North Park home. Bottin, his chauffeur/man-servant for as many years as anyone could remember, showed me in.

"Had lunch yet?" the judge wanted to know.

I shook my head. "As a matter of fact, no."

"Bottin, how about a tray of sandwiches and some cold beer?"

The tall, painfully thin manservant gave an almost imper-ceptible nod, spun on his heel, and glided from the room.

In sharp contrast to his faithful employee, the judge was built considerably thicker and closer to the ground. He moved with the bulky grace of a former athlete who wasn't exactly winning his battle of the bulge but hadn't thrown in the towel yet, either. I look in the mirror a time or two each day and see another guy, twenty years younger and a little taller, you could describe pretty much the same way.

"Well?"

The question was abrupt, almost demanding. It irritated me.

"Well what?" I said.

"Did you meet with her?"

"Yeah, I met with her."

"And?"

"And I agreed to look into the mess. To try and help her. And you. You damn fool."

His facial muscles pulled tight, and his eyes narrowed for an instant. Then the quick anger was past, and his mouth curved in a rueful smile. "Yeah, I guess I am at that. No fool like an old fool, right?"

"No fool like a guy who makes a chump of himself over a dame."

"Ah, there's where you're wrong, Joe. You're still a relatively young man, still have some of the fire and cockiness of youth left in you. When you're a little older, then you'll know, too. There is nothing—absolutely nothing on this earth, my friend—*better* to make a fool of yourself over than a woman."

"Christ," I growled. "Are you drunk?"

"Drunk? Naw, I've got the flu, that's all. Why else would I not be at the courthouse performing my judicial duties? Home sick with the flu, that's me. The fact that I can't quite bring myself to put on those grand old robes and pretend to dispense wisdom and justice while there's a killer running loose—a killer I fed a victim to—hasn't a goddamn thing to do with it!"

He was standing near a massive fireplace. Suddenly he pivoted and smacked his right fist against the flat stone face of the hearth. The sound of the impact made me wince.

Bottin entered at that moment, carrying a tray of sand-

wiches stacked around a silver bucket of ice in which a half
dozen bottles of Michelob were nestled. If he'd seen or heard
the punch, he made no indication.

"Your food and drink, sir," he said calmly.

Hugh Farrow stood facing the hearth with his fist still
pressed against the gunmetal gray stone. Without turning,
he said, "That'll be all for now, Bottin. Thanks."

When Bottin had withdrawn, I sat down before the tray of
eats and twisted open a bottle of Michelob. I drained a third
of it, then tried one of the sandwiches. Turkey. Delicious.
Over my shoulder I said, "If you need help pulling your fist
out of that stone, you'll have to wait until I'm finished here."

After a minute or so, the judge came over and sat down
across from me. The knuckles of his right hand were scraped
and bleeding. We both pretended not to notice.

Halfway through our second bottles of beer, he was ready
to talk about it.

"You've met her," he said. "Unless you're made of wood,
you certainly felt the impact she can have on a man. What
can I say? She's been a great comfort to me over the past few
years, ever since Margaret passed away. Even some before
that, to be perfectly frank about it. I was almost grateful for
the chance to do something for her in return." He paused,
watching the carbon bubbles rise behind the dark glass of
one of the bottles. When he spoke again, it was in a slightly
quieter, huskier voice. "Even if I'd known the truth about
Mardix when she first came to me, I think I still would have
been willing to do what I did."

I let that lie there.

"Tell me about Max Cobb," I said.

He shrugged. "What's to tell? You knew him."

"Knew of him," I corrected.

"He was a strongarm artist, a legbreaker from way back.
No spring chicken anymore, middle fifties but still rough as a
cob, just like his name. That was his boast, and he could

back it up. He would have been damned hard to take, Joe. That makes this Mardix a very dangerous character."

"What do you know about him? Anything?"

"Zip so far. A man of mystery. I ran some checks that yielded nothing, and I've got some more going now. I know people in all the right places and I know how to pull their strings, but it takes time to get it done with discretion. As soon as I turn up anything, I'll let you know."

"That leaves me with only one possible lead on him."

"What's that?"

"Myra only saw new customers on recommendation. Who do you think originally recommended Earl Mardix?"

"I give. Who?"

"Albert Renman, his first victim."

"Ironic."

"Yeah. Or is it more than that? At any rate, wives tend to know their husband's friends, right? I'm going to pay Renman's widow a visit this afternoon. Maybe she can point me toward Mardix."

We talked until the beer and sandwiches were polished off. I told him about stashing Myra at the St. George. I also gave him my spiel about going to the cops if I had to.

When I stood to leave, I said, "One more thing."

"What's that?"

"What you said before about those grand old judicial robes? They'll still fit if you give them half a chance. One mistake shouldn't cancel out a lifetime of making the right moves. You're a judge, not God. You're human, just like the rest of us. Give yourself the same break you'd give any first-time offender."

Roberta Renman turned out to be a frail-looking woman of about forty, with stringy blonde hair and nervous, birdlike movements. To give her her due, she was probably pretty enough under normal circumstances, but right now she was going through the worst period of widowhood, the hollow, empty time that hits a couple weeks after the funeral, when the relatives and friends have quit dropping by and all that's left is the sense of loss.

I fed her a line about working for some big security outfit and checking out the employment application of one Earl Mardix.

"His previous job record looks good," I explained. "But my company places a good deal of importance on character references. Unfortunately, this Mardix seems to be a bit of a loner, and one of the few personal references he provided was your late husband. I really hate to bother you at a time like this, but I thought you might also be acquainted with Mr. Mardix and could help me out."

"Mardix . . . Mardix . . ." She tried the name out loud a couple times to jog her memory.

"First name Earl," I said, then offered the description Myra had provided me with. "About thirty, medium height and build, straw-colored hair worn on the longish side."

She frowned over it a minute or so more and then gave an apologetic little smile. "I'm sorry, but Albert met so darn many people at the auto dealership . . . I couldn't begin to remember them all."

I thanked her for her time and went back out into the rain. My mood was as gray as the overcast sky.

I returned to the city, remembering to swing by my bank and deposit Myra Caine's retainer check, then decided it was time to pay a visit to my office. I hadn't bothered to check in that morning, so I had to wade through a pile of mail (eighty percent bills, twenty percent circulars, zero percent anything important) that had been shoved through the mail slot. I wadded the whole works into a ball and slam-dunked it into the wastebasket on the way by. Eat your heart out, Darryl Dawkins.

While a pot of day-old coffee was reheating, I punched the

playback on the phone answering machine. Some little old lady wanted me to find her pet parakeet that had flown out the window of her tenth-floor apartment; a horseplayer I knew wanted to borrow some money to bet on a "sure thing"; and a lavender-voiced individual named Floyd wanted me to find his dear friend Marcus and convince him that all was forgiven and he should come home. I mentally took care of all three requests in the same manner as the day's mail.

The coffee was just this side of unbearable, but I managed to down a couple cups as I went over my notes on the Caine case and wrapped up the loose ends on a few other matters. It was dusk by the time I finished.

Before leaving the office, I took care of one more piece of business. The well-oiled old .45 came out of its resting place in the desk drawer and the shoulder rig came off its hook in the closet and, together, they ended up on my person. The .22 magnum derringer I wear clipped inside the rim of my right boot is adequate for emergencies and everyday walk-around business, but when I recognize in advance that a situation could turn hairy—like this one—then it's time to strap on the heavy artillery.

I picked Myra up around seven and took her out for supper at a little steak house I frequent. Over two of the best sirloins in Rockford, I reported on my afternoon's activities and then worked my way into some other things I had on my mind.

"A couple things have been bugging me," I said. "For one, it's obvious Mardix has had you under pretty close surveillance ever since he swore he wouldn't allow another man to touch you. Any idea why you were able to give him the slip this morning?"

She shook her head. "No. I never really thought about it."

"Then it wasn't anything you did intentionally. Did you change your regular routine in some way?"

"Well, sure. I went to meet you. Otherwise, I'm almost never up before noon."

I nodded. "Okay, it's probably as simple as that. He has to sleep and eat just like everybody else, and he'd have been doing it to fit your schedule. You changed your routine and threw him off."

"What else? You said a couple things."

"Any idea what made him fall so hard for you, become so possessive in the first place?"

She shrugged. "Because I helped him over his sexual hang-ups, I guess. When he first came to me, he had a lot of problems. It's not uncommon for guys like that to fall in love with a hooker who has the patience and expertise to help them in ways a straight chick wouldn't—or couldn't."

"Sort of like falling in love with your psychiatrist or a doctor who's saved your life."

"You make it sound corny but, yeah, something like that."

"Was he over his hang-ups completely, or just with you?"

"I'm not sure. If I had to guess, I'd say just with me." Her mouth curved in a dubious little smile. "Is all this really necessary, or are you being a teeny bit voyeuristic?"

I shook my head. "I'm just trying to get a feel for the guy, that's all. We know so damn little about him. Where does he live? What does he do? Hell, Earl Mardix apparently isn't even his real name. There's no phone listing, published or private, for anyone by that name. And from what Mrs. Renman said it sounds as if her husband met him at a car dealership, yet there's no vehicle registration or city sticker issued to a Mardix. The judge sure as hell hit it on the head when he called him a man of mystery."

"There's one thing that might help."

"What's that?"

"I think he was in the war. You know, Vietnam. He had a

bad dream one night, and he called out some things in his sleep. I couldn't make sense of what he said, but there were a lot of Asian-sounding names and phrases, you know? When I tried to ask him about it later, he got really uptight."

I made a mental note to pass that bit of info along to the judge. It could be another angle for him to have checked.

"I'll take you back to the St. George when we're finished here," I told Myra, "and then I'm going to spend the night at your place."

"What on earth for?"

"If we're right, if your change-up maneuver is what gave Mardix the slip this morning, then by now he's got to know he lost you. It's a safe bet that that will have him riled. With any luck it could rattle him enough to make him do something dumb. Like maybe break into your apartment and try to find some clue as to where you went."

"And you'll be there waiting for him?"

"Exactly."

"Won't that be dangerous for you?"

"Could be. But if I play it right, it'll be a lot more dangerous for him."

We finished our meal, passed on dessert, and I drove her back to the St. George. On the way she asked me to stop somewhere so she could pick up some overnight things. When I turned into a K Mart, she commented dryly: "Gee, Hannibal, you take me to all the finest places." I saw her to her room, and as we stood facing each other in the doorway, I was again acutely aware of her raw sexuality. I fantasized briefly about saying to hell with Earl Mardix, sweeping her up in my arms, carrying her into the room, and hanging out the "Do Not Disturb" sign for the rest of the week.

Instead I settled for a quick peck on the cheek from her and a huskily whispered, "For luck."

Myra Caine's apartment was on the third floor of a luxury condo just off East State. I went up the back way from the parking garage and used every trick I know to make sure I wasn't observed. It was a little before nine when I let myself in.

I locked the door behind me and left the lights off. Guided by the thin beam of a pencil flash, I made a tour of the apartment, familiarizing myself with the layout. She lived very well. Elegance without extravagance.

By half past nine I was ready to take up my post. Early in my tour I'd noted the doors to a large walk-in closet just off the living room and had decided on that as a likely spot. It was centrally located without being readily visible to anyone entering the apartment. I plucked a couple sofa pillows from the couch and carried them over along with the thermos of coffee I'd brought. I slid the doors open.

He exploded out of the closet with a nerve-freezing combat cry. He threw three lightning kicks to my chest, knocking me back, then a fourth wiped my legs out from under me. I crashed down across the end of the couch. I rolled, trying to escape his stamping feet. An end table got in the way, and I turned it into splinters. His face was just a blur in the darkness, but I knew it had to be Mardix. The sneaky sonofabitch had gotten in ahead of me somehow and had lain in hiding all the while I was prowling. I could hear his grunts of effort and feel the breeze as his heels whistled past my face in near misses.

I managed to get my knees under me, then my feet, and lunged up into him. We bounced off the wall in a clinch. I tried to throw a knee into his groin, but he blocked it with his hip. He head-butted me in the face and jerked away. I swung a roundhouse right that hit nothing but air.

I lost him in the dark. I stood in the center of the room with fists balled and eyes watering from the head butt, and the only thing I could hear was the puff of my own labored breathing. I felt as if I were fighting a goddamn shadow.

And then he was behind me. The bloodcurdling cry again,

and in the same instant a length of piano wire slipped down over my face and bit into my throat. He slammed a foot against the nape of my neck and pulled into it. I bridged and thrust back like a man hit by high voltage, but he moved expertly with me, never lessening the pressure. I sank to my knees with a strange sound filling my ears. I realized it was a roar of pain and rage and panic trying to escape from deep inside me.

I had only seconds before the piano wire did its trick. It was already embedded so deeply in my flesh that I could barely feel it with my clawing fingertips. I reached for the .45, but my hand found nothing but an empty holster. The big gun had fallen out sometime during the struggle. And the derringer was out of reach now with my legs pinned under Mardix as he rode me down. I sagged forward. My head felt ready to explode, and my throat burned like fire as the wire bit deeper and deeper.

On the carpet just ahead of me something glinted dully in the almost nonexistent light. My thermos. The one I'd brought along, filled with coffee to keep me awake through what might have turned out to be a long, uneventful night. I reached out and gripped it with rubbery fingers, slipping my right hand through the plastic handle. I had time enough and strength enough for one attempt. If it failed, I'd never get another chance.

I whipped the metal-cased cylinder up over my head, then back and down. I heard the sharp crack of metal striking flesh and bone and felt the shock of the impact vibrate through my wrist. Mardix emitted a different kind of cry this time as he released his grip on the wire ends and toppled off my back. I fell forward, flames flooding down through my chest as I sucked in great mouthfuls of air. I tore away the wire and spun to face him. We were both on our hands and knees. Dark blood ran down over his left eye, and he was poised catlike, as if ready to pounce on me. I lashed out with the thermos again. His reflexes were still good, and I managed only to graze the top of his head. I belly-flopped with the effort. He rolled away, scrambled to his feet, fumbled for a moment with the door lock, then ran out. Bright light poured in from the hallway, stinging my eyes as I lay there and listened to the sound of his retreat.

I hauled myself up, relocked the door, turned on every light I could get my hands on. I found the .45 amidst the rubble of the destroyed end table. I sat for a long time with it resting in my lap while I caught my breath and gently rubbed my scraped, bleeding throat.

It was well past ten when I killed the lights and quit the apartment. I walked down to the parking garage with my hands thrust deep in my jacket pockets, the right one firmly gripping the .45. I felt restless and angry. Angry with myself. I'd had Mardix right in my hands and let him get away. Damn it all. But at the same time a part of me was in no hurry to meet up with him again. Twice I jumped at shadows and silently cursed my skittishness.

The city was a kaleidoscope of rain-blurred neon, with cars hissing across the shiny pavement like darting reptiles. I drove without knowing exactly where I wanted to go, until, abruptly it seemed, I found myself in front of the St. George. I parked and went in with my collar flipped up to hide my bloodied throat. I called Myra's room from the lobby to let her know I was coming up.

She was waiting for me in her doorway, wrapped in a powder-blue quilted robe. She hadn't been to sleep yet, but her hair was pinned up and her only makeup was a touch of fresh lipstick. She looked more gorgeous than ever. I told her what had happened, coloring my narrative with plenty of four-lettered adjectives. When she saw my throat, she called down to the desk for a first-aid kit and, at my insistence, a bottle of bourbon.

When they arrived, I belted down some of the whiskey

while Myra played Florence Nightingale. I don't know exactly how what happened next came about, or even who made the first move. It wasn't what I had gone there for. Or maybe, on some subconscious level, it was. I don't know. But suddenly I had her in my arms. The robe slipped away, and beneath it she was even more splendid than I'd imagined. We fell back across the bed and, for a frenzied span of time, lost ourselves in each other and the immediate needs of our flesh.

"What was that?" Myra said afterward. "Reaffirmation of life after nearly dying in that dark apartment?"

"It was just sex," I replied. "No need to read anything more into it."

"Well, it doesn't seem to have cheered you up a whole hell of a lot."

I sat on the edge of the bed and reached for a cigarette. "That sonofabitch is still out there somewhere," I said. "I know next to nothing about him, and the one chance I had to get my hands on him, I blew. I'm not likely to get real cheery until I rectify some of that."

"That reminds me," Myra said, sitting up behind me. "The judge called just after you left. He said he'd learned some things about Mardix that you should know. I explained to him that you'd be at my apartment with the phone switched off, so he said if I heard from you before he did, to have you get in touch with him right away."

I smoked my cigarette. The restlessness and anger hadn't abated much, not even with the help of booze and sex. The latter, in fact, had added a twinge of guilt to my already tangled emotions. I knew I wasn't ready for sleep.

I got up and walked over to the phone, dialed Hugh Farrow's number. A busy signal burped in my ear. I tried four more times in the next twenty minutes with the same results. A nagging fear crawled through me. It was past midnight, hardly the hour for lengthy phone conversations. I began pulling on my clothes.

"Where are you going?" Myra wanted to know.

"Out," I told her. "Keep the lights low and stay away from the windows. Lock the door when I leave, and don't open it for anyone but me."

I pulled the derringer from my boot and handed it to her. Her eyes flicked down to the weapon, then back up, wide with uncertainty and a trace of fear.

I said, "Mardix is running scared now, maybe completely out of control. At best, there's a fine line between love and hate. There's a good chance he's crossed that line, and that means his obsession for you may have changed from lust to fury."

"You mean he blames me for the trouble he's in?"

"I've seen it happen that way."

"Jesus."

"I'll wake Grissom and put him right outside the door. I'll be back as quick as I can. Try to relax, but remember everything I said."

It was a twenty-minute drive from the St. George to North Park. I spotted the Farrow house from six blocks away. Every light in it was on.

I slammed the old Mustang to a halt in the middle of the driveway, left it rocking back and forth on worn springs with headlights still on and the door hanging open as I raced through the stinging rain up to the front door. I went in with the .45 in my fist.

There was blood on the walls of the front hall, and Bottin lay at the foot of the open stairway with his throat slit open like a second mouth. He was beyond help. I leaped over him and went bounding up the stairs.

I found the judge in his bedroom, on the bed, feet and hands lashed to the cornerposts with torn strips of sheeting.

His chest was a crisscross of black and red welts, and I could smell the burned flesh. A poker from the smoldering fireplace lay nearby on a patch of singed carpet.

He rolled his head and looked up at me through pain-dulled eyes. "Jesus Christ, Joe," he said hoarsely. "Jesus . . . Christ."

I knelt at the edge of the bed and began untying his hands. "Easy, old buddy," I said. "Everything's going to be okay. Don't try to talk."

But he had things he wanted me to know. "His real name is Evan Maddox," he said. "He was a Special Forces war hero in Vietnam. He was part of an elite penetration team that specialized in assassination and subversive tactics behind enemy lines. He became an artist with silent weapons—garrote, knife, bow and arrow, bare hands, you name it. They thought they had him deprogrammed after the war and sent him home to his family in Michigan. Everything went okay for a few years, but then something snapped in the winter of 1980. He killed his parents and wife of six months and three neighbors before fleeing in a stolen car. The Army formed a special team to track him down. They came close a few times but never could close the lid. They learned he hired out for mercenary work, using aliases such as Earl Mardix. Nine months ago they lost all track of him. My inquiries came to their attention, and the team is on its way here now."

"Swell," I said. "They can take over this whole mess. Nobody's better than those military boys when it comes to smoothing things over."

The judge grabbed my sleeve. "You don't understand. We can't wait for them now."

"Why not?"

"Don't you see? Why do you think Mardix came here tonight and did this? He must have been following Myra when she first contacted me. After you spooked him at her place, he returned here and forced me to tell him where she is."

"Damn!" I exploded.

"I tried to hold out, but I . . . I couldn't."

"Nobody can blame you for that. How long ago did he leave here?"

"I'm not sure. I think he left me for dead. I sort of . . . drifted in and out."

"Listen, can you hang on long enough to make a phone call?"

"Damn right I can."

"Call Bill Grissom at the St. George; he's the house dick there. Tell him what's coming down. Tell him to get Myra out of there if he can. Then call the cops and anybody else you can think of. I'm on my way, and I'll take all the help I can get!"

On the return trip, I cut my previous time in half. The Mustang's half-bald tires wouldn't grip the rain-slick pavement, and the front end jumped the curb in front of the St. George before the brakes held. I bailed out, repeating my door-left-open-and-lights-on routine, plunged into the lobby with the .45 drawn and ready.

The desk clerk was sprawled half in, half out of his chair, with his neck twisted in an impossible way. Déjà vu. I pounded up the stairs and down the second-floor hall toward Myra's room. Grissom lay on the floor outside the shattered door. An old revolver lay beside him and I could smell the stink of cordite, so at least he'd gotten off a shot. But it hadn't done him much good. He was as dead as the plaster on the walls.

I went into the room with my heart thumping up in my throat. I was half afraid of what I would find and half afraid of what I wouldn't.

Nothing. The room in shambles but nobody there.

And then I spotted the open window.

They were out there, on the flat, tar-papered roof that stretched out over the hotel's single-storied dining and kitchen unit. Myra, naked except for satiny briefs, was backing up with the derringer, gripped in both hands, held at arm's length in front of her. I could hear the repeated snap of the firing pin falling on an empty chamber. Mardix was moving slowly but relentlessly toward her. He seemed slightly unsteady on his feet. I guessed that at least one of those bullets—either from the derringer or from Grissom's old revolver—had found its mark.

I went over the windowsill and cat-footed across the roof, moving to a point where Myra was out of my line of fire.

Mardix was talking. The wind caught his words and tossed them around, but I could hear most of what he was saying.

"All I wanted was to love you," he told Myra. "Do you know how long it's been since I felt love? Why couldn't you try to return it? . . . Why make me do those things?"

"Mardix!" I called out.

He spun to face me. I could see the crimson stains on the front of him now. He'd taken two slugs and was losing a lot of blood.

"She's not the one who made you do those things," I said. "You're sick, you need help. It has to end right here. One way or another."

"I shouldn't have left you alive," he snarled.

"Maybe not," I replied evenly. "But I won't make the same mistake. This is a .45 in my fist. Take a good look at it. One wrong move and it will blow you in half."

I could hear the whine of sirens now, not far off. Mardix heard them, too. His eyes flicked around, scanning the rooftop.

"You don't have a prayer," I warned.

The eyes came back to me. And then he did a strange

thing. He smiled. And in a flat, emotionless voice he said, "Yeah, I know."

Even with two bullets in him, his speed and reflexes were incredible. His right hand blurred up, reaching behind his neck, and the arm snapped down in a throwing motion. I caught the glint of the blade as it whirled from his fingertips, and in the same instant I fired. I saw his body jerk and hurtle backward as if yanked by invisible wires before the knife thunked into my shoulder and spun me around.

I went to one knee with fiery pain boiling down across my back and through my left arm. My head swam, and for a minute I thought I was going to black out. Myra's screams gave me something else to focus on, helped me cling to consciousness. When my head cleared, I stood up.

Mardix lay in a heap near the edge of the roof. I walked toward him with the knife handle jutting out ahead of me like the jib boom of a listing schooner. The .45 was still in my hand, and I kept it trained on him every step of the way. He'd nearly killed me twice this night; I half expected him to leap up and try again. But the gaping hole over his heart convinced me I had nothing more to fear from him. No one did.

Myra's screams had deteriorated to ragged sobs. I put my good arm around her. "It's okay," I said. "It's over."

We stood there leaning on each other until the cops arrived.

LOREN D. ESTLEMAN

I'M IN THE BOOK

When I finally got in to see Alex Wynn of Reiner, Switz, Galsworthy & Wynn, the sun was high over Lake St. Clair outside the window behind his desk and striking sparks off the choppy steel-blue surface with sailboats gliding around on it cutting white foam, their sharkfin sails striped in broad bright bikini colors. Wynn sat with his back to the view and never turned to look at it. He didn't need to. On the wall across from him hung a big framed color photograph of bright-striped sailboats cutting white foam on the steel-blue surface of Lake St. Clair.

Wynn was a big neat man with a black widow's peak trimmed tight to his skull and the soft gray hair at his temples worn long over the tops of his ears. He had on aviator glasses with clear plastic rims and a suit the color and approximate weight of ground fog, that fit him like no suit will ever fit me if I hit the Michigan Lottery tomorrow. He had deep lines in his Miami-brown face and a mouth that turned down like a shark's to show a bottom row of caps as white and even as military monuments. It was a predator's face. I liked it fine. It belonged to a lawyer and in my business lawyers mean a warm feeling in the pit of the bank account.

"Walker, Amos," he said, as if he were reading roll call. "I like the name. It has a smoky strength to it."

"I've had it a long time."

He looked at me with his strong white hands folded on top of his absolutely clean desk. His palms didn't leave marks on the glossy surface the way mine would have. "I keep seeing your name on reports. The Reliance people employ your services often."

"Only when the job involves people," I said. "Those big investigation agencies are good with computers and diamonds and those teeny little cameras you can hide in your left ear. But when it comes to stroking old ladies who see things and leaning on supermarket stock boys who smuggle sides of beef out the back door, they remember us little shows."

"How big is your agency?"

"You're looking at it. I have an answering service," I added quickly.

"Better and better. It means you can keep a secret. You have a reputation for that, too."

"Who told?"

"The humor I can take or let alone." He refolded his hands the other way. "I don't like going behind Reliance's back like this. We've worked together for years and the director's an old friend. But this is a personal matter, and there are some things you would prefer to have a stranger know than someone you play poker with every Saturday night."

"I don't play poker," I said. "Whoops, sorry." I got out a cigarette and smoothed it between my fingers. "Who's missing, your wife or your daughter?"

He shot me a look he probably would have kept hooded in court. Then he sat back, nodding slightly. "I guess it's not all that uncommon."

"I do other work but my specialty is tracing missing persons. You get so you smell it coming." I waited.

"It's my wife. She's left me again."

"Again?"

"Last time it was with one of the apprentices here, a man named Lloyd Debner. But they came back after three days. I fired him, naturally."

"Naturally."

A thin smile played around with his shark's mouth, gave it up and went away. "Seems awfully Old Testament, I know. I tried to be modern about it. There's really no sense in blaming the other man. But I saw myself hiding out in here to avoid meeting him in the hall, and that would be grotesque. I gave him excellent references. One of our competitors snapped him up right away."

"What about this time?"

"She left the usual note saying she was going away and I was not to look for her. I called Debner but he assured me he hadn't seen Cecelia since their first . . . fling. I believe him. But it's been almost a week now and I'm concerned for her safety."

"What about the police?"

"I believe we covered that when we were discussing keeping secrets," he said acidly.

"You've been married how long?"

"Six years. And yes, she's younger than I, by fourteen years. That was your next question, wasn't it?"

"It was in there. Do you think that had anything to do with her leaving?"

"I think it had everything to do with it. She has appetites that I've been increasingly unable to fulfill. But I never thought it was a problem until she left the first time."

"You quarreled?"

"The normal amount. Never about that. Which I suppose is revealing. I rather think she's found a new boyfriend, but I'm damned if I can say who it is."

"May I see the note?"

He extracted a fold of paper from an inside breast pocket and passed it across the desk. "I'm afraid I got my finger-prints all over it before I thought over all the angles."

"That's okay. I never have worked on anything where prints were any use."

It was written on common drugstore stationery, tinted blue with a spray of flowers in the upper right hand corner. A hasty hand full of sharp points and closed loops. It said what he'd reported it said and nothing else. Signed with a C.

"There's no date."

"She knew I'd read it the day she wrote it. It was last Tuesday."

"Uh-huh."

"That means what?" he demanded.

"Just uh-huh. It's something I say when I can't think of anything to say." I gave back the note. "Any ideas where she might go to be alone? Favorite vacation spot, her hometown, a summer house, anything like that? I don't mean to insult you. Sometimes the hardest place to find your hat is on your head."

"We sublet our Florida home in the off-season. She grew up in this area and has universally disliked every place we've visited on vacation. Really, I was expecting something more from a professional."

"I'm just groping for a handle. Does she have any hobbies?"

"Spending my money."

I watched my cigarette smoke drifting toward the window. "It seems to me you don't know your wife too well after six years, Mr. Wynn. When I find her, if I find her, I can tell you where she is, but I can't make her come back, and from the sound of things she may not want to come back. I wouldn't be representing your interests if I didn't advise you to save your money and set the cops loose on it. I can't give you guarantees they won't give."

"Are you saying you don't want the job?"

"Not me. I don't have any practice at that. Just being straight with a client I'd prefer keeping."

"Don't do me any favors, Walker."

"Okay. I'll need a picture. And what's her maiden name? She may go back to it."

"Collier." He spelled it. "And here." He got a wallet-size color photograph out of the top drawer of the desk and skidded it across the glossy top like someone dealing a card.

She was a redhead, and the top of that line. She looked like someone who would end up married to a full partner in a weighty law firm with gray temples and an office overlooking Lake St. Clair. It would be in her high school yearbook under "Predictions."

I put the picture in my breast pocket. "Where do I find this Debner?"

"He's with Paxton & Ring on West Michigan. But I told you he doesn't know where Cecelia is."

"Maybe he should be asked a different way." I killed my stub in the smoking stand next to the chair and rose. "You'll be hearing from me."

His eyes followed me up. All eight of his fingers were lined up on the near edge of his desk, the nails pink and perfect. "Can you be reached if I want to hear from you sooner?"

"My service will page me. I'm in the book."

A Japanese accent at Paxton & Ring told me over the telephone that Lloyd Debner would be tied up all afternoon in Detroit Recorder's Court. Lawyers are always in court the way executives are always in meetings. At the Frank Murphy Hall of Justice a bailiff stopped spitting on his handkerchief and rubbing at a spot on his uniform to point out a bearded man in his early thirties with a mane of black hair smoking a pipe and talking to a gray-headed man in the corridor outside one of the courtrooms. I went over there and introduced myself.

"Second," he said, without taking his eyes off the other man. "Tim, we're talking a lousy twenty bucks over the fifteen hundred. Even if you win, the judge will order probation. The kid'll get that anyway if we plead Larceny Under, and there's no percentage in mucking up his record for life just to fatten your win column. And there's nothing saying you'll win."

I said, "This won't take long."

"Make an appointment. Listen, Tim—"

"It's about Cecelia Wynn," I said. "We can talk about it out here in the hall if you like. Tim won't mind."

He looked at me then for the first time. "Tim, I'll catch you later."

"After the sentencing." The gray-headed man went into the courtroom, chuckling.

"Who'd you say you were?" Debner demanded.

"Amos Walker. I still am, but a little older. I'm a P.I. Alec Wynn hired me to look for his wife."

"You came to the wrong place. That's all over."

"I'm interested in when it wasn't."

He glanced up and down the hall. There were a few people in it, lawyers and fixers and the bailiff with the stain that wouldn't go away from his crisp blue uniform shirt. "Come on. I can give you a couple of minutes."

I followed him into a men's room two doors down. We stared at a guy combing his hair in front of the long mirror over the sinks until he put away his comb and picked up a brown leather briefcase and left. Debner bent down to see if there were any feet in the stalls, straightened, and knocked out his pipe into a sink. He laid it on a soap canister to cool and moved his necktie a centimeter to the right.

"I don't see Cecelia when we pass on the street," he said, inspecting the results in the mirror. "I had my phone number changed after we got back from Jamaica so she couldn't call me."

"That where you went?"

"I rented a bungalow outside Kingston. Worst mistake I ever made. I was headed for a junior partnership at Reiner when this happened. Now I'm back to dealing school board presidents' sons out of jams they wouldn't be in if five guys ahead of me hadn't dealt them out of jams just like them starting when they were in junior high."

"How'd you and Cecelia get on?"

"Oh, swell. So good we crammed two weeks' reservations into three days and came back home."

"What went wrong?"

"Different drummers." He picked up his pipe and blew through it.

"Not good enough," I said.

He grinned boyishly. "I didn't think so. To begin with, she's a health nut. I run and take a little wheat germ myself sometimes, you don't even have to point a gun at me, but I draw the line at dropping vitamins and herb pills at every meal. She must've taken sixteen capsules every time we sat down to eat. It can drive you blinkers. People in restaurants must've figured her for a drug addict."

"Sure she wasn't?"

"She was pretty open about taking them if she was. She filled the capsules herself from plastic bags. Her purse rattled like a used car."

A fat party in a gray suit and pink shirt came in and smiled and nodded at both of us and used the urinal and washed his hands. Debner used the time to recharge his pipe.

"Still not good enough," I said when the fat party had gone. "You don't cut a vacation short just because your bed partner does wild garlic."

"It just didn't work out. Look, I'm due back in court."

"Not at half past noon." I waited.

He finished lighting his pipe, dropped the match into the sink where he'd knocked his ashes earlier, grinned around the stem. I bet that melted the women jurors. "If this gets around, I'm washed up with every pretty legal secretary in the building," he said.

"Nothing has to get around. I'm just looking for Cecelia Wynn."

"Yeah. You said." He puffed on the pipe, took it out, smoothed his beard and looked at it in the mirror. "Yeah. Well, she said she wasn't satisfied."

"Uh-huh."

"No one's ever told me that before. I'm not used to complaints."

"Uh-*huh*."

He turned back toward me. His eyes flicked up and down. "We never had this conversation, okay?"

"What conversation?"

"Yeah." He put the pipe back between his teeth, puffed. "Yeah."

We shook hands. He squeezed a little harder than I figured he did normally.

I dropped two dimes into a pay telephone in the downstairs lobby and fought my way through two secretaries before Alec Wynn came on the line. His voice was a full octave deeper than it had been in person. I figured it was that way in court too.

"Just checking back, Mr. Wynn. How come when I asked you about hobbies you didn't tell me your wife was into herbs?"

"Into *what?*"

I told him what Debner had said about the capsules. He said, "I haven't dined with my wife in months. Most legal business is conducted in restaurants."

"I guess you wouldn't know who her herbalist is, then."

"Herbalist?"

"Sort of an oregano guru. They tell their customers which herbs to take in the never-ending American quest for a healthy body. Not a few of the runaways I've traced take their restlessness to them first."

"Well, I wouldn't know anything about that. Trina might. Our maid. She's at the house now."

"Would you call her and tell her I'm coming?"

He said he would and broke the connection.

It was a nice place if you like windows. There must have been fifty on the street side alone, with ivy or something just as green crawling up the brick wall around them and a courtyard with a marble fountain in the center and a black chauffeur with no shirt on washing a blue Mercedes in front. They are always washing cars. A white-haired Puerto Rican woman with muddy eyes and a faint mustache answered my ring.

"Trina?"

"Yes. You are Mr. Walker? Mr. Wynn told me to expect you."

I followed her through a room twice the size of my living room but designed just for following maids through, and down a hall with dark paintings on the walls to a glassed-in porch at the back of the house containing ferns in pots and lawn furniture upholstered in a floral print. The sliding glass door leading outside was ajar and a strong chlorine stench floated in from an outdoor crescent-shaped swimming pool. She slid the door shut.

"The pool man says alkali is leaking into the water from an underground spring," she explained. "The chlorine controls the smell."

"The rich suffer too." I told her what I wanted.

"Capsules? Yes, Mrs. Wynn has many bottles of capsules in her room. There is a name on the bottles. I will get one."

"No hurry. What sort of woman is Mrs. Wynn to work for?"

"I don't know that that is a good question to answer."

"You're a good maid, Trina." I wound a five-dollar bill around my right index finger.

She slid the tube off the finger and flattened it and folded it over and tucked it inside her apron pocket. "She is a good employer. She says please and does not run her fingers over the furniture after I have dusted, like the last woman I worked for."

"Is that all you can tell me?"

"I have not worked here long, sir. Only five weeks."

"Who was maid before that?"

"A girl named Ann Foster, at my agency. Multi-Urban Services. She was fired." Her voice sank to a whisper on the last part. We were alone.

"Fired why?"

"William the chauffeur told me she was fired. I didn't ask why. I have been a maid long enough to learn that the less you know the more you work. I will get one of the bottles."

She left me, returning a few minutes later carrying a glass container the size of an aspirin bottle, with a cork in the top. It was half full of gelatin capsules filled with fine brown powder. I pulled the cork and sniffed. A sharp, spicy scent. The name of a health foods store on Livernois was typewritten on the label.

"How many of these does Mrs. Wynn have in her bedroom?" I asked.

"Many. Ten or twelve bottles."

"As full as this?"

"More, some of them."

"That's a lot of capsules to fill and then leave behind. Did she take many clothes with her?"

"No, sir. Her closets and drawers are full."

I thanked her and gave her back the bottle. It was getting

to be the damnedest disappearing act I had covered in a long, long time.

The black chauffeur was hosing off the Mercedes when I came out. He was tall, almost my height, and the bluish skin of his torso was stretched taut over lumpy muscle. I asked him if he was William.

He twisted shut the nozzle of the hose, watching me from under his brows with his head down, like a boxer. Scar tissue shone around his eyes. "Depends on who you might be."

I sighed. When you can't even get their name out of them, the rest is like pulling nails. I stood a folded ten-spot on the Mercedes' hood. He watched the bottom edge darken as it soaked up water. "Ann Foster," I said.

"What about her?"

"How close was she to Cecelia Wynn?"

"I wouldn't know. I work outside."

"Who fired her, Mr. or Mrs. Wynn?"

He thought about it. Watched the bill getting wetter. Then he snatched it up and waved it dry. "She did. Mrs. Wynn."

"Why?"

He shrugged. I reached up and plucked the bill out of his fingers. He grabbed for it but I drew it back out of his reach. He shrugged again, wringing the hose in his hands to make his muscles bulge. "They had a fight of some kind the day Ann left. I could hear them screaming at each other out here. I don't know what it was about."

"Where'd she go after she left here?"

He started to shrug a third time, stopped. "Back to the agency, maybe. I don't ask questions. In this line—"

"Yeah. The less you know the more you work." I gave him the ten and split.

The health foods place was standard, plank floor and hanging plants and stuff you can buy in any supermarket for a fraction of what they were asking. The herbalist was a small, pretty woman of about thirty, in a gypsy blouse and a floor-length denim skirt with bare feet poking out underneath and a bandanna tied around her head. She also owned the place. She hadn't seen Mrs. Wynn since before she'd turned up missing. I bought a package of unsalted nuts for her trouble and ate them on the way to the office. They needed salt.

I found Multi-Urban Services in the Detroit metropolitan directory and dialed the number. A woman whose voice reminded me of the way cool green mints taste answered.

"We're not at liberty to give out information about our clients."

"I'm sorry to hear that," I said. "I went to a party at the Wynn place in Grosse Pointe about six weeks ago and was very impressed with Miss Foster's efficiency. I'd heard she was free and was thinking of engaging her services on a full-time basis."

The mints melted. "I'm sorry, Miss Foster is no longer with this agency. But I can recommend another girl just as efficient. Multi-Urban prides itself—"

"I'm sure it does. Can you tell me where Miss Foster is currently working?"

"Stormy Heat Productions. But not as a maid."

I thanked her and hung up, thinking about how little it takes to turn mint to acid. Stormy Heat was listed on Mt. Elliott. Its line was busy. Before leaving the office, I broke the Smith & Wesson out of the desk drawer and snapped the holster onto my belt under my jacket. It was that kind of neighborhood.

The outfit worked out of an old gymnasium across from Mt. Elliott Cemetery, a scorched brick building as old as the eight-hour day with a hand-lettered sign over the door and a concrete stoop deep in the process of going back to the land. The door was locked. I pushed a sunken button that grated in its socket. No sound issued from within. I was about to knock when a square panel opened in the door at head level and a mean black face with a beard that grew to a point looked into mine.

"You've got to be kidding," I said.

"What do you want?" demanded the face.

"Ann Foster."

"What for?"

"Talk."

"Sorry." The panel slid shut.

I was smoking a cigarette. I dropped it to the stoop and crushed it out and used the button again. When the panel shot back I reached up and grasped the beard in my fist and yanked. His chest banged the door.

"You white—!"

I twisted the beard in my fist. He gasped, and tears sprang to his eyes. "Joe sent me," I said. "The goose flies high. May the Force be with you. Pick the password you like, but open the door."

"Who—?"

"Jerk Root, the Painless Barber. Open."

"Okay, okay." Metal snapped on his side. Still hanging on to his whiskers, I reached down with my free hand and tried the knob. It turned. I let go and opened the door. He was standing just inside the threshold, a big man in threadbare jeans and a white shirt open to the navel Byron-fashion, smoothing his beard with thick fingers. He had a Colt magnum in his other hand pointed at my belt buckle.

"Nice," I said. "The nickel plating goes with your eyes. You got a permit for that?"

He smiled crookedly. His eyes were still watering. "Why didn't you say you was cop?" He reached back and jammed the revolver into a hip pocket. "You got paper?"

"Not today. I'm not raiding the place. I just want to talk to Ann Foster."

"Okay," he said. "Okay. I don't need no beef with the laws. You don't see nothing on the way, deal?"

I spread my hands. "I'm blind. This isn't an election year."

There was a lot not to see. Films produced by Stormy Heat were not interested in the Academy Award or even feature billing at the all-night grindhouses on Woodward Avenue. Its actors were thin and ferretlike, and its actresses used powder to fill the cavities in their faces and cover their stretch marks. The lights and cameras were strictly surplus, their cables frayed and patched all over like old garden hoses. We walked past carnal scenes, unnoticed by the grunting performers or the sweat-stained crews, to a scuffed steel door at the rear that originally led into a locker room. My escort went through it without pausing. I followed.

"Don't they teach you to knock in the jungle?"

I'd had a flash of a naked youthful brown body, and then it was covered by a red silk kimono that left a pair of long legs bare to the tops of the thighs. She had her hair cut very short and her face with its upturned nose and lower lip thrust out in a belligerent pout was boyish. I had seen enough to know she wasn't a boy.

"What's to see that I ain't already seen out on the floor?" asked the Beard. "Man to see you. From the Machine."

Ann Foster looked at me quickly. The whites of her eyes had a bluish tinge against her dark skin. "Since when they picking matinee idols for cops?"

"Thanks," I said. "But I've got a job."

We stared at the guy with the beard until he left us, letting the door drift shut behind him. The room had been converted into a community dressing room, but without much conviction. A library table littered with combs and brushes and pots of industrial strength makeup stood before a long mirror, but the bench on this side had come with the place and the air smelled of mildew and old sweat. She said, "Show me you're cop."

I flashed my photostat and honorary sheriff's star. "I'm private. I let Lothar out there think different. It saved time."

"Well, you wasted it all here. I don't like rental heat any more than the other kind. I don't even like men."

"You picked a swell business not to like them in."

She smiled, not unpleasantly. "I work with an all-girl cast."

"Does it pay better than being a maid?"

"About as much. But when I get on my knees it's not to scrub floors."

"Cecelia Wynn," I said.

Her face moved as if I'd slapped her. "What about her?" she barked.

"She's missing. Her husband wants her back. You had a fight with her just before you got fired. What started it?"

"What happens if I don't answer?"

"Nothing. Now. But if it turns out she doesn't want to be missing, the cops get it. I could save you a trip downtown."

She said, "Hell, she's probably off someplace with her lawyer boyfriend, like the last time."

"No, he's accounted for. Also she left almost all her clothes behind, as well as the herbs she spent a small country buying and a lot of time stuffing into capsules. It's starting to look like leaving wasn't her idea, or that where she was going she wouldn't need those things. What was the fight about?"

"I wouldn't do windows."

I slapped her for real. It made a loud flat noise off the echoing walls and she yelled. The door swung open. Beard stuck his face inside. Farther down the magnum glittered. "What?"

I looked at him, looked at the woman. She stroked her burning cheek. My revolver was behind my right hipbone, a thousand miles away. Finally she said, "Nothing."

"Sure?"

She nodded. The man with the beard left his eyes on me a moment longer, then withdrew. The door closed.

"It was weird," she told me. "Serving dinner this one night, I spilled salad oil down the front of my uniform. I went to my room to change. Mrs. Wynn stepped inside to ask for something, just like you walked in on me just now. She caught me naked."

"So?"

"So she excused herself and got out. A half hour later I was fired. For spilling the salad oil. I yelled about it, as who wouldn't? But it wasn't the reason."

"What was?"

She smoothed the kimono across her pelvis. "You think I don't know that look on another woman's face when I see it?"

We talked some more, but none of it was for me. On my way out I laid a twenty on the dressing table and stood a pot of cold cream on top of it. I hesitated, then added one of my cards to the stack. "In case something happens to change your mind about rental heat," I said. "If you lose the card, I'm in the book."

Back in civilization, I gassed up and used the telephone in the service station to call Alec Wynn at his office. I asked him to meet me at his home in Grosse Pointe in twenty minutes.

"I can't," he said. "I'm meeting a client at four."

"He'll keep. If you don't show up, you may be one yourself." We stopped talking to each other.

Both William the chauffeur and the Mercedes were gone from the courtyard, leaving only a puddle on the asphalt to reflect the window-studded facade of the big house. Trina let me in and listened to me and escorted me back to the enclosed porch. When she left I slid open the glass door and stepped outside to the pool area. I was there when Wynn came out five minutes later. His gray suit looked right, even in those surroundings. It always would.

"You've caused me to place an important case in the hands of an apprentice," he announced. "I hope this means you've found Cecelia."

"I've found her. I think."

"What's that supposed to signify? Or is this the famous Walker sense of humor at work?"

"Cut it, Mr. Wynn. We're just two guys talking. How long have you been holding on to your wife's good-bye note, since the first time she walked out?"

"You're babbling."

"It worried me that it wasn't dated," I said. "A thing like that comes in handy too often. Being in corporate law, you might not know that the cops have ways to treat writing in ink with chemicals that can prove within a number of weeks when it was written."

His face was starting to match his suit. I went on.

"Someone else knew you hadn't been able to satisfy Cecelia sexually, or you wouldn't have been so quick to tell me. Masculine pride is a strong motive for murder, and in case something had happened to her, you wanted to be sure you were covered. That's why you hired me, and that's why you dusted off the old note. She didn't leave one this time, did she?"

"You have found her."

I said nothing. Suddenly he was an old man. He shuffled blindly to a marble bench near the pool and sank down onto it. His hands worked on his knees.

"When I didn't hear from her after several days I became frightened," he said. "The servants knew we argued. She'd told Debner of my . . . shortcomings. Before I left criminal law, I saw several convictions obtained on flimsier evidence. Can you understand that I had to protect myself?"

I said, "It wasn't necessary. Debner was just as unsuccessful keeping her happy. Any man would have been. Your wife was a lesbian, Mr. Wynn."

"That's a damn lie!" He started to rise. Halfway up, his knees gave out and he sat back down with a thud.

"Not a practicing one. It's possible she didn't even realize what her problem was until about five weeks ago, when she accidentally saw your former maid naked. The maid is a lesbian and recognized the reaction. Was Cecelia a proud woman?"

"Intensely."

"A lot of smoke gets blown about the male fear of loss of masculinity," I said. "No one gives much thought to women's fears for their femininity. They can drive a woman to fire a servant out of hand, but she would just be removing temptation from her path for the moment. After a time, when the full force of her situation struck home, she might do something more desperate.

"She would be too proud to leave a note."

Wynn had his elbows on his knees and his face in his hands. I peeled cellophane off a fresh pack of Winstons.

"The cops can't really tell when a note was written, Mr. Wynn. I just said that to hear what you'd say."

"Where is she, Walker?"

I watched my reflection in the pool's turquoise-colored surface, squinting against the chlorine fumes. The water was clear enough to see through to the bottom, but there was a recessed area along the north edge with a shelf obscuring it from above, a design flaw that would trap leaves and twigs and other debris that would normally be exposed when the pool was drained. Shadows swirled in the pocket, thick and dark and full of secrets.

WILLIAM CAMPBELL GAULT

APRIL IN PERIL

It was a Sunday morning. Jan was reading the entertainment pages at breakfast, and I was reading the sports pages. She looked up to say, "I see that April Fielding is having her hands imprinted in the cement on Hollywood Boulevard. Wasn't she your second client?"

"I think so."

"Didn't you meet me on your first case?"

"Yes. You have that suspicious look again, madame. We weren't married then."

"But we were lovers."

"Not that week. You were at a decorators' convention in New York with your handsome friend Richard Delmark."

"We went on a plane together, if that's what you mean. But we didn't share a room. And I'm sure you know that Richard is . . . well, not interested in girls."

"The word I have on him is that he's a switch hitter. But, of course, I didn't know him as intimately as you did."

"We were business associates, that's all!"

"Jan," I said firmly, "please don't play the village virgin with me. Let's drop the subject."

"Let's not," she said, and gave me her sunniest smile. "Tell me about it. You know, for auld lang syne?"

I gave her a bowdlerized version of it at the table in placid San Valdesto. It was another country, so to speak, but the wench was not dead. Here is the way it really was:

I was in my second-floor office in Beverly Hills that muggy March morning, trying to balance my checkbook, when this vision walked in. Her hair was short and blonde, her figure medium-height and slim. Her eyes had a hint of green in them; her dress was a dark tan rough linen.

"Mr. Callahan?" she asked.

I stood up and nodded.

"My name is April Fielding," she told me. "Perhaps you've heard of me?"

"Not by name," I said. "But I'm sure I saw you on the tube Tuesday night. What was the name of that show?"

"'Fletcher's Folly,'" she said. "Did you like it?"

I shook my head. "Only you. You deserve better."

"Thank you! May I sit down?"

"Of course."

She sat down and said, "Manny told me that if you have to tell people you're famous you're not. I should have listened. Do you know him—Manny Adler?"

"He's a good friend of mine," I said. "Is he your agent?"

She nodded. "He suggested I go to Joe Puma and I did. Do you know him?"

"Yes. He's a very competent investigator. Did Joe suggest you come to me?"

"No way! He kept coming on to me, and he's not my type. Besides, he's married, isn't he?"

"Not to my knowledge. What is your problem, Miss Fielding?"

"It's kind of complicated," she said.

"Which could mean it's not something you could take to the police."

She frowned. "I don't like the way you said that."

I shrugged.

"But I suppose it's true," she admitted.

I smiled. "Tell me your problem."

She studied me. "Are you expensive?"

"My non-coming-on rate is fifty dollars a day and expenses."

"Manny told me you were cheaper than that."

"I'm sure you meant to say less expensive. Miss Fielding, those are my current rates—if I accept your business. Perhaps you would like to consult with Manny first. You may use my phone."

"I'm having lunch with him," she said. "Will you be in the office this afternoon?"

"Either I or my answering machine. Whatever your problem is, I hope you solve it."

She sighed. She looked around my little pine-paneled office and took a deep breath. Finally, she said, "I suppose I'd better talk with Manny first. He's also my business manager. This is a crazy town, isn't it?"

I nodded.

She left.

When I had finished balancing my checkbook, it was time for lunch. I walked over to Heinie's for that. His lunches were not exactly gourmet, but his draft Einlicher was. I was halfway through a beaker of it when Joe Puma walked in. I waved him over to my booth.

He slid onto the bench across from me and asked, "You buying?"

"A beer. You can buy your own lunch. One of your former clients just left my office. April Fielding."

"That teaser?" he scoffed. "She's flaky!"

"She thought you were married. Are you?"

"Next week," he said. "Our boy is almost five now, and we figured it's time for wedding bells. When are you and Jan going to hitch up?"

"When I get solvent. What's Miss Fielding's problem?"

"Didn't she tell you?"

I shook my head. "She hasn't hired me—yet."

"Then it's privileged information. You know that, Brock."

"Okay. Buy your own beer."

He sighed and slid out of the booth. "Same old chintzy Callahan!" He went to the bar.

He had labeled April a teaser. Horny Joe Puma cherished the chauvinistic fantasy that any woman who smiled in his presence was begging for action. Jan thought he was the handsomest male since Adonis, an opinion I didn't share.

I had another beaker of beer with my corned beef sandwich and went out into the mist, which had now turned into a drizzle. A block from Heinie's it turned into rain. Two blocks from my office it turned into a downpour.

I hung my wet jacket on a hanger in the office, stuffed my shoes with pages from the morning *Times*, and hung my sodden socks over the back of a chair.

The rain had stopped and I was halfway through the crossword puzzle when the door opened for the second time that day. I looked up, expecting April.

It wasn't. It was Al Peregrine, a lanky, swarthy, slimy gent who used to hang around Heinie's until Heinie gave him the word and the bounce. He had been arrested twice for pandering and now called himself a talent scout. Which he was—for stag party porno films.

He smiled at me. I glared at him.

"I hear you had a visitor this morning," he said.

"I may have. What makes it your business?"

"That's why I'm here," he said, "for business. I thought maybe you'd like to pick up a few dollars."

"I couldn't stoop low enough to pick up your kind of dollars, Al."

"You don't look that rich to me," he said. "Puma dumped her. He's smart."

"Is that where you heard about my visitor, from Puma?"

He shook his head. He asked, "Could you stoop low enough to pick up a grand?"

"Nope. In ten seconds, though, I'm picking up the phone and calling the law."

"No kidding? What would you tell 'em?"

"I can dream up something. And whose word do you think they'd believe?"

He stared at me doubtfully. I reached for the phone. He left.

I had the crossword puzzle finished when Manny Adler phoned. April, he explained, had forgotten she had an appointment at MGM this afternoon, and that's why she hadn't come to the office. "I know that Jan is out of town," he said, "and Sarah thought maybe you'd like to have dinner with us tonight. Then you and I can talk."

"I'll be there. What time?"

"Around seven?"

"Fine."

It was now 3:30. The prospect of another potential client paying me a visit today was remote. April had been my first in a week. I went home to my little Westwood pad and took a long, hot shower.

Stag party films and a rising starlet; the connection was obvious. Peregrine thought he had something to sell. So many of those young hopefuls who come to tinsel town wind up working in drive-ins, massage parlors, or stag party films.

But why Joe Puma? Manny and I were friends. He had been an ardent Rams fan in my playing days.

The rain had moved south and the night was clear when I drove to the Adler's old two-story house near the Brentwood Country Club.

Sarah opened the door to my ring. "It's been a long time, you Irish bastard," she said, and hugged me.

My arms were almost long enough to hug her in return. Sarah was a lot of woman. "I apologize. I haven't seen Manny at Heinie's lately."

"He hasn't been well," she said. "Reuben really runs the office these days."

Reuben was their only son. They had three daughters, all safely married.

I've forgotten what we ate for dinner, but it had to be good. The Adlers had a housekeeper, but Sarah did the cooking.

We talked about this and that at dinner, small talk, with no mention of Al Peregrine or April Fielding. Before Manny and I went to his study, Sarah gave me her standard lecture on the imminent necessity of marrying Jan before some wiser and better man beat me to the punch.

She had told me that Manny was not well. He looked worse than that; he looked *sick*. His face was sunken, his eyes dull, his step faltering.

Which I mentioned in his study.

"I don't want to talk about it," he said. "If I get weaker, I'll see a doctor. It's probably just old age, Brock."

I didn't press him; Manny shared my cynical view of doctors. I said, "Al Peregrine paid me a visit this afternoon. What is it, blackmail?"

He nodded.

"Some stag films he's trying to sell you?"

"Yes."

"And you suggested Puma. Why?"

"Because he carries a gun. You don't."

"I have one. I rarely carry it. A fly swatter should be weapon enough for Al Peregrine."

He shook his head. "Not anymore. He's working with Dutch Kronen now. Dutch is looking for seed money. He's taken over the old Art Cinema studio on Ivar Street. He wants to expand."

"Dutch is heavy," I admitted. "Why don't you pay him off?"

"We paid him five thousand dollars for the first can. We thought that was the end of it. Now he has found some others and he wants more." He took a deep breath. "You can imagine what that would do to April's future, with the industry as scared as it is today."

"How much more does he want?"

"More than we can afford. But that's not my major worry. Dutch sent a couple of his punks to harass April. One of them was high. Lucky for her, a prowl car was going by at the time and it scared them off." He paused. "She lives in Santa Monica. I thought, well, maybe you could move in with her for a couple of days until we can work out a deal we can afford."

"She works days. You meant nights, I suppose."

"Both," he said.

"Okay. But please don't tell Sarah. It could get back to Jan."

"There is very little that I tell Sarah," he told me. "Which is why we have been happily married for fifty years."

He phoned April before I left to clear it with her. He gave me five twenty-dollar bills as a retainer, and I went home for some clothes and my trusty Colt .38 caliber Police Special, vintage unknown.

The ancient stucco cottage that housed the lovely April Fielding was on a side street in Santa Monica, two blocks from Wilshire Boulevard and about five blocks from the ocean.

The front door opened directly into the living room. She was wearing a long black velveteen robe and a towel around her hair. Her face was devoid of makeup now, but just as beautiful.

"We meet again," she said. "Come in."

The furniture was mostly discount house maple, the open studio bed upholstered in a tan plastic.

She closed the door and said, "There's only the one bedroom. I hope that couch is long enough for you."

"It'll do. Any new threats I don't know about?"

She shook her head. "Would you like a drink of something?"

"Cocoa, if you have it. I usually drink a cup of it before I go to bed, and it's almost that time."

"I have it," she said. "I like it, too."

We drank it together in our separate maple chairs, and she told me her sad story, the innocent from Milwaukee who had come to lotusland. I had heard it too often before, but this was the first time from Milwaukee. The plot was as full of clichés as a TV script: clerking at The May Company, working in the amateur theaters at night, and then the meeting with Al Peregrine.

"That's enough." I stopped her. "I don't want to hear about him. I have a weak stomach. Just remember that Manny Adler does not ever handle any beginners unless they have one hell of a talent. Let's think about now and from now on."

She nodded. "I'm trying to. I'm glad you're here, Brock Callahan. Why didn't Manny suggest you first?"

"Because Puma carries a gun and I usually don't."

She made a face. "Macho Joe! He really thinks he's God's gift to women, doesn't he?"

I shrugged. "You'll have to admit he's handsome."

She shook her head. "Not to me. He doesn't hold a candle to you!"

"Lady," I told her, "you've got it all, talent and beauty and discernment. And now, if you don't mind, I'll hit the hay. Who's first in the bathroom?"

"It's all yours," she said. "I've had my bath and washed my hair. What would you like for breakfast?"

Just you across the table from me, I thought. I said, "I'll have whatever you have. I don't want to be a bother."

"You're no bother," she said. "You're a comfort."

I dreamed of Jan that night, and somewhere in the dream the handsome face of her New York companion, Richard Delmark, appeared. But I forget now what they were doing.

We ate breakfast in the breakfast nook that served as a dining room. It was an exceptionally small cottage. We had bacon and scrambled eggs and toasted English muffins.

"That," I told her, "was one fine breakfast, Miss Milwaukee. Where do we go today, MGM, Paramount, Columbia Pictures?"

She shook her head. "Manny's still dickering with that producer at Metro. The sun is out. Why don't we go to the beach?"

"I didn't bring my swimming trunks."

"You don't need any. Can't we just walk barefoot through the shallow water? I could pack a lunch."

"Don't bother. We'll have hot dogs on me. Your car or mine?"

"Let's walk," she suggested. "It's only a few blocks."

We walked to the beach and along the beach to Muscle Beach in Venice and back. We had hot dogs in the shade of the beach umbrella she had brought, and potato chips and a pair of double-dip chocolate ice cream cones and later two Cokes.

She told me about her mother, who had died when she was fourteen, and her father and brother, who both worked at the Miller Brewery. She told me about her one year at the University of Wisconsin, where she had planned to study drama but had decided Hollywood might be a better place for that.

"Why not New York?" I asked. "Why not the stage?"

She shook her head. "I'm not that good."

"Like hell you aren't! If you weren't, Manny never would have handled you. Don't be too modest."

"I'm not. Tell me about you."

I told her about my young days in Long Beach, about Stanford and the Rams, and my policeman father, who had been killed by a hoodlum.

"Is that," she asked, "why you're doing . . . what you're doing? Couldn't you have been a coach or a sports announcer or something like that after you left the Rams?"

I shrugged.

"I know what you are," she said. "You are a militant moralist." She smiled. "You hate the bad guys, don't you?"

"Not all of them. April, I am what I am. Maybe we'd better get back to the house. Manny might have phoned."

There was no message on her answering machine. I was bushed from the sun and the walk. I took a nap when we came home. She wrote a letter to her father and another to her married brother.

Manny phoned at 5:30 to tell her they had an appointment at MGM the following morning for contract signing.

"Which means," she said, "that I can now afford to buy your dinner. You bought our lunch."

"And then we'll go to a movie on me," I said. "There's a great one at the Westwood Theatre."

"What's the name of it?" she asked.

"I don't know. But John Wayne is in it."

"My kind of man," she agreed. "I like to see the bad guys get it where it hurts."

Long Beach and Milwaukee are distant only geographically. We were kindred souls.

We had home cooking at Bess Eiler's and made the first show at the Westwood. Big John took care of every bad guy, each in his own time, and went riding off into the western sunset. We had chocolate cake with ice cream at The Chatam to top off an all-around great day.

We were about half a block from her house when she said hoarsely, "That's them. That's their car. That's the same one they were driving that night."

I pulled over to the curb and stopped. About three houses past hers, a chopped and channeled black Ford coupe was parked. "The punks?" I asked.

"Yes."

I turned off the lights. "They're not in the car. They could be in the house. Stay here and keep the doors locked. I'll go take a look."

"Wouldn't it be wiser to call the police?"

"For punks? Would John Wayne call the police?"

"That's not funny," she said. "One of them had a knife."

I took out my .38. "And I have this. Stay in the car."

"Brock—!"

"Stay here," I repeated.

The moon was out and the night bright. I walked across the lawns of the houses this side of hers and into her side lot. I peered in the side window and saw two blobs in the maple chairs.

I crouched low and walked quietly to her small front porch and tried the knob gently. The door was locked; they must have come in through a window or possibly picked the lock and locked it again once they were inside.

The living room light switch was next to the door, and it was an old and fragile door. I stepped back and crashed my right foot into it just below the knob.

They were halfway out of their chairs when I snapped on the light, two pale youths in chinos and T-shirts, both sporting flattop haircuts.

"On the floor, belly down and arms outstretched," I told them. "*Move!*"

They looked at the .38 and at each other.

"Damn you, move!"

They did as requested. I picked up the phone on the table

next to the couch and called the Santa Monica Police Department.

April came in with the prowl officers. One was young and sinewy, the other stout and middle-aged.

The young one went over to cuff the punks. The stout one studied me. "Aren't you Brock Callahan? Didn't you play with the Rams?"

I nodded.

He looked at April. "And you're Mrs. Callahan?"

"Not yet," she said. Her chin lifted. "My name is April Fielding."

He took out his ballpoint pen. "How is that last name spelled?"

She sighed and spelled it out for him. The two youths were standing now, cuffed to each other.

We would have to appear in court, they told us before they left; we would be notified. And the stout one told me quietly, "You'd better marry her soon, Brock. She won't be on the market long."

They left. I went to get my car and park it in her driveway. When I came into the house, she said acidly, "How is that last name spelled!"

"They have to get it straight for the record," I explained, and added what the older man had told me.

"But he knew *you!*"

"Someday, April," I assured her, "people all over the world will know you and not even football fans will remember me. Are you too stuffed for cocoa?"

She nodded.

"So am I. Let's see what's on the eleven o'clock news and then hit the sack."

Which we did, she in her bedroom, me on the studio couch. I couldn't get to sleep. I tried to convince myself that it was because of my afternoon nap, but I knew that was a lie.

I was still awake when she came into the moonlit living room and slid in next to me. "I'm scared," she said. "Hold me tight."

Over waffles and small pork sausages in the breakfast nook she averted her eyes every time I looked at her.

"What's wrong?" I asked.

"I'm embarrassed. You must think I'm a tramp."

"No way. I think you are a lovely, talented, and wonderful woman."

"I'll bet! For your information, footballer, it was purely therapeutic."

"I know."

"And for your further information, I was never in the . . . the action scenes in those awful movies. They used a double for that, a professional."

"They often do," I said. "Don't spoil our night, April."

She stared at me for seconds, and then she smiled. "Do you really think I'll be famous someday?"

"I'd make book on it," I said. "When are we due at MGM?"

"We have time. Do you think those two kids will tell the police they were working for Dutch Kronen?"

"Not if they want to live."

"Poor Manny!" she said. "He's been so loyal!" She paused. "You know he has leukemia, don't you?"

"Hell, no! I noticed he looked sick, and Sarah told me he wasn't well. How does he know he has it? He told me two nights ago that he hadn't seen a doctor."

"He lied. And he tells Sarah nothing that might trouble her. He's her buffer in this crazy world out here."

Never complain and never explain, that was Manny Adler, a fortress of integrity in wasteland west.

The guard at the gate at MGM smiled at April and waved us through.

"He knew you," I said. "You're big in Culver City."

"Shut up, smartass. What do you plan to do while Manny argues terms with the producer? It could be a while."

"I'll sit and wait. That's what I get paid for. Maybe I'll see Lana Turner."

I sat in the car in the parking lot. Manny's Rolls rumbled in about two minutes later and parked at the far end. I was going to get out and intercept him—until I saw he was talking to somebody down there. It was a lanky, swarthy man who looked like Al Peregrine from where I stood. I got back into the car and slumped low in the seat.

About five minutes later a gray Chevrolet went by with Al at the wheel. There was no way the creep could have got past the guard without an okay from within. Was the fortress crumbling? Not Manny, no, never!

I turned on the radio to a Dixieland station and sat and wished I hadn't given up smoking.

April came out shortly before noon. "We won," she said. "Lunch is on me. Or would you rather go to the beach?"

"The beach," I said. "I don't like the climate around here." I hesitated before telling her about Manny's meeting with Peregrine.

"He told me," she said. "I guess he dickered for a price we can pay. He said it should all be cleared up by tonight."

"I can't believe Manny would trust those two to honor an agreement," I said.

She smiled. "If they don't, we always have you. Let's get to the beach for our last romp in the sun. Will you miss me, footballer?"

"I'll remember you until the day I die, lady. Move!"

It was all right. It wasn't like yesterday and nothing close to last night, but it was all right. We splashed and laughed and switched to hamburgers and milk shakes for a change.

We came home around five o'clock. "If Manny calls early

enough," she said, "maybe you can sleep in your own bed tonight."

"I am not Joe Puma, ma'am."

"I wasn't worried about you," she said. "I was worried about me. You're a lot of man, Callahan."

"With a semi-steady girlfriend who earns a hell of a lot more than I do. But she's in New York with another fella."

"She's a damned fool!"

"And I'm a dumb and stubborn jock. Do you play gin rummy?"

"Very well," she assured me. "I'll get the cards."

Three dollars and twelve cents into the red later, I asked, "Are we going to eat out tonight?"

"Manny might call," she said, "and I want to hear the good news firsthand. Why don't I make us some sandwiches?"

Manny phoned a little before nine. The deal had been made. She no longer needed my protection.

"You can stay over if you want," she said. "I promise to be good."

I shook my head. "I'd better get home, where I can sulk. Do we kiss good-bye?"

She nodded. I kissed her. "I'll miss you," she said.

"Thank you. It's mutual. Good night, star."

Back to the pad, back to the humdrum. My apartment smelled musty. I opened a couple of windows and took a bottle of Einlicher out of my midget fridge. I drank it. I dozed. It was close to eleven o'clock when I came back to the here and now.

I turned on the boob tube and caught the opening story. Al Peregrine and Dutch Kronen had been found dead in the studio of Mr. Kronen's converted Art Cinema building on Ivar Street. There was evidence of ransacking, but the police did not believe that robbery was the motive. It was their current view that the local mob had finally resented Dutch's entry into the porno field they planned to dominate.

They picked up a few suspects in the following week but eventually put the case into their permanent unsolved crime file. It wasn't likely that the death of either creep would be bad news to the Los Angeles Police Department.

Manny died three days after the double murder. He is now residing at Forest Lawn next to his beloved Sarah. The police can burn their file. Manny had done as he had promised, he had finally got a deal he and April could afford.

SUE GRAFTON

THE PARKER SHOTGUN

The Christmas holidays had come and gone, and the new year was underway. January, in California, is as good as it gets—cool, clear, and green, with a sky the color of wisteria and a surf that thunders like a volley of gunfire in a distant field. My name is Kinsey Millhone. I'm a private investigator, licensed, bonded, insured; white, female, age thirty-two, unmarried, and physically fit. That Monday morning, I was sitting in my office with my feet up, wondering what life would bring, when a woman walked in and tossed a photograph on my desk. My introduction to the Parker shotgun began with a graphic view of its apparent effect when fired at a formerly nice-looking man at close range. His face was still largely intact, but he had no use now for a pocket comb. With effort, I kept my expression neutral as I glanced up at her.

"Somebody killed my husband."

"I can see that," I said.

She snatched the picture back and stared at it as though she might have missed some telling detail. Her face suffused with pink, and she blinked back tears. "Jesus. Rudd was killed five months ago, and the cops have done shit. I'm so sick of getting the runaround I could scream."

She sat down abruptly and pressed a hand to her mouth, trying to compose herself. She was in her late twenties, with a gaudy prettiness. Her hair was an odd shade of brown, like cherry Coke, worn shoulder length and straight. Her eyes were large, a lush mink brown; her mouth was full. Her complexion was all warm tones, tanned, and clear. She didn't seem to be wearing makeup, but she was still as vivid as a magazine illustration, a good four-color run on slick paper. She was seven months pregnant by the look of her; not voluminous yet, but rotund. When she was calmer, she identified herself as Lisa Osterling.

"That's a crime lab photo. How'd you come by it?" I said when the preliminaries were disposed of.

She fumbled in her handbag for a tissue and blew her nose. "I have my little ways," she said morosely. "Actually I know the photographer and I stole a print. I'm going to have it blown up and hung on the wall just so I won't forget. The police are hoping I'll drop the whole thing, but I got news for *them*." Her mouth was starting to tremble again, and a tear splashed onto her skirt as though my ceiling had a leak.

"What's the story?" I said. "The cops in this town are usually pretty good." I got up and filled a paper cup with water from my Sparklett's dispenser, passing it over to her. She murmured a thank you and drank it down, staring into the bottom of the cup as she spoke. "Rudd was a cocaine dealer until a month or so before he died. They haven't said as much, but I know they've written him off as some kind of small-time punk. What do they care? They'd like to think he was killed in a drug deal—a double cross or something like that. He wasn't, though. He'd given it all up because of this."

She glanced down at the swell of her belly. She was wearing a kelly green T-shirt with an arrow down the front. The word "Oops!" was written across her breasts in machine embroidery.

"What's your theory?" I asked. Already I was leaning toward the official police version of events. Drug dealing isn't synonymous with longevity. There's too much money involved and too many amateurs getting into the act. This was Santa Teresa—ninety-five miles north of the big time in L.A., but there are still standards to maintain. A shotgun blast is the underworld equivalent of a bad annual review.

"I don't have a theory. I just don't like theirs. I want you to look into it so I can clear Rudd's name before the baby comes."

I shrugged. "I'll do what I can, but I can't guarantee the results. How are you going to feel if the cops are right?"

She stood up, giving me a flat look. "I don't know why Rudd died, but it had nothing to do with drugs," she said. She opened her handbag and extracted a roll of bills the size of a wad of socks. "What do you charge?"

"Thirty bucks an hour plus expenses."

She peeled off several hundred-dollar bills and laid them on the desk.

I got out a contract.

My second encounter with the Parker shotgun came in the form of a dealer's appraisal slip that I discovered when I was nosing through Rudd Osterling's private possessions an hour later at the house. The address she'd given me was on the Bluffs, a residential area on the west side of town, overlooking the Pacific. It should have been an elegant neighborhood, but the ocean generated too much fog and too much corrosive salt air. The houses were small and had a temporary feel to them, as though the occupants intended to move on when the month was up. No one seemed to get around to painting the trim, and the yards looked like they were kept by people who spent all day at the beach. I followed her in my car, reviewing the information she'd given me as I urged my ancient VW up Capilla Hill and took a right on Presipio.

The late Rudd Osterling had been in Santa Teresa since the sixties, when he migrated to the West Coast in search of sunshine, good surf, good dope, and casual sex. Lisa told me he'd lived in vans and communes, working variously as a roofer, tree trimmer, bean picker, fry cook, and forklift operator—never with any noticeable ambition or success. He'd started dealing cocaine two years earlier, apparently netting more money than he was accustomed to. Then he'd met and married Lisa, and she'd been determined to see him clean up his act. According to her, he'd retired from the drug trade and was just in the process of setting himself up in a landscape maintenance business when someone blew the top of his head off.

I pulled into the driveway behind her, glancing at the frame and stucco bungalow with its patchy grass and dilapidated fence. It looked like one of those households where there's always something under construction, probably without permits and not up to code. In this case, a foundation had been laid for an addition to the garage, but the weeds were already growing up through cracks in the concrete. A wooden outbuilding had been dismantled, the old lumber tossed in an unsightly pile. Closer to the house, there were stacks of cheap pecan wood paneling, sunbleached in places and warped along one edge. It was all hapless and depressing, but she scarcely looked at it.

I followed her into the house.

"We were just getting the house fixed up when he died," she remarked.

"When did you buy the place?" I was manufacturing small talk, trying to cover my distaste at the sight of the old linoleum counter, where a line of ants stretched from a crust of toast and jelly all the way out the back door.

"We didn't really. This was my mother's. She and my stepdad moved back to the Midwest last year."

"What about Rudd? Did he have any family out here?"

"They're all in Connecticut, I think, real la-di-dah. His parents are dead, and his sisters wouldn't even come out to the funeral."

"Did he have a lot of friends?"

"All cocaine dealers have friends."

"Enemies?"

"Not that I ever heard about."

"Who was his supplier?"

"I don't know that."

"No disputes? Suits pending? Quarrels with the neighbors? Family arguments about the inheritance?"

She gave me a "no" on all four counts.

I had told her I wanted to go through his personal belongings, so she showed me into the tiny back bedroom, where he'd set up a card table and some cardboard file boxes. A real entrepreneur. I began to search while she leaned against the doorframe, watching.

I said, "Tell me about what was going on the week he died." I was sorting through canceled checks in a Nike shoe box. Most were written to the neighborhood supermarket, utilities, telephone company.

She moved to the desk chair and sat down. "I can't tell you much because I was at work. I do alterations and repairs at a dry cleaner's up at Presipio Mall. Rudd would stop in now and then when he was out running around. He'd picked up a few jobs already, but he really wasn't doing the gardening full time. He was trying to get all his old business squared away. Some kid owed him money. I remember that."

"He sold cocaine on *credit*?"

She shrugged. "Maybe it was grass or pills. Somehow the kid owed him a bundle. That's all I know."

"I don't suppose he kept any records."

"Nuh-uh. It was all in his head. He was too paranoid to put anything down in black and white."

The file boxes were jammed with old letters, tax returns, receipts. It all looked like junk to me.

"What about the day he was killed? Were you at work then?"

She shook her head. "It was a Saturday. I was off work, but I'd gone to the market. I was out maybe an hour and a half, and when I got home, police cars were parked in front, and the paramedics were here. Neighbors were standing out on the street." She stopped talking, and I was left to imagine the rest.

"Had he been expecting anyone?"

"If he was, he never said anything to me. He was in the garage, doing I don't know what. Chauncy, next door, heard the shotgun go off, but by the time he got here to investigate, whoever did it was gone."

I got up and moved toward the hallway. "Is this the bedroom down here?"

"Right. I haven't gotten rid of his stuff yet. I guess I'll have to eventually. I'm going to use his office for the nursery."

I moved into the master bedroom and went through his hanging clothes. "Did the police find anything?"

"They didn't look. Well, one guy came through and poked around some. About five minutes' worth."

I began to check through the drawers she indicated were his. Nothing remarkable came to light. On top of the chest was one of those brass and walnut caddies, where Rudd apparently kept his watch, keys, loose change. Almost idly, I picked it up. Under it there was a folded slip of paper. It was a partially completed appraisal form from a gun shop out in Colgate, a township to the north of us. "What's a Parker?" I said when I'd glanced at it. She peered over the slip.

"Oh. That's probably the appraisal on the shotgun he got."

"The one he was killed with?"

"Well, I don't know. They never found the weapon, but the homicide detective said they couldn't run it through ballistics, anyway—or whatever it is they do."

"Why'd he have it appraised in the first place?"

"He was taking it in trade for a big drug debt, and he needed to know if it was worth it."

"Was this the kid you mentioned before or someone else?"

"The same one, I think. At first, Rudd intended to turn around and sell the gun, but then he found out it was a collector's item so he decided to keep it. The gun dealer called a couple of times after Rudd died, but it was gone by then."

"And you told the cops all this stuff?"

"Sure. They couldn't have cared less."

I doubted that, but I tucked the slip in my pocket anyway. I'd check it out and then talk to Dolan in homicide.

The gun shop was located on a narrow side street in Colgate, just off the main thoroughfare. Colgate looks like it's made up of hardware stores, U-haul rentals, and plant nurseries; places that seem to have half their merchandise outside, surrounded by chain link fence. The gun shop had been set up in someone's front parlor in a dinky white frame house. There were some glass counters filled with gun paraphernalia, but no guns in sight.

The man who came out of the back room was in his fifties, with a narrow face and graying hair, gray eyes made luminous by rimless glasses. He wore a dress shirt with the sleeves rolled up and a long gray apron tied around his waist. He had perfect teeth, but when he talked I could see the rim of pink where his upper plate was fit, and it spoiled the effect. Still, I had to give him credit for a certain level of good looks, maybe a seven on a scale of ten. Not bad for a man his age. "Yes ma'am," he said. He had a trace of an accent, Virginia, I thought.

"Are you Avery Lamb?"

"That's right. What can I help you with?"

"I'm not sure. I'm wondering what you can tell me about this appraisal you did." I handed him the slip.

He glanced down and then looked up at me. "Where did you get this?"

"Rudd Osterling's widow," I said.

"She told me she didn't have the gun."

"That's right."

His manner was a combination of confusion and wariness. "What's your connection to the matter?"

I took out a business card and gave it to him. "She hired me to look into Rudd's death. I thought the shotgun might be relevant since he was killed with one."

He shook his head. "I don't know what's going on. This is the second time it's disappeared."

"Meaning what?"

"Some woman brought it in to have it appraised back in June. I made an offer on it then, but before we could work out a deal, she claimed the gun was stolen."

"I take it you had some doubts about that."

"Sure I did. I don't think she ever filed a police report, and I suspect she knew damn well who took it but didn't intend to pursue it. Next thing I knew, this Osterling fellow brought the same gun in. It had a beavertail fore-end and an English grip. There was no mistaking it."

"Wasn't that a bit of a coincidence? His bringing the gun in to you?

"Not really. I'm one of the few master gunsmiths in this area. All he had to do was ask around the same way she did."

"Did you tell her the gun had showed up?"

He shrugged with his mouth and a lift of his brows. "Before I could talk to her, he was dead and the Parker was gone again."

I checked the date on the slip. "That was in August?"

"That's right, and I haven't seen the gun since."

"Did he tell you how he acquired it?"

"Said he took it in trade. I told him this other woman showed up with it first, but he didn't seem to care about that."

"How much was the Parker worth?"

He hesitated, weighing his words. "I offered him six thousand."

"But what's its value out in the marketplace?"

"Depends on what people are willing to pay."

I tried to control the little surge of impatience he had sparked. I could tell he'd jumped into his crafty negotiator's mode, unwilling to tip his hand in case the gun showed up and he could nick it off cheap. "Look," I said, "I'm asking you in confidence. This won't go any further unless it becomes a police matter, and then neither one of us will have a choice. Right now, the gun's missing anyway, so what difference does it make?"

He didn't seem entirely convinced, but he got my point. He cleared his throat with obvious embarrassment. "Ninety-six."

I stared at him. "Thousand dollars?"

He nodded.

"Jesus. That's a lot for a gun, isn't it?"

His voice dropped. "Ms. Millhone, that gun is priceless. It's an A-1 Special 28-gauge with a two-barrel set. There were only two of them made."

"But why so much?"

"For one thing, the Parker's a beautifully crafted shotgun. There are different grades, of course, but this one was exceptional. Fine wood. Some of the most incredible scroll-work you'll ever see. Parker had an Italian working for him back then who'd spend sometimes five thousand hours on the engraving alone. The company went out of business around 1942, so there aren't any more to be had."

"You said there were two. Where's the other one, or would you know?"

"Only what I've heard. A dealer in Ohio bought the one at auction a couple years back for ninety-six. I understand some fella down in Texas has it now, part of a collection of Parkers. The gun Rudd Osterling brought in has been missing for years. I don't think he knew what he had on his hands."

"And you didn't tell him."

Lamb shifted his gaze. "I told him enough," he said carefully. "I can't help it if the man didn't do his homework."

"How'd you know it was the missing Parker?"

"The serial number matched, and so did everything else. It wasn't a fake, either. I examined the gun under heavy magnification, checking for fill-in welds and traces of markings that might have been overstamped. After I checked it out, I showed it to a buddy of mine, a big gun buff, and he recognized it, too."

"Who else knew about it besides you and this friend?"

"Whoever Rudd Osterling got it from, I guess."

"I'll want the woman's name and address if you've still got it. Maybe she knows how the gun fell into Rudd's hands."

Again he hesitated for a moment, and then he shrugged. "I don't see why not." He made a note on a piece of scratch paper and pushed it across the counter to me. "I'd like to know if the gun shows up," he said.

"Sure, as long as Mrs. Osterling doesn't object."

I didn't have any other questions for the moment. I moved toward the door, then glanced back at him. "How could Rudd have sold the gun if it was stolen property? Wouldn't he have needed a bill of sale for it? Some proof of ownership?"

Avery Lamb's face was devoid of expression. "Not necessarily. If an avid collector got hold of that gun, it would sink out of sight, and that's the last you'd ever see of it. He'd keep it in his basement and never show it to a soul. It'd be enough if he knew he had it. You don't need a bill of sale for that."

I sat out in my car and made some notes while the information was fresh. Then I checked the address Lamb had given me, and I could feel the adrenaline stir. It was right back in Rudd's neighborhood.

The woman's name was Jackie Barnett. The address was two streets over from the Osterling house and just about parallel; a big corner lot planted with avocado trees and bracketed with palms. The house itself was yellow stucco with flaking brown shutters and a yard that needed mowing. The mailbox read "Squires," but the house number seemed to match. There was a basketball hoop nailed up above the two-car garage and a dismantled motorcycle in the driveway.

I parked my car and got out. As I approached the house, I saw an old man in a wheelchair planted in the side yard like a lawn ornament. He was parchment pale, with baby-fine white hair and rheumy eyes. The left half of his face had been disconnected by a stroke, and his left arm and hand rested uselessly in his lap. I caught sight of a woman peering through the window, apparently drawn by the sound of my car door slamming shut. I crossed the yard, moving toward the front porch. She opened the door before I had a chance to knock.

"You must be Kinsey Millhone. I just got off the phone with Avery. He said you'd be stopping by."

"That was quick. I didn't realize he'd be calling ahead. Saves me an explanation. I take it you're Jackie Barnett."

"That's right. Come in if you like. I just have to check on him," she said, indicating the man in the yard.

"Your father?"

She shot me a look. "Husband," she said. I watched her

cross the grass toward the old man, grateful for a chance to recover from my gaffe. I could see now that she was older than she'd first appeared. She must have been in her fifties—at that stage where women wear too much makeup and dye their hair too bold a shade of blonde. She was buxom, clearly overweight, but lush. In a seventeenth-century painting, she'd have been depicted supine, her plump naked body draped in sheer white. Standing over her, something with a goat's rear end would be poised for assault. Both would look coy but excited at the prospects. The old man was beyond the pleasures of the flesh, yet the noises he made—garbled and indistinguishable because of the stroke—had the same intimate quality as sounds uttered in the throes of passion, a disquieting effect.

I looked away from him, thinking of Avery Lamb instead. He hadn't actually told me the woman was a stranger to him, but he'd certainly implied as much. I wondered now what their relationship consisted of.

Jackie spoke to the old man briefly, adjusting his lap robe. Then she came back and we went inside.

"Is your name Barnett or Squires?" I asked.

"Technically it's Squires, but I still use Barnett for the most part," she said. She seemed angry, and I thought at first the rage was directed at me. She caught my look. "I'm sorry," she said, "but I've about had it with him. Have you ever dealt with a stroke victim?"

"I understand it's difficult."

"It's impossible! I know I sound hard-hearted, but he was always short-tempered and now he's frustrated on top of that. Self-centered, demanding. Nothing suits him. Nothing. I put him out in the yard sometimes just so I won't have to fool with him. Have a seat, hon."

I sat. "How long has he been sick?"

"He had the first stroke in June. He's been in and out of the hospital ever since."

"What's the story on the gun you took out to Avery's shop?"

"Oh, that's right. He said you were looking into some fellow's death. He lived right here on the Bluffs, too, didn't he?"

"Over on Whitmore . . ."

"That was terrible. I read about it in the papers, but I never did hear the end of it. What went on?"

"I wasn't given the details," I said briefly. "Actually, I'm trying to track down a shotgun that belonged to him. Avery Lamb says it was the same gun you brought in."

She had automatically proceeded to get out two cups and saucers, so her answer was delayed until she'd poured coffee for us both. She passed a cup over to me, and then she sat down, stirring milk into hers. She glanced at me self-consciously. "I just took that gun to spite *him*," she said with a nod toward the yard. "I've been married to Bill for six years and miserable for every one of them. It was my own damn fault. I'd been divorced for ages and I was doing fine, but somehow when I hit fifty, I got in a panic. Afraid of growing old alone, I guess. I ran into Bill, and he looked like a catch. He was retired, but he had loads of money, or so he said. He promised me the moon. Said we'd travel. Said he'd buy me clothes and a car and I don't know what all. Turns out he's a penny-pinching miser with a mean mouth and a quick fist. At least he can't do that anymore." She paused to shake her head, staring down at her coffee cup.

"The gun was his?"

"Well, yes, it was. He has a collection of shotguns. I swear he took better care of them than he did of me. I just despise guns. I was always after him to get rid of them. Makes me nervous to have them in the house. Anyway, when he got sick, it turned out he had insurance, but it only paid eighty percent. I was afraid his whole life savings would go up in smoke. I figured he'd go on for years, using up all the money, and then I'd be stuck with his debts when he died. So I just picked up one of the guns and took it out to that gun place to sell. I was going to buy me some clothes."

"What made you change your mind?"

"Well, I didn't think it'd be worth but eight or nine hundred dollars. Then Avery said he'd give me six thousand for it, so I had to guess it was worth at least twice that. I got nervous and thought I better put it back."

"How soon after that did the gun disappear?"

"Oh, gee, I don't know. I didn't pay much attention until Bill got out of the hospital the second time. He's the one who noticed it was gone," she said. "Of course, he raised pluperfect hell. You should have seen him. He had a conniption fit for two days, and then he had another stroke and had to be hospitalized all over again. Served him right if you ask me. At least I had Labor Day weekend to myself. I needed it."

"Do you have any idea who might have taken the gun?"

She gave me a long, candid look. Her eyes were very blue and couldn't have appeared more guileless. "Not the faintest."

I let her practice her wide-eyed stare for a moment, and then I laid out a little bait just to see what she'd do. "God, that's too bad," I said. "I'm assuming you reported it to the police."

I could see her debate briefly before she replied. Yes or no. Check one. "Well, of course," she said.

She was one of those liars who blush from lack of practice.

I kept my tone of voice mild. "What about the insurance? Did you put in a claim?"

She looked at me blankly, and I had the feeling I'd taken her by surprise on that one. She said, "You know, it never even occurred to me. But of course he probably would have it insured, wouldn't he?"

"Sure, if the gun's worth that much. What company is he with?"

"I don't remember offhand. I'd have to look it up."

"I'd do that if I were you," I said. "You can file a claim, and then all you have to do is give the agent the case number."

"Case number?"

"The police will give you that from their report."

She stirred restlessly, glancing at her watch. "Oh, lordy, I'm going to have to give him his medicine. Was there anything else you wanted to ask while you were here?" Now that she'd told me a fib or two, she was anxious to get rid of me so she could assess the situation. Avery Lamb had told me she'd never reported it to the cops. I wondered if she'd call him up now to compare notes.

"Could I take a quick look at his collection?" I said, getting up.

"I suppose that'd be all right. It's in here," she said. She moved toward a small paneled den, and I followed, stepping around a suitcase near the door.

A rack of six guns was enclosed in a glass-fronted cabinet. All of them were beautifully engraved, with fine wood stocks, and I wondered how a priceless Parker could really be distinguished. Both the cabinet and the rack were locked, and there were no empty slots. "Did he keep the Parker in here?"

She shook her head. "The Parker had its own case." She hauled out a handsome wood case from behind the couch and opened it for me, demonstrating its emptiness as though she might be setting up a magic trick. Actually, there was a set of barrels in the box, but nothing else.

I glanced around. There was a shotgun propped in one corner, and I picked it up, checking the manufacturer's imprint on the frame. L. C. Smith. Too bad. For a moment I'd thought it might be the missing Parker. I'm always hoping for the obvious. I set the Smith back in the corner with regret.

"Well, I guess that'll do," I said. "Thanks for the coffee."

"No trouble. I wish I could be more help." She started easing me toward the door.

I held out my hand. "Nice meeting you," I said. "Thanks again for your time."

She gave my hand a perfunctory shake. "That's all right. Sorry I'm in such a rush, but you know how it is when you have someone sick."

Next thing I knew, the door was closing at my back and I was heading toward my car, wondering what she was up to.

I'd just reached the driveway when a white Corvette came roaring down the street and rumbled into the drive. The kid at the wheel flipped the ignition key and cantilevered himself up onto the seat top. "Hi. You know if my mom's here?"

"Who, Jackie? Sure," I said, taking a flyer. "You must be Doug."

He looked puzzled. "No, Eric. Do I know you?"

I shook my head. "I'm just a friend passing through."

He hopped out of the Corvette. I moved on toward my car, keeping an eye on him as he headed toward the house. He looked about seventeen, blond, blue-eyed, with good cheekbones, a moody, sensual mouth, lean surfer's body. I pictured him in a few years, hanging out in resort hotels, picking up women three times his age. He'd do well. So would they.

Jackie had apparently heard him pull in, and she came out onto the porch, intercepting him with a quick look at me. She put her arm through his, and the two moved into the house. I looked over at the old man. He was making noises again, plucking aimlessly at his bad hand with his good one. I felt a mental jolt, like an interior tremor shifting the ground under me. I was beginning to get it.

*   *   *

I drove the two blocks to Lisa Osterling's. She was in the backyard, stretched out on a chaise in a sunsuit that made her belly look like a watermelon in a laundry bag. Her face and arms were rosy, and her tanned legs glistened with tanning oil. As I crossed the grass, she raised a hand to her eyes, shading her face from the winter sunlight so she could look at me. "I didn't expect to see you back so soon."

"I have a question," I said, "and then I need to use your phone. Did Rudd know a kid named Eric Barnett?"

"I'm not sure. What's he look like?"

I gave her a quick rundown, including a description of the white Corvette. I could see the recognition in her face as she sat up.

"Oh, him. Sure. He was over here two or three times a week. I just never knew his name. Rudd said he lived around here somewhere and stopped by to borrow tools so he could work on his motorcycle. Is he the one who owed Rudd the money?"

"Well, I don't know how we're going to prove it, but I suspect he was."

"You think he killed him?"

"I can't answer that yet, but I'm working on it. Is the phone in here?" I was moving toward the kitchen. She struggled to her feet and followed me into the house. There was a wall phone near the back door. I tucked the receiver against my shoulder, pulling the appraisal slip out of my pocket. I dialed Avery Lamb's gun shop. The phone rang twice.

Somebody picked up on the other end. "Gun shop."

"Mr. Lamb?"

"This is Orville Lamb. Did you want me or my brother, Avery?"

"Avery, actually. I have a quick question for him."

"Well, he left a short while ago, and I'm not sure when he'll be back. Is it something I can help you with?"

"Maybe so," I said. "If you had a priceless shotgun—say, an Ithaca or a Parker, one of the classics—would you shoot a gun like that?"

"You could," he said dubiously, "but it wouldn't be a good idea, especially if it was in mint condition to begin with. You wouldn't want to take a chance on lowering the value. Now if it'd been in use previously, I don't guess it would matter much, but still I wouldn't advise it—just speaking for myself. Is this a gun of yours?"

But I'd hung up. Lisa was right behind me, her expression anxious. "I've got to go in a minute," I said, "but here's what I think went on. Eric Barnett's stepfather has a collection of fine shotguns, one of which turns out to be very, very valuable. The old man was hospitalized, and Eric's mother decided to hock one of the guns in order to do a little something for herself before he'd blown every asset he had on his medical bills. She had no idea the gun she chose was worth so much, but the gun dealer recognized it as the find of a lifetime. I don't know whether he told her that or not, but when she realized it was more valuable than she thought, she lost her nerve and put it back."

"Was that the same gun Rudd took in trade?"

"Exactly. My guess is that she mentioned it to her son, who saw a chance to square his drug debt. He offered Rudd the shotgun in trade, and Rudd decided he'd better get the gun appraised, so he took it out to the same place. The gun dealer recognized it when he brought it in."

She stared at me. "Rudd was killed over the gun itself, wasn't he?" she said.

"I think so, yes. It might have been an accident. Maybe there was a struggle and the gun went off."

She closed her eyes and nodded. "Okay. Oh, wow. That

feels better. I can live with that." Her eyes came open, and she smiled painfully. "Now what?"

"I have one more hunch to check out, and then I think we'll know what's what."

She reached over and squeezed my arm. "Thanks."

"Yeah, well, it's not over yet, but we're getting there."

When I got back to Jackie Barnett's, the white Corvette was still in the driveway, but the old man in the wheelchair had apparently been moved into the house. I knocked, and after an interval, Eric opened the door, his expression altering only slightly when he saw me.

I said, "Hello again. Can I talk to your mom?"

"Well, not really. She's gone right now."

"Did she and Avery go off together?"

"Who?"

I smiled briefly. "You can drop the bullshit, Eric. I saw the suitcase in the hall when I was here the first time. Are they gone for good or just for a quick jaunt?"

"They said they'd be back by the end of the week," he mumbled. It was clear he looked a lot slicker than he really was. I almost felt bad that he was so far outclassed.

"Do you mind if I talk to your stepfather?"

He flushed. "She doesn't want him upset."

"I won't upset him."

He shifted uneasily, trying to decide what to do with me. I thought I'd help him out. "Could I just make a suggestion here? According to the California penal code, grand theft is committed when the real or personal property taken is of a value exceeding two hundred dollars. Now that includes domestic fowl, avocados, olives, citrus, nuts, and artichokes. Also shotguns, and it's punishable by imprisonment in the county jail or state prison for not more than one year. I don't think you'd care for it."

He stepped away from the door and let me in.

The old man was huddled in his wheelchair in the den. The rheumy eyes came up to meet mine, but there was no recognition in them. Or maybe there was recognition but no interest. I hunkered beside his wheelchair. "Is your hearing okay?"

He began to pluck aimlessly at his pant leg with his good hand, looking away from me. I've seen dogs with the same expression when they've done pottie on the rug and know you've got a roll of newspaper tucked behind your back.

"Want me to tell you what I think happened?" I didn't really need to wait. He couldn't answer in any mode that I could interpret. "I think when you came home from the hospital the first time and found out the gun was gone, the shit hit the fan. You must have figured out that Eric took it. He'd probably taken other things if he'd been doing cocaine for long. You probably hounded him until you found out what he'd done with it, and then you went over to Rudd's to get it. Maybe you took the L. C. Smith with you the first time, or maybe you came back for it when he refused to return the Parker. In either case, you blew his head off and then came back across the yards. And then you had another stroke."

I became aware of Eric in the doorway behind me. I glanced back at him. "You want to talk about this stuff?" I asked.

"Did he kill Rudd?"

"I think so," I said. I stared at the old man.

His face had taken on a canny stubbornness, and what was I going to do? I'd have to talk to Lieutenant Dolan about the situation, but the cops would probably never find any real proof, and even if they did, what could they do to him? He'd be lucky if he lived out the year.

"Rudd was a nice guy," Eric said.

"God, Eric. You *all* must have guessed what happened," I said snappishly.

He had the good grace to color up at that, and then he left the room. I stood up. To save myself, I couldn't work up any righteous anger at the pitiful remainder of a human being hunched in front of me. I crossed to the gun cabinet.

The Parker shotgun was in the rack, three slots down, looking like the other classic shotguns in the case. The old man would die, and Jackie would inherit it from his estate. Then she'd marry Avery and they'd all have what they wanted. I stood there for a moment, and then I started looking through the desk drawers until I found the keys. I unlocked the cabinet and then unlocked the rack. I substituted the L. C. Smith for the Parker and then locked the whole business up again. The old man was whimpering, but he never looked at me, and Eric was nowhere in sight when I left.

The last I saw of the Parker shotgun, Lisa Osterling was holding it somewhat awkwardly across her bulky midriff. I'd talk to Lieutenant Dolan all right, but I wasn't going to tell him everything. Sometimes justice is served in other ways.

STUART M. KAMINSKY

BUSTED BLOSSOMS

Darkness. I couldn't see, but I could hear someone shouting at me about Adolf Hitler. I opened my eyes. I still couldn't see. Panic set in before memory told me where I was. I pushed away the jacket covering my head. After a good breath of stale air, I realized where I was, who I was, and what I was doing there.

It was 1938, February, a cool Sunday night in Los Angeles, and I was Toby Peters, a private investigator who had been hired to keep an eye on a washed-up movie director who had come in from out of town and picked up a few death threats. I was getting fifteen dollars a day, for which I was expected to stay near the target and put myself in harm's way if trouble came up. I was not being paid to fall asleep.

My mouth tasted like ragweed pollen. I reached over to turn off the radio. When I had put my head back to rest on the bed and pulled my suede zipped jacket over me, Jeanette MacDonald had been singing about Southern moons. I woke up to the news that Reichsführer Hitler had proclaimed himself chief of national defense and had promoted Hermann Wilhelm Göring, minister of aviation, to field marshal. I was just standing when the door opened and D. W. Griffith walked in.

"Mr. Peters," he said, his voice deep, his back straight, and, even across the room, his breath dispensing the Kentucky fumes of bourbon.

"I was on my way down," I said. "I was listening to the news."

Griffith eyed me from over his massive hawk of a nose. He was about five-ten, maybe an inch or so taller than me, though I guessed he weighed about 180, maybe twenty pounds more than I did. We both seemed to be in about the same shape, which says something good for him or bad for me. I was forty-one, and he was over sixty. He was wearing a black suit over a white shirt and thin black tie.

"I have something to tell you," Griffith said.

So, I was canned. It had happened before, and I had a double sawbuck in my wallet.

"I really was coming down," I said, trying to get some feeling in my tongue.

"You were not," Griffith said emphatically. "But that is of little consequence. A man has been murdered."

"Murdered?" I repeated.

I am not the most sophisticated sight even when I'm combed, shaved, and operating on a full stomach. My face is dark and my nose mush, not from business contacts, but from an older brother who every once in a while thought I needed redefinition. I sold that tough look to people who wanted a bodyguard. Most of my work was for second-rate clothing stores that had too much shoplifting, hard-working bookies whose wives had gone for Chiclets and never came back, and old ladies who had lost their cats, who were always named Sheiba. That's what I usually did, but once in a while I spent a night or a few days protecting movie people who got themselves threatened or were afraid of getting crushed in a crowd. D.W. had no such fears. No one was looking for his autograph anymore. No one was hiring him. He seemed to have plenty of money and a lot of hope; that was why he had driven up from Louisville. He hoped someone would pick up the phone and call him to direct a movie, but in the week I had worked for him, no one had called, except the guy who threatened to lynch him with a Ku Klux Klan robe. D.W. had explained that such threats had not been unusual during the past two decades since the release of *Birth of a Nation*, which had presented the glories of the Ku Klux Klan. D.W. had tried to cover his prejudice with *Intolerance* and a few more films, but the racism of *Birth* wouldn't wash away.

"Mr. Peters." He tried again, his voice now loud enough to be heard clearly in the back row if we were in a Loews theater. "You must rouse yourself. A man has been murdered downstairs."

"Call the police," I said brilliantly.

"We are, you may recall, quite a distance from town," he reminded me. "A call has been placed, but it will be some time before the constabulary arrives."

Constabulary. I was in a time warp. But that was the way I had felt since meeting Griffith, who now touched his gray sideburns as if he were about to be photographed for *Click* magazine.

"Who's dead?" I asked.

"Almost everyone of consequence since the dawn of time," Griffith said, opening the door. "In this case, the victim is Jason Sikes. He is sitting at the dinner table with a knife in his neck."

"Who did it?" I began.

"That, I fear, is a mystery," Griffith said. "Now let us get back to the scene."

I walked out the door feeling that I was being ushered from act one to act two. I didn't like the casting. Griffith was directing the whole thing, and I had the feeling he wanted to cast me as the detective. I wanted to tell him that I had been hired to protect his back, not find killers. I get double time for finding killers. But one just didn't argue with Dave Griffith. I slouched ahead of him, scratched an itch on my right arm, and slung my suede jacket over my shoulder so I could at least straighten the wrinkled striped tie I was wearing.

What did I know? That I was in a big house just off the California coast about thirty miles north of San Diego. The house belonged to a producer named Korites, who Griffith hoped would give him a directing job. Korites had gathered his two potential stars, a comic character actor, and a potential backer, Sikes, to meet the great director. I had come as Griffith's "associate." D.W. had left his young wife back at the Roosevelt Hotel in Los Angeles, and we had stopped for drinks twice on the way in his chauffeur-driven Mercedes. In the car Griffith had talked about Kentucky, his father, his mother, who had never seen one of his films—"She did not approve of the stage," he explained—and about his comeback. He had gone on about his youthful adventures as an actor, playwright, boxer, reporter, and construction worker. Then, about ten minutes before we arrived, he had clammed up, closed his eyes, and hadn't said another word.

Now we were going silently down the stairs of the house of Marty Korites, stepping into a dining room, and facing five well-dressed diners, one of whom lay with his face in a plate of Waldorf salad with a knife in his back.

The diners looked up when we came in. Korites, a bald, jowly man with Harold Lloyd glasses, was about fifty and looked every bit of it and more. His eyes had been resting angrily on the dead guest, but they shot up to us as we entered the room. On one side of the dead guy was a woman, Denise Giles, skinny as ticker tape, pretty, dark, who knows what age. I couldn't even tell from the freckles on her bare shoulders. On the other side of the dead guy was an actor named James Vann, who looked like the lead in a road-show musical, blond, young, starched, and confused.

He needed someone to feed him lines. Griffith was staring at the corpse. The great director looked puzzled. The last guest sat opposite the dead man. I knew him, too, Lew Dollard, a frizzy-haired comedian turned character actor who was Marty Korites' top name, which gives you an idea of how small an operator Marty was and what little hope Griffith had if he had traveled all the way here in the hope of getting a job from him.

"Mr. Griffith says you're a detective, not a film guy," Korites said, his eyes moving from the body to me for an instant and then back to the body. I guessed he didn't want the dead guy to get away when he wasn't looking.

"Yeah, I'm a detective," I said. "But I don't do windows and I don't do corpses."

Dollard, the roly-poly New York street comic in a rumpled suit, looked up at me.

"A comedy writer," he said with a smile showing big teeth. I had seen one of Dollard's movies. He wasn't funny.

"Someone killed Sikes," Korites said with irritation.

"Before the main course was served, too," I said. "Some people have no sense of timing. Look. Why don't we just sit still, have a drink or two, and wait till the police get here. We can pass the time by your telling me how someone can get killed at the dinner table and all of you not know who did it. That must have been some chicken liver appetizer."

"It was," said Griffith, holding his open palm toward the dead man, "like a moment of filmic chicanery, a magic moment from Méliès. I was sipping an aperitif and had turned to Miss Giles to answer a question. And then, a sound, a groan. I turned, and there sat Mr. Sikes."

We all looked at Sikes. His face was still in the salad.

"Who saw what happened?" I asked.

They all looked up from the corpse and at each other. Then they looked at me. Dollard had a cheek full of something and a silly grin on his face. He shrugged.

"A man gets murdered with the lights on with all of you at the table and no one knows who did it?" I asked. "That's a little hard to believe. Who was standing up?"

"No one," said Vann, looking at me unblinking.

"No one," agreed Griffith.

There was no window behind the body. One door to the room was facing the dead man. The other door was to his right. The knife couldn't have been thrown from either door and landed in his back. The hell with it. I was getting paid to protect Griffith, not find killers. I'd go through the motions till the real cops got there. I had been a cop back in Glendale before I went to work for Warner Brothers as a guard and then went into business on my own. I knew the routine.

"Why don't we go into the living room?" Korites said, starting to get up and glancing at the corpse. "I could have Mrs. Windless—"

"Sit down," I said. "Mrs. Windless is . . . ?"

"Housekeeper," Korites said. "Cook."

"Was she in here when Sikes was killed?"

I looked around. All heads shook no.

"Anyone leave the room before or after Sikes was killed?" I went on.

"Just Mr. Griffith," said Vann. The woman still hadn't said anything.

"We stay right here till the police arrive. Anyone needs the toilet, I go with them, even the dragon lady," I said, trying to get a rise out of Denise Giles. I got none.

"What about you?" said Dollard, rolling his eyes and gurgling in a lousy imitation of Bert Lahr.

"I wasn't in the room when Sikes took his dive into the salad," I said. "Look, you want to forget the whole thing and talk about sports? Fine. You hear that Glenn Cunningham won the Wanamaker mile for the fifth time yesterday?"

"With a time of 4:11," said Denise Giles, taking a small sip of wine from a thin little glass.

I looked at her with new respect. Griffith had sat down at the end of the table, the seat he had obviously been in when murder interrupted the game. Something was on his mind.

"Who was Sikes?" I asked, reaching down for a celery stick.

"A man of means," said Griffith, downing a slug of bourbon.

"A backer," said Korites. "He was thinking of bankrolling a movie D.W. would direct and I would produce."

"With Vann here and Miss Giles as stars?" I said.

"Right," said Korites.

"Never," said Griffith emphatically.

"You've got no choice here," Korites shouted back. "You take the project the way we give it to you or we get someone else. Your name's got some curiosity value, right, but it doesn't bring in any golden spikes."

"A man of tender compassion," sighed Griffith, looking at me for understanding. "It was my impression that the late Mr. Sikes had no intention of supplying any capital. On the contrary, I had the distinct impression that he felt he was in less than friendly waters and had only been lured here with the promise of meeting me, the wretched director who had once held the industry in his hand, had once turned pieces of factory-produced celluloid into art. As I recall, Sikes also talked about some financial debt he expected to be paid tonight."

"You recall?" Korites said with sarcasm, shaking his head. "You dreamed it up. You're still back in the damn nineteenth century. Your movies were old-fashioned when you made them. You don't work anymore because you're an anachronism."

"Old-fashioned?" said Griffith with a smile. "Yes, old-fashioned, a romantic, one who respects the past. I would rather die with my Charles Dickens than live with your Hemingway."

Dollard finished whatever he had in his mouth and said, "You think it would be sacrilegious to have the main course? Life goes on."

"Have a celery stick," I suggested.

"I don't want to eat a celery stick," he whined.

"I wasn't suggesting that you put it in your mouth," I said.

This was too much for Dollard. He stood up, pushing the chair back.

"I'm the comic here," he said. "Tell him."

He looked around for someone to tell me. The most sympathetic person was Sikes, and he was dead.

"So that's the way it is," Dollard said, looking around the room. "You want me to play second banana."

"This is a murder scene," shouted Korites, taking his glasses off, "not a night club, Lew. Try to remember that." His jowls rumbled as he spoke. He was the boss, but not mine.

"Someone in this room murdered the guy in the salad," I reminded them.

"My father," said Griffith.

"Your father killed Sikes?" I asked, turning to the great director. Griffith's huge nose was at the rim of his almost empty glass. His dark eyes were looking into the remaining amber liquid for an answer.

"My father," he said without looking up, "would have known how to cope with this puzzle. He was a resourceful man, a gentleman, a soldier."

"Mine was a grocer," I said.

"This is ridiculous," said Denise Giles throwing down her napkin.

"Not to Sikes," I said. Just then the door behind me swung open. I turned to see a rail of a woman dressed in black.

"Are you ready for the roast?" she asked.

"Yes," said Dollard.

"No," said Korites, "we're not having any more food."

"I have rights here," Dollard insisted.

Now I had it. This was an Alice in Wonderland nightmare and I was Alice at the Mad Hatter's tea party. We'd all change places in a few seconds and the Dormouse, Sikes, would have to be carried.

"What," demanded Mrs. Windless, "am I to do with the roast?"

"You want the punch line or can I have it?" Dollard said to me.

"Sikes already got the punch line," I reminded him.

Mrs. Windless looked over at Sikes for the first time.

"Oh my God," she screamed. "That man is dead."

"Really?" shouted Dollard leaping up. "Which one?"

"Goddamn it," shouted Korites. "This is serious." His glasses were back on now. He didn't seem to know what to do with them.

Griffith got up and poured himself another drink.

"We know he's dead, Mrs. Windless," Korites said. "The police are on the way. You'll just have to stick all the food in the refrigerator and wait."

"What happened?" Mrs. Windless asked, her voice high, her eyes riveted on Sikes. "Who did this? I don't want anything to do with murder."

"You don't?" said Dollard. "Why didn't you tell us that before we killed him? We did it for you." He crossed his eyes but didn't close them in time to block out the wine thrown in his face by the slinky Denise.

Dollard stood up sputtering and groped for a napkin to wipe his face. Purple tears rolled down his cheeks.

"Damn it," he screamed. "What the hell? What the hell?" His hand found a napkin. He wiped his eyes. The stains were gone, but there was now a piece of apple from the Waldorf salad on his face.

"Mrs. Windless," said D.W., standing and pointing at the door. "You will depart and tell my driver, Mr. Reynolds, that

Mr. Peters and I will be delayed. Mr. Dollard. You will sit down and clean your face. Miss Giles, you will refrain from outbursts, and Mr. Vann, you will attempt to show some animation. It is difficult to tell you from Mr. Sikes. Mr. Peters will continue the inquiry."

Vann stood up now, kicking back his chair. Griffith rose to meet him. They were standing face to face, toe to toe. Vann was about thirty years younger, but Griffith didn't back away.

"You can't tell us what to do. You can't tell anyone what to do. You're washed up," Vann hissed.

"As Bluebeard is rumored to have said," whispered Griffith, "I am merely between engagements."

"See, see," grouched Dollard, pointing with his fork at the two antagonists. "Everyone's a comic. I ask you."

I sighed and stood up again.

"Sit down," I shouted at Vann and Griffith. The room went silent. The mood was ruined by my stomach growling. But they sat and Mrs. Windless left the room. "Who called the police?"

"I did," said Korites.

"I thought no one left the room but Griffith?" I said.

"Phone is just outside the door, everyone could see me call. I left the door open," Korites said. He pushed his dirty plate away from him and then pulled it back. "What's the difference?"

"Why didn't you all start yelling, panic, accuse each other?" I asked.

"We thought it was one of Jason's practical jokes," said Denise Giles. "He was fond of practical jokes."

"Rubber teeth, joy buzzers, ink in the soup," sighed Dollard. "A real amateur, a putz. Once pretended he was poisoned at a lunch in . . ."

"Lew," shouted Korites. "Just shut up."

"All right you people," I said. "None of you liked Sikes, is that right?"

"Right," Korites said, "but that's a far cry from one of us . . ."

"How about hate?" I tried. "Would hate be a good word to apply to your feelings about the late dinner guest?"

"Maybe," said Korites, "there was no secret about that among our friends. I doubt if anyone who knew Jason did anything less than hate him. But none of us murdered him. We couldn't have."

"And yet," Griffith said, "one of you had to have done the deed. In *The Birth of a Nation*—"

"This is death, not birth," hissed Vann. "This isn't a damn movie."

Griffith drew his head back and examined Vann over his beak of a nose.

"Better," said Griffith. "Given time I could possibly motivate you into a passable performance. Even Richard Barthelmess had something to learn from my humble direction."

There was a radio in the corner. Dollard had stood up and turned it on. I didn't stop him. We listened to the radio and watched Sikes and each other while I tried to think. Griffith was drawing something on the white tablecloth with his fork.

Dollard found the news, and we learned that Hirohito had a cold but was getting better, King Farouk of Egypt had just gotten married, Leopold Stokowski was on his way to Italy under an assumed name, probably to visit Greta Garbo, and a guy named Albert Burroughs had been found semiconscious in a hotel room in Bloomington, Illinois. The room was littered with open cans of peas. Burroughs managed to whisper to the ambulance driver that he had lived on peas for nine days even though he had $77,000 in cash in the room.

I got up and turned off the radio.

"You tell a story like that in a movie," said Korites, "and they say it isn't real."

"If you tell it well, they will believe anything," said Griffith, again doodling on the cloth.

The dinner mess, not to mention Sikes' corpse, was beginning to ruin the party.

"Things are different," Griffith said, looking down at what he had drawn. He lifted a long-fingered hand to wipe out the identations in the tablecloth.

"Things?" I asked, wondering if he was going to tell us tales about his career, his father, or the state of the universe.

"I am an artist of images," he explained, looking up, his eyes moving from me to each of the people around the table. "I kept the entire script of my films, sometimes 1,500 shots, all within my head." He pointed to his head in case we had forgotten where it was located.

"This scene," he went on, "has changed. When I left this room to find Mr. Peters, Mr. Sikes had a knife in his neck, not his back, and it was a somewhat different knife."

"You've had three too many D.W.," Dollard said with a smile.

I got up and examined Sikes. There was no hole in his neck or anywhere else on his body that I could find.

"No cuts, bruises, marks . . ." I began, and then it hit me. My eyes met Griffith's. I think it hit him at the same moment.

"We'll just wait for the police," Korites said, removing his glasses again.

"Go on Mr. G.," I said. "Let's hear your script."

Griffith stood again, put down his glass, and smiled. He was doing either Abe Lincoln or Sherlock Holmes.

"This scene was played for me," he said. "I was not the director. I was the audience. My ego is not fragile, at least not too fragile to realize that I have witnessed an act. I can see each of you playing your roles, even the late Mr. Sikes. Each of you in an iris, laughing, silently enigmatic, attentive. And then the moment arrives. The audience is distracted by a pretty face in close-up. Then a cut to body, or supposed body, for Sikes was not dead when I left this room to find Mr. Peters."

"Come on . . ." laughed Dollard.

"Of all . . ." sighed Denise Giles.

"You're mad . . ." counterpointed Vann.

But Korites sat silent.

"He wasn't dead," I said again, picking up for Griffith, who seemed to have ended his monologue. All he needed was applause. He looked good, but he had carried the scene as far as he could. It was mine now.

"Let's try this scenario," I said. "Sikes was a practical joker, right?"

"Right," Dollard agreed, "but—"

"What if you all agreed to play a little joke on D.W.? Sikes pretends to be dead with a knife in his neck when Denise distracts Griffith. Sikes can't stick the fake knife in his back. He can't reach his own back. He attaches it to his neck. Then you all discover the body, Griffith comes for me, Sikes laughs. You all laugh, then one of you, probably Korites, moves behind him and uses a real knife to turn the joke into fact. You're all covered. Someone did it. The police would have a hell of a time figuring out which one, and meanwhile, it would make a hell of a news story. Griffith a witness. All of you suspects. Probably wind up with a backer who'd cash in on your morbid celebrity."

"Ridiculous," laughed Korites.

"I was the audience," Griffith repeated with a rueful laugh.

"Even if this were true," said Denise Giles, "you could never prove it."

"Props," I said. "You didn't have time to get rid of that fake knife, at least not to get it hidden too well. D.W. was with me for only a minute or two, and you didn't want to get too far from this room in case we came running back here. No, if we're right, that prop knife is nearby, where it can be found, somewhere in this room or not far from it."

"This is ridiculous," said Vann, standing up. "I'm not staying here for any more of this charade." He took a step toward the door behind Griffith, giving me a good idea of where to start looking for the prop knife, but the director was out of his chair and barring his way.

"Move," shouted Vann.

"Never," cried Griffith.

Vann threw a punch, but Griffith caught it with his left and came back with a right. Vann went down. Korites started to rise, looked at my face, and sat down again.

"We can work something out here," he said, his face going white.

A siren blasted somewhere outside.

"Hell of a practical joke," Dollard said, dropping the radish in his fingers. "Hell of a joke."

No one moved while we waited for the police. We just sat there, Vann on the floor, Griffith standing. I imagined a round iris closing in on the scene, and then a slow fade to black.

ROB KANTNER

FLY AWAY HOME

The pigeons descend in twos and threes, lighting on the short ledge at the edge of the roof. They flutter and strut among the debris and droppings, warbling deep in their throats. Occasionally two or three collide, and there is a squawking, flap-winged argument, with the loser taking wing in a shallow dive off the ledge.

I watch them intently, a cigarette smoldering in one hand, a coffee cup steaming black in the other. It is early summer and early in the morning in Detroit. The city comes awake with increasing sounds of traffic from fourteen floors below. To the south the heavily industrialized Zug Island sends smoke into the air to war with the haze. To the east freighters bay on the Detroit River. Up here I am alone with my coffee and my cigarette, dressed as always in white shirt, neatly clipped tie, dark pants, and black wing-tipped shoes. I look like a clerk, which I am; and I look like I'm about to begin another routine work day, which I am not.

The pigeons descend in twos and threes, lighting on the ledge at the edge of the roof. The turnover is constant, new birds descending to the ledge, others dropping away. Where do they go? A phrase comes to mind from nowhere: fly away home. Fly away home. I think it's a nursery rhyme. Probably recited to me by my grandmother many years ago. I cannot remember the rest of the poem. I do remember my grandmother, and I see her fresh in my mind's eye, kneeling at her flower bed, short spade in hand, straightening and smiling and rising as she watches me approach. . . .

Footsteps sound from behind me, ascending the seldom-used stairwell that rises from the guts of the building to the roof. I turn impatiently, waiting to see who is coming. It was the sound of footsteps like these that started the mess, just a week ago. . . .

I turned as the footsteps reached the top of the stairs and crushed out my cigarette as Connie came through the door. She was a big, beefy bull of a woman, dressed in an immense purple balloon of a dress, with dark brown hair permed high on her head. She had a happy, goofy, angelic face, except when she was forced to talk to me. "Someone to see you," she said flatly, standing at the door to the stairway as if afraid to come out on the roof toward me.

I glanced at my watch. "Well, *who*, Connie? The work day doesn't start for fifteen minutes."

"Maurie's lawyer," she said through a pinched mouth. "And she's brought some kind of detective with her. You'd better get down there. They're going to interview everybody today, in alphabetical order."

That put me first on the list. Bad luck. I huffed a sigh and followed Connie down the dark stairwell. As we approached the heavy fire door leading into our company's suite of offices, she turned to me, face softer and somewhat scared, and said, "You don't think Maurie did it, do you?"

"I'm sure of it," I said sincerely.

Connie's meaty, clownish face looked somber. "Mo was such a nice girl. Maurie is, too. I just can't believe Maurie would kill her. Think there's a chance the lawyer can get her off?"

"There's always a chance, Connie," I said heavily. We entered the suite, air-conditioning gushing coolly against my hot, moist skin. "Where are they waiting?"

Before my eyes, as if she realized who she was talking to, Connie's face changed back to that look, that look that women always had for me: suspicion, contempt, loathing. "Conference B," she answered through pinched lips, and swept away from me.

I headed over there.

I entered the room, closed the door behind me, and stood still, feet apart, hands clasped at my waist in front of me, a polite smile on my face. To my left, at the head of the conference table, sat a tall blonde woman in her mid-thirties, dressed in a navy-blue skirt, matching jacket, and white blouse with spaghetti-thin ties down the front. She had dark eyes, a creamy complexion, and a snub nose, plus a look of competent self-importance. A thin hand-tooled leather brief-case sat open on the table in front of her.

To her right sat a broad-shouldered, very tan, very fit-looking man in his early forties. His full head of thick black hair swept back along the sides and down to the collar. His dark blue eyes shone brightly from the deep tan of his face, and he had a variety of laugh and squint lines to go with the broken nose, broad forehead, and squarish jaw; but mostly he looked sleepy, cynical, contemptuous, inimical. His short-sleeved chambray shirt revealed hard, tanned, heavily muscled arms matted thickly with black hair; intermittently, whitish scars showed against the tan. Below, he wore jeans. In appearance and dress he looked better suited to mowing lawns or digging graves than to presenting himself for discussions in a professional place of business.

Taking the bit in my teeth, I introduced myself and went on. "The lawyer and the detective. Which, may I ask, is which?"

The man looked bored, the woman amused. "I'm Carole Somers, Maureen Frye's attorney." She tipped her head toward the man. "This is the private detective I've retained to assist me in the case. Ben Perkins."

The detective's eyes locked on mine, and instantly I knew him. I knew those men, all of them. Muscled and tanned, with full heads of hair, big white smiles, hearty laughs, and slaps on the rump, jokes and repartee that turned English into a foreign language. Oh, yes, I knew those men. The high school jocks who stared through their intellectual superiors as if they were bugs, who drove fast cars, joked easily with big-busted girls, and were handy with tools. I knew those men, all right. The slow-moving, lazy hunks who cluttered dark after-hours bars, who bought lottery tickets and cheap beer in dozen lots, who wolfed down ground rounds and watched big-TV sports with packs of their fellows in bowling alley cocktail lounges.

If Perkins read anything in my face—something I worked hard to avoid—he didn't show it. He nodded at me, extracted a short cork-tipped cigar from his shirt pocket, and with the snap of a wood match on his thumbnail began filling the conference room with an evil stench.

Carole Somers said briskly, "Please be seated. We'll try not to take up too much of your time."

I took a chair and composed myself neatly, watching the two as Somers took a yellow legal pad out of her briefcase and Perkins smoked his cigar. I wondered if they had gone to bed together, and then I was sure they had, probably many times.

Somers looked at me, face expectant, professional. "Maureen Stevens: 'Mo.' Maureen Frye: 'Maurie.'" She paused. "Tell me about them, please."

I shrugged. Under the stares of the lawyer and the detective, my palms became moist; to dry them off, I placed them on the padded arms of the chair. "I don't know much.

They worked here together. They shared an apartment. They were close friends and well enough liked by everyone who knew them. This past Monday, Mo was found bludgeoned to death here in the office. The police have arrested Maurie and charged her with murder." I smiled indulgently. "Maurie has retained you to help her. You have retained this man to help you." I raised my now-dry hands palms up. "Not much help, I'm afraid."

"You're doing fine," Somers said without raising her eyes from her notes. "Do you personally believe that Maurie killed Mo?"

"No." Palms dry now, heart pounding steadily, mind icily calm, I felt gutsy, daring, brave. "I am convinced she did not."

Somers' eyes met mine. "The police have what they believe is a strong case. During nonworking hours, only authorized personnel are permitted access to the offices. They must sign in at the security guard's desk downstairs. Mo was here very early in the morning, as was her habit; and during the time she was here, only Maurie signed in downstairs. Further, the police theorize, there was some competition between the two—competition for men, leading possibly to a motive of jealousy."

"Certainly Maurie denies that," I said stoutly.

"Of course." Far as Somers was concerned, the detective, Perkins, was not in the room, which would have been fine with me. She was cute. "Maurie says she stopped at the office to pick up some proofs that had to be at the printer first thing in the morning. She swears that Mo was alive when she got there, that she talked with her, that Mo was alive and well when she left. She saw no one else in the office or elsewhere in the building except for the security guard. Further, while both women were single and, ah, fairly active in their involvement with men, there was total openness and communication between the two, and no jealousy between them as far as Maurie was concerned."

I ignored the vacant stare of the beefy detective and kept my eyes candid and friendly on the luscious Carole Somers. "That is consistent with my observations," I said. As usual, particularly when talking to a woman, I felt I sounded stilted and pompous, but Carole did not seem to notice.

She leaned back in her chair and studied me. "In your observation, would you characterize Mo and Maurie as, shall we say, fast women?"

"Nice girls, both of them," I retorted.

She smiled. "Please. There is already evidence on record attesting to a certain level of what some would characterize as promiscuity. It speaks well for you that you defend your friends, but what I think of you personally is irrelevant. I remind you that Maurie is charged with first-degree murder, and if I'm to defend her adequately, I must have the truth."

"Well." I adjusted myself in my chair, studied the backs of my hands, found the detective's flat, vacant stare, and turned my eyes to the lawyer. "You're interviewing everyone in the office today, so I might as well be the one to tell you. Mo and Maurie were—how shall I phrase this?—cheerfully voracious where men were concerned. One heard . . . jokes about them. Some referred to them as 'The Maureens.' As in, 'The Maureens are looking for a few good men.'" I smiled sadly. "I felt that such jokes were in the worst possible taste. Not at all what I consider appropriate in a professional setting." I felt perfectly composed now, strong, confident, secure.

Ben Perkins began to stub out his filthy-smelling cigar in an ashtray and spoke for the first time. "You get any of that?"

"I'm sorry?" I asked politely.

His eyes stayed on his cigar as he crushed it. "Either one of them. Or both."

I played dumb. "I'm afraid I don't follow you."

Perkins finished snuffing his cigar and rubbed his jaw with the back of a heavily knuckled hand as he fixed his blue eyes on me. "What I'm asking you is, was one of those 'few good men' you?"

Irrelevantly, I detected a trace of a Southern accent in his heavy, husky voice. I brought myself up straight in my chair and looked at Carole Somers. Rather than giving Perkins an annoyed look, she was watching me expectantly. So.

"I'm a married man," I said, allowing some heat to enter my voice.

"So?" Perkins responded, the syllable a Neanderthal grunt.

I gnawed my lip impatiently. "Certainly not."

Perkins did not change expression. He leaned forward, elbows on knees, eyes on me. "Worked here long?"

"Many years."

"Associate with either Maureen away from the office?"

"I believe it imprudent to develop personal relationships with co-workers. That is my rule."

Paper ripped as Carole Somers tore a blank sheet of paper off her pad. She slid it over to me, along with a pen. "Write something."

Smooth team. Smooth team. But so stupid. They watched me as I selected a pen from the plastic carrier in my pocket and, without a word of protest, wrote the standard "quick brown fox" sentence on the paper. "Satisfied?"

"Right-handed," Perkins told Carole Somers.

"Brilliant deduction, Ben," she answered sarcastically.

That would have angered me, but Perkins only grinned. To me he said with infuriating jauntiness, "Medical examiner says whoever beat Mo to death was left-handed. How they figure that kind of thing I'll never know."

"And you suspect *me*," I said stiffly.

Carole Somers said evenly, "I have an obligation to my client to conduct a full investigation."

"Seems to me that's a job for the police."

Perkins snorted. "Police already figure they got their perp. Maurie's left-handed. She can be placed at the scene at the approximate time of the murder. Motive can be presumed. Detroit's finest are overworked, understaffed; they'll grab the path of least resistance and go for it."

I consciously steadied myself down, forced myself to relax in the chair. Somers and Perkins watched me blandly. I made a smile and said, "Certainly no one would be more happy to see Maurie cleared than myself. I do not doubt that she is innocent." I scratched the bare skin on the side of my head. "But, Mister Perkins, what makes *you* think she's innocent?"

Perkins leaned back in his chair and crossed an ankle over his knee. Eyes empty, he answered quite lazily, "Yeah, well, number one, I'm being paid to think so. Plus, I've talked to her, and I really do believe it."

Carole Somers had her elegant hands folded over her pad. Obviously she was finished questioning me, and I wanted to be gone, but Perkins kept talking. "Anyway, these things generally get sorted out if someone who gives a damn goes to work on 'em. Guys like me, who make a living asking around and checking up, get a feel for this stuff, get experience, whereas guys who do murder tend not to do it but once, so they don't get experience, and they leave tracks. See? I'll mess with it awhile and get it sorted out."

The big, hard-muscled man sounded so matter-of-fact, so confident, so strong, that I felt loathing rise in me like a gorge. I consciously willed it from showing on my face. Of Somers I asked, "Is there any other way I can be of service?"

"No. You're excused. And many thanks for your help." She gave me a sincere, radiant smile, but it was too late; my interest in her was gone; she'd blown it; anybody who'd go to bed with a man like Perkins could be of no use to me.

"Thank *you*." I went to the conference room door and,

before leaving, turned back toward Perkins. "Any theories as to the actual murderer?"

Perkins was lighting another filthy cigar. "Nary a one." He puffed. "I don't work that way; I start out clean. One thing, though." He pulled the cigar from his mouth and looked at me. "Judging from the pics of the stiff, whoever did her must have had one hell of a reason."

He was certainly right about that. But where did it begin?

Perhaps at home, with Pam. Married eleven years; friends for, perhaps, the first seven. It did not change overnight. As our jobs got worse, and the money tighter, the economy sank its teeth into us. We got older and heavier, less vigorous and more bored. Friends and colleagues moved up in their careers and away to the coasts, leaving us behind; or they bought houses in the suburbs, began to rear fat babies, and preferred to associate with others like them rather than us.

And the guerrilla warfare began. The ambushes. From in the kitchen, or over the phone, or in bed at night. "Why don't you get a better job? Why don't you fight for a promotion? When are you going to stand up for yourself? That piece-of-junk car of mine is going; what are you going to do about *that*? I need *money*. We'll *never* be able to buy a house, *never*. Everybody has nice houses. Everybody has nice cars. Everybody goes on nice vacations. Everybody else but *us*. And all *you* do is sit here with your nose stuck in a book. When are you going to *do* something? When? When? When?"

I was a good husband and provider. I changed jobs and worked desperately hard to improve my position and advance myself. I did it all for her and it was never enough. And the time came when I realized that if there was to be a reward, I would have to get it for myself. I had earned it, and I was going to get it.

That was when I decided on Mo Stevens. Everyone else enjoyed her. Why not me?

As the two-day computer seminar in Cleveland drew near, I made it a point to stop by her desk frequently. I was clumsy and shy, as always, but she, unlike the other women at the company, was off-hand and friendly, with lots of secretive smiles and casual, seemingly accidental brushings.

On the first day of the seminar, we sat at opposite sides of the classroom. Among the forty other attendees and the droning instructor, in the hot, stuffy August heat, our glances met many times. I felt alone with her. I felt eager and energized for the first time in years.

That night I asked her to dinner. She pleaded a headache and said she'd stay in her room, but she smiled regretfully and, before retiring, gave my arm a warm squeeze that lasted the rest of the night.

The second evening—our last in Cleveland—we had drinks and then dinner. We talked about everything but the real subject. I strolled back to her room with her. She got out her key. I reached for the key and took her hand instead, awkwardly. She faced me, a searching, speculative look on her face. Then she leaned forward and kissed me. I moved against her and kissed her hard. Her arms went around me, the key clinking against my back. She pulled back, a secretive, knowing smile on her face, and said, "B plus." Then she unlocked her door, swung it open, and beckoned me in.

Back home in Detroit, I spent the next two days—Saturday and Sunday—waiting for Monday, waiting to see Mo at the office. It was terribly hot, and Pam was at her vicious best, but for once she didn't get to me. Because now I had Mo. I wanted to call her right away but didn't dare; I respected the fact that she'd want our relationship to be kept a deadly secret. So I waited, strung out with happy, excited anticipation.

On Monday morning I found her at her desk. She smiled at me but kept her manner cool and professional. Good lass, I thought; good lass. Casually I invited her to lunch. She declined, pleading a doctor's appointment.

On Tuesday I went out during my lunch hour and rented a room at the Sheraton Cadillac. I called home and informed Pam that a business emergency required me to go to Toledo that night. Back at the office I wrote a brief note, sealed it in an envelope, and left it on Mo's desk. At quitting time I fairly flew to the Sheraton, ate a quick dinner, then went to the room and waited. I waited till past eleven o'clock, and Mo never arrived.

Mo wasn't at her desk much on Wednesday. I finally encountered her emerging from the conference room. Placing myself between her and the others, I clumsily asked her what had gone wrong the night before. Her face froze, she stared through me, then she made an icy smile, shook her head, and walked away.

She didn't come to work on Thursday. I did my work in a state of nervous, preoccupied dread. At lunchtime I called Mo's apartment. When she heard my voice, she hung up.

The next day I felt none of the usual end-of-the-week relief. I stayed in my cubicle, sorting and shuffling my papers and typing my forms, feeling strangely immobile and detached, dreading going home, dreading staying in the office. Just before lunchtime, I heard voices in the passageway outside my cubicle, and Mo glanced in at me. She turned to her companion, excused herself, then entered, set a file down on the table before me, opened it, and bent down as if to discuss something in the file with me.

But what she said, in a voice light and airy enough to have caused no interest in anyone who couldn't understand the words, was: "Listen, you warped little creep, maybe Cleveland gave you the wrong idea. That was a one-shot, you understand? A whim. The fact is, you make my skin crawl. There is no way it will ever happen again, because even standing this close to you makes me want to puke. Is that clear? Have I made myself very, very clear now?" She closed the file, gave me a casual wave for public consumption, and left. I sat there, a noise like a waterfall roaring in my head.

The noise roared in my head through the weekend and was still there the following Monday, very, very early in the morning, as I stood with my back to the wall, around the corner from Mo and Maurie as they chatted lightly in the deserted office. When Maurie left, I walked around the corner and toward Mo's desk. She jumped when she saw me, her eyes flashed briefly, then her face paled as I brought the short length of lead pipe from behind me and tapped its end lightly in my palm.

I asked, "Am I too close now, Mo? You feel like puking, maybe?"

She slowly rolled on her chair back from her desk. Her eyes grew and grew, and she started to say something, but her mouth was too dry.

I kept approaching her, tapping the pipe. "How about your skin? Is it crawling now, Mo?"

She lunged clumsily up from her chair. I took a final step, gripped the pipe with both hands, and swung in a flat, arm's-length arc. I didn't feel the impact, but she flew back as if jerked off her feet by a rope around her neck and sprawled with a blaze of tan legs and white underwear over her chair. The roaring in my head built suddenly to full gain as I kicked her chair aside, straddled her like a runner in the starting blocks, and dealt her the two-handed swing again, again, again, again. Over the roaring I heard my own voice: "Made myself clear now, Mo? How about it, Pam? Have I made myself clear? How about it, Mo?" And then it was just the two names, Mo, Pam, Mo, Pam, as if I didn't know who it was.

In the days that followed my interview with Carole Somers and Ben Perkins, I saw the detective around a few times.

I saw him one afternoon in the pub on the ground floor of our building, drinking beer (naturally) and chatting with a handful of people from our company. He gave me a sober-faced wave and nod, nothing more.

I saw him in one of the back halls of our office suite as I was sweeping up the shards of a coffee carafe that one of our clumsy secretaries had dropped on the way to the conference room. As he passed me, Perkins gave me a crooked grin and a nod, nothing more.

I saw him at the curb of Congress Street, leaning out the window of his souped-up blue Mustang (naturally), chatting with Bernie, an elderly, hump-backed man who from time immemorial had been a private message runner and one-man delivery service for downtown companies. Perkins didn't see me that time.

Otherwise I knew nothing about Perkins' "investigation." And I didn't think about it. My plan had been sound, the execution flawless. No subeducated, inarticulate grunt was going to make a case on me. Besides, my thoughts centered on my other problem. The one with Pam's name on it.

I stare impatiently at the stairwell as Ben Perkins emerges onto the sun-drenched roof. He squints from the light but seems unsurprised to see me. He says, "Told you I'd sort it out."

Does he really think I'm such a fool? "I don't want to hear about it." I flick away my half-smoked cigarette.

"Sure you do." Perkins grins. "They all do." Today he's as well-dressed as he probably ever gets, in a blue blazer, matching slacks, open-collar white dress shirt. The warm morning breeze whips his thick black hair as the pigeons wheel in the air above us, light on the ledge to my left, and drop into space to fly away home.

Perkins glances around the roof, probably looking for a place to sit. There is none, except the ledge, so instead he leans against the wall and with a big, knuckly hand fetches one of his short cigars out of his blazer pocket. "I found that other way into the building, the one you used to get past the security guard."

I stare at him. The front of my face feels numb. "You think *I* killed Mo?"

He flares a wood match on his thumbnail, applies the flame to the end of his cigar, and nods as he puffs. "Oh yeah," he answers casually, waving the match out and tossing it. "See, I talked to old Bernie, the delivery fella. He's been working these buildings for years, knows 'em better than the rats. This building wasn't always secure; used to be a passageway on the sixth floor between the Olivetti firm's offices and this building. Hardly anybody remembers it now. But you used to work for Olivetti, right?"

I deny him the satisfaction of changing expression. He shrugs easily. "Show me how you bat," he says casually.

Defiantly I start into the stance, then freeze and straighten again. Perkins' eyes are cold and assured. "Lefty," he murmurs. "You write right-handed, sure. But I saw you swinging a broom the other day. You're sort of ambidextrous. For some reason, lefty's the way you swing a bat, a broom, an ax—and a club. Right?"

I hear the pigeons flapping off the ledge. Traffic noise builds from fourteen floors below as the morning rush hour begins. I sneer at Perkins. "Not precisely what I'd call hanging evidence, Perkins."

"Hey, man's got to try." He puffs on his cigar, studying me. "That Mo, she liked action, right? What'd she do? Turn you down? Or tumble and then dump you? It's an old story, man. A real old story."

As if Perkins cares. I notice that he has positioned himself near the door, as if to intercept me should I try to escape. Fool.

Perkins folds his arms across his chest with his cigar jutting from two fingers, and yawns. "Anyway, I talked it over with the detectives. They got a search warrant last night for your house. They're there right now. Checking your clothes and stuff. For evidence and that. Routine."

My eyes close for just an instant, and in that instant I see what the police will find. Mo, Pam! Mo, Pam!

I turn and stroll casually to the ledge. Pigeons glare and scatter with fluttering squawks as I sit on the ledge with my forearms on my knees, facing the detective. He's stood and taken a couple of steps toward me, eyes narrow. I smile at him. The narrow, tense expression wipes away, and he says, "Well, that about covers it. Come on, let's go downstairs. It's getting right hot up here."

I feel the empty air behind me. Now I can hear the traffic much clearer from the street fourteen floors down. Perkins stands fifteen, twenty feet away from me, waiting for an answer that does not come. Through my mind runs the litany: fly away, fly away, fly away home. Then I remember: it's about a ladybug. Figures. Helpless insect, eaten alive by stronger ones.

Perkins says in a low, calm voice, "You know, once some wise men got together to come up with an absolutely universal truth, and what they came up with was, 'This, too, shall pass.'"

"So?"

He smiles in what I imagine to be a friendly fashion, but I know better; he's no friend. Men like him never are. He says, "You can get past this, pal."

I'm too tired to argue. I simply say, "No."

"You don't want to die. No matter how bad things are, you don't really want to die. Nobody does. You know why? Because there's nothing then. No rushing wind, no blinding light, no incredible feeling of peace, no welcoming faces of the previously departed. There's absolute, stone-cold nothing."

Fresh in my mind's eye I see my grandmother, kneeling at her flower bed, short spade in hand, straightening and smiling and rising as she watches me approach. I snarl at Perkins, "Spare me your supermarket-tabloid shrink shtick, Perkins."

His voice was still gentle. "Come on, walk back over here."

"No."

His face changes, goes dark and angry, the tendons showing against the tan skin as his jaw tightens. "Okay, so what the hell do *I* care? Go ahead, jump. World could sure use one less sniveling, twisted, four-eyed pukebag. Only thing, I hope you don't land on some innocent citizen down there. Be a real shame if a normal person got hurt by a sick piece of worthless garbage like you. Go ahead, jump! Have a nice trip!"

I grin with contempt at this futile stratagem. He wants to anger me, make me attack him so he can drag me away from the ledge. Even if I hadn't seen *Dirty Harry* and known how the con is supposed to work, it wouldn't have, because all my rage is gone. I am harmless now and know what I am going to do, and no one can stop me, most particularly this son of a bitch.

In the long pause, the traffic noise builds from the amphitheater far, far below. Perkins knots his fists. "What are ya, chicken? Need a hand? Well, buddy, happy to oblige. Call me a public-spirited citizen." He starts for me.

I tease him and play with him and tempt him, sitting still, letting him think I'm so stupid I'll let him grab me and pull me away from the ledge. Just as he lunges for me, I tumble over backward and leave the ledge.

And get just a glimpse of Perkins' reaction, which fills me with joy. His face is a mask of shock, horror, fear, despair.

The wind tears at my clothes and blinds my eyes as I laugh soundlessly. I've beaten him! I've won! I've—

Grandmother?

GRANDMOTHER?

JOHN LUTZ

THE THUNDER OF GUILT

It didn't begin as anything unusual. The big guy, Arthur Leland, came into Nudger's office and hired him to follow his wife, Beatrice. Nudger got a lot of that kind of work; his seedy address seemed to attract it. Even if clients had plenty of money, like Leland, and lived in a good part of town, also like Leland, they seemed to think they should hire a private investigator they considered to be from the unwashed underside of life to follow an errant spouse. Dirty folks for dirty work.

Leland owned and managed a construction company specializing in commercial projects. There was real agony on his veiny, ruddy face as he told Nudger, "Bea is a good woman. She's had some strain lately. We're both forty-one, Nudger. She became pregnant six months ago and had an abortion. It went against her grain, and I guess I talked her into it. A week later our youngest child, Alice, was killed in an automobile crash. She was our last child at home. It . . . ruined both of us for a while. We didn't know what to do. The church didn't seem to help. I tried to talk Bea into professional counseling, but she wouldn't go. We suffered a lot. We came out of it different people."

"And now you think she's seeing another man," Nudger

said. He picked up the pity in his voice and was embarrassed; he felt sorry for both the Lelands, with their dead child and their dead or dying marriage. He didn't like the idea of following the wife to some motel, where she'd meet a man, they'd have a few drinks in the lounge, and then rent a room at the four-hour rate. The prospect of watching and reporting that made Nudger feel like the cheap goods Leland probably thought he was.

"She goes out at odd hours during the day, doesn't tell anyone where she's going. And she lies to me at times; I know because the odometer on her car doesn't register the mileage it would if she was telling me the truth." Leland shifted his husky frame awkwardly. "I'm not looking for ammunition for a divorce, Nudger. I'm worried about Bea; I just want to know what's going on. I need to know, damn it!"

"And you will know," Nudger told him, trying to spike the man's anger with the old positive approach.

He thought Leland was going to snap the ballpoint pen in half when he signed a contract for Nudger's services. Leland's jaw muscles were working as if he were chewing raw leather, and when he leaned near, he smelled like desperation. It was tough, the tricks love played on some people.

The big man counted out the retainer in cash almost absently and left it on Nudger's desk, then buttoned his overcoat to the neck and left the office.

Beatrice Leland was middle-aged plump but still attractive, with a head of thick, wavy dark hair and pale blue, gentle eyes. There was a subtle sadness to her, even at first glance. She would appeal to those men who could sense a vague helplessness in women; predators who picked off the cripples.

At three o'clock on the afternoon of her husband's visit to Nudger's office, she got into her blue Toyota sedan and drove from the driveway of her comfortably plush home in Des Peres. She was wearing a gray dress and red high heels, carrying a large red purse. There was a jacket-length fur draped over her shoulders. Nudger classified her as dressed up, not just on her way to pick up some crackers and dip. She wasn't running errands; the lady was going somewhere that meant something.

He followed as she headed south, then as she turned east on Manchester, back toward Nudger's office. For a moment Nudger wondered inanely if she were on her way to hire him to follow her husband.

Her first stop surprised him. She parked on Sutton Avenue in Maplewood and crossed the street to enter a plumbing supply company. She had a graceful, alluring walk despite her extra ten or fifteen pounds. Nice ankles and proportioned curve of hip. Maybe she was having an extramarital affair with a plumber, Nudger mused, as he sat in his dented Volkswagen Beetle and shivered in the January cold.

But ten minutes later she came out of the plumbing supply place, carrying her purse as if it were heavier. She got back into the Toyota and U-turned to head north on Sutton. Nudger followed her as she made a left and drove west on Manchester, away from the city.

At the Holiday Inn on Craigshire, she parked and walked directly to a second-floor door. She knocked lightly twice, as if whoever was in the room was expecting her. The door opened almost immediately, and she disappeared inside. The number 201 was visible in a glint of sunlight when the door swung closed.

Keeping an eye on her parked car, Nudger left the Volkswagen nestled out of sight behind a van and walked into the office. He tried to slip the pimply-faced young desk clerk ten dollars of Arthur Leland's money to give him the name of whoever was in 201. The desk clerk was a guy who probably never went to the movies or read detective novels.

He told Nudger to go to hell, the motel's guests were entitled to their privacy. Nudger shrugged and slunk back to his car. It was much colder there than in hell.

Beatrice Leland emerged from the room an hour later. She looked the same as when she'd entered; hair not mussed, clothes still unwrinkled. There were too many cars parked in the lot for Nudger to be able to tell which belonged with room 201, so he didn't write down a license number before following her out of the parking lot.

He expected her to go home. Instead, she drove for twenty minutes and made a left turn into the Howard Johnson's Motel on South Lindbergh. She was staying with franchises.

Again she went directly to one of the rooms. This time the desk clerk was more cooperative because Nudger didn't discourage the impression that he was a policeman. The man in the room had registered an hour ago as James Smith. Actually Smith.

But this time there was little doubt which car went with the room. Business was slow today; the only car parked on that side of the lot was a dark gray Lincoln with black-tinted windows. Nudger jotted down its license plate number in his spiral pocket notebook.

Apparently Beatrice Leland had done enough of whatever it was she was doing. When she left Howard Johnson's and Mr. Smith, she drove straight home. She looked upset when she went into the house, and she didn't leave again that day. Nudger waited in the stifling little Volkswagen until he saw Arthur Leland arrive home from work, then he went home himself and had a high old time with a frozen turkey dinner and a cold beer.

After supper he watched a "Barney Miller" rerun on TV and thought about Beatrice Leland and the woman in his own life, Claudia Bettencourt, who was in Chicago for a week-long teachers' convention. If the husband was the last to know, could it be that the boyfriend never found out at all?

*   *   *

In the morning he phoned Lieutenant Jack Hammersmith at the Third District police station and asked him please, please if he'd run a check with the Department of Motor Vehicles to see who owned the gray Lincoln. Hammersmith didn't like it, or pretended he didn't like it, as he puffed and smacked his lips on his foul cigar over the phone and copied the license number Nudger read to him. Then Nudger went down to Danny's Donuts, directly below his second-floor office, and had a Dunker Delite, coffee, and an antacid tablet for breakfast.

Forced by Danny to accept a free second cup of acidic coffee, he sat at the stainless steel counter and wondered about Beatrice Leland. Was this a flare-up of middle-aged sexuality? He'd seen it before, in women as well as men. Maybe Beatrice Leland was having a final sexual fling, or maybe her daughter's death had inspired some sort of nymphomaniacal clinging to sex as a symbol of life. Nudger had seen that before, too, this compulsion for sex after having dealings with death; he'd felt that one and knew how powerful it might be to a lonely, bereaved woman like Beatrice Leland.

Danny looked at Nudger with his doleful brown eyes and nodded toward the grease-spotted frosty window beyond the low counter. "Looks like business, Nudge," he said.

Nudger swiveled on his stool just in time to see Arthur Leland open the door next to the doughnut shop; he heard the door swing shut and the heavy tramp of Leland's footfalls as he climbed the narrow stairs to the door to Nudger's office.

"I guess I'd better be in," Nudger said. He carried his coffee with him so as not to offend Danny and joined Leland on the second-floor landing outside the door.

"She left the house yesterday and lied to me about where

she went," Leland said without preliminaries. "Where did she go?"

Nudger unlocked the door and ushered Leland inside. Leland stood with his arms crossed while Nudger opened the drapes to let in more winter gloom, then turned up the valve on the steam radiator and sat down behind his desk. "She drove to the Holiday Inn on Craigshire," Nudger said, "then to the Howard Johnson's motel on South Lindbergh. Both times she stayed in a room about an hour."

A sheen Nudger didn't like slid into Leland's hard eyes. Leland uncrossed his arms and unbuttoned his bulky overcoat. "Who did she see in these rooms?"

"I don't know yet. I'm finding out who she met at Howard Johnson's; I got the license number of his car."

"You saw him?" Leland asked, a sharp edge to his voice.

"No, I saw his name on the registration card. James Smith."

Leland grunted and began to pace.

"Don't jump to conclusions," Nudger cautioned, wondering at the value of that advice.

Leland grinned. It had nothing to do with humor. "My wife sees two men at motels in the middle of the afternoon and one of them registered under the name Smith, and you tell me not to draw any conclusion?"

"We don't even know if the person at the Holiday Inn was a man."

"Worse still," Leland said, his imagination really taking hold. "You know how to cheer up a client, Nudger."

"All I'm doing is passing on what I've learned," Nudger said. "That's why you hired me. I'm also advising you not to waste your anger and frustration yet, because we don't know the story."

"You telling me my wife is supplying these motels with Gideon Bibles, Nudger?"

"Somebody does."

"Don't smart off," Leland said. "That I didn't hire you for." He sighed and wiped a hand over his forehead, gazed at his fingers as if to see if they were soiled by his thoughts. "I'm not upset for the usual reason, Nudger. If my wife needs professional help, I want to see that she gets it. She's entering menopause, and she's suffering a terrible grief and strain." He looked at Nudger, his beefy face contorted by agony. "I can forgive her, whatever she's done."

"Do you want me off the case?" Nudger asked. "You get a refund. Maybe you don't want to learn anything more."

Leland shook his big head. "No, find out the rest of it." He walked heavily to the door, staring at the floor. "You have my work number; call me if anything urgent comes up."

"I'll phone you when I learn anything else," Nudger said, and watched Leland wedge his wide body through the doorframe. He listened to the big man's steps as Leland descended the stairs to the street. Cold air stirred briefly around Nudger's ankles a moment after he heard the outside door open and close. He picked up his foam coffee cup from the desk, took a sip, and was about to get up and pour the rest of the coffee down the washbasin in the office's half bath when the telephone rang.

It was Hammersmith. "What are you up to with this one, Nudge?" he asked around his cigar.

"Errant spouse case. Why?"

Hammersmith chuckled and slurped at the cigar. "You might be a bit errant yourself this time."

Nudger knew Hammersmith relished the dramatic pause. He waited patiently, silently, listening to the wheeze of the cigar being smoked, glad he was talking to Hammersmith by phone and not in person in Hammersmith's clouded office. He'd expected only a name and address out of this conversation, and Hammersmith knew it. Nudger thought about the big, fancy Lincoln. It crossed his mind that James Smith might be a known pimp, and Beatrice Leland was working for him, turning over her share of the profits. Arthur Leland would be thrilled to learn that.

"That license plate you asked me to run for you," Hammersmith said, "it belongs to a new Lincoln, gray on gray, registered to the Archdiocese of St. Louis."

"What?"

"The Church," Hammersmith said. "A priest drives it. Father Adam Tooley of St. Luke's Parish; the address is St. Luke's Cathedral over on Hanley." Hammersmith wheezed and chuckled again around the fat cigar. "I think you got the wrong car, Nudge."

He hung up, still chuckling.

But Nudger wasn't even smiling.

He followed Beatrice Leland again that afternoon. This time she was wearing jeans and a red quilted ski jacket. She appeared nervous; maybe she'd had a talk with her husband and suspected she was being followed. She drove around most of the afternoon, going nowhere, stopping only once, to buy gas.

When Nudger reported this to Arthur Leland that evening, Leland seemed relieved. He shouldn't have been; Beatrice surely was hiding something from him.

Nudger slept uneasily that night, nagged by his subconscious. He was up at 1:00 A.M. with heartburn and didn't fall asleep again until almost 2:30, an antacid tablet dissolving on his tongue.

He felt better at 8:30 after a shower and shave. As he sat eating the leathery omelet he'd prepared for breakfast, sipping coffee, he watched the morning local news on the black and white portable Sony in his apartment kitchen. Another mugging in the West End, the pretty blonde anchorwoman said disconsolately, as a shot of some buildings that might have been anywhere in town came on the screen. She was happier about the mayor's new cleanup campaign to get unemployed youths off the street. There was a piece of videotape of a surly kid spearing a crumpled paper bag with a spiked pole. Nudger wondered if he might be the one doing the mugging in the West End.

After a commercial the news came back on with tape of a group of people picketing an abortion clinic and tying up yesterday evening's downtown rush-hour traffic. A concerned-looking doctor inside the clinic was interviewed and said that tomorrow was the thirteenth anniversary of the Supreme Court's decision to legalize abortion, and he feared there might be violence. The right-to-lifers outside didn't look violent to Nudger. The newsman was talking to a fiftyish, balding man in a trenchcoat now. One of the picketers. His gentle gaze was firm, and he didn't blink once as he spoke. The wintry breeze blew his coat partly open and revealed a white clerical collar. After the interview, which Nudger didn't bother listening to, the newsman referred to the man as "Father Tooley, the militant priest."

Nudger dropped the piece of toast he was buttering. Then he realized the "tomorrow" the clinic doctor had referred to was today.

He went into the living room and picked up the phone.

Arthur Leland sounded as if he'd been awakened by the call. Nudger didn't care. He quickly identified himself and said, "Mr. Leland, this question might not make much sense to you, but are you having plumbing problems?"

"Is this a joke, Nudger?"

"No."

"All right, then. No. No plumbing problems—of any kind."

"Is your wife home?"

"No. She went shopping with her sister, early, before the stores get crowded. At least, that's what I was told."

"Did you see your sister-in-law?"

"No, Bea took our car and picked her up. Listen, Nudger—"

Nudger hung up the phone, then lifted the receiver again and dialed Hammersmith at the Third.

Then he left the apartment. Fast.

He tried to sort things out as he drove along Manchester in the bouncing Volkswagen, hoping he was wrong, knowing he wasn't. The first person Beatrice Leland had met was probably a demolitions expert—or more likely an amateur who thought he was an expert—a member of a violent anti-abortion organization. The second person, Father Tooley, possibly gave her exact instructions, or simply fortified her with faith.

There was nothing Nudger could do. Or Hammersmith and the power of the law. It had been too late when Nudger phoned.

Ten minutes from the apartment the news came over the car radio. The Woman's Clinic Downtown had been destroyed by a bomb blast. Apparently it was assumed that the building would be empty, but staff members had early abortions and consultations scheduled. Two staff members were killed, and three patients. Along with a woman thought to be carrying the bomb, who was seen entering the clinic with a large red purse a few minutes before the explosion. Police speculated that something had gone wrong with the explosive device. They were still trying to determine the identity of the woman with the purse, and what kind of explosive device was used.

Nudger knew who the woman was: Beatrice Leland. And he knew what kind of explosive device had been in her purse: a pipe bomb. Assembled at the Holiday Inn on Craigshire.

The bomb was supposed to stop abortions at the clinic and to draw attention to the anti-abortion cause. No one was supposed to die. Right-to-life groups didn't stand for death. Priests didn't stand for death. Six people were dead.

Nudger pulled the Volkswagen to the curb and sat still for

a long time, staring out the windshield at nothing beyond the car's sloping, dented hood. He felt angry, guilty for not having figured out everything sooner. That guilt was unreasonable, maybe, but there it was, resting heavily on him like a pall, and he couldn't do anything about it.

Eventually he realized he was cold.

He started the engine, jammed the car into gear, and drove on toward St. Luke's Cathedral.

The massive church's parking lot was almost empty when Nudger left the Volkswagen in a No Parking area near the front entrance. He hurried up veined marble steps and through ornate doors, then down the wide, carpeted center aisle of the cavernous cathedral. Above him towered ancient Gothic arches, carved stone, and softly glowing stained glass. Statuary was set in the walls on each side of the wide rows of dark-stained wooden pews; St. Luke himself on Nudger's right, on Nudger's left a stone Holy Mother and Child. Spiraling organ pipes rose on one side of the pulpit, where a young altar boy stood near wooden stairs. Except for half a dozen worshipers seated or kneeling in the vastness of the church, the altar boy seemed to be the only one around.

"Where can I find Father Tooley?" Nudger asked.

"In the rectory," the boy stammered, seeing the intensity in Nudger's face.

An elderly, gray man Nudger hadn't noticed stood up from the organ bench and said, "He's in his office, I believe. I saw him go in there earlier this morning." He pointed to a door behind the pulpit. "You'll have to check with Miss Hammond."

Nudger nodded and walked through the door, then down a richly paneled hall to a tall closed oak door.

He opened the door to find himself in a large outer office. The walls were lined with books and paintings. Behind a massive carved-wood desk sat a dark, fiftyish woman with stern eyes and a severe skinned-back hairdo. Miss Hammond, no doubt.

"I want to see Father Tooley," Nudger said.

Miss Hammond didn't like the way he'd asked. Her sharp eyes darted to a closed door on her left, back to Nudger. "He's preparing for Mass. I'm afraid—"

She stood up as Nudger ignored her and strode to the office door, his rage building. He wasn't sure what he was going to say once he got in to see Father Tooley. He figured that would take care of itself. Before the capable Miss Hammond could stop him, he opened the door and stepped inside.

Behind him Miss Hammond gasped. Then her harsh intake of air exploded outward in a scream.

Father Tooley was hanging motionless by a red sash looped around his distended neck. He was in his full and colorful priest's vestments, eyes bulging and grotesquely swollen purple tongue protruding. He resembled a huge, exotic tropical bird that had been garroted; bird of paradise profaned.

Miss Hammond seemed to be screaming from far away, though she was standing right next to Nudger. He turned and left her, and with that slight distance her shrieks became almost deafeningly loud. The altar boy and the gray old organist rushed past Nudger at exactly the same pace, as if drawn magnetically by the screams; several people who had joined the worshipers in the church passed him indistinctly, moving more slowly, hesitantly, sensing the worst, shadow figures in a dark dream.

Nudger's stomach was kicking around violently. He staggered up the wide center aisle toward the doors. The Holy Mother's calm stone eyes seemed to follow him as he passed. From high on the cross behind the altar, a crucified Christ gazed down on the scene through His suffering.

The echoing wails and cries of the parishioners racketed off the high arches and stone and stained glass of the great cathedral as Nudger found his way outside. He felt the stinging coldness of tears on his cheeks as he slumped on the marble steps.

He knew he wasn't crying for the dead at the clinic or for Father Tooley, but for everyone left behind in the wilderness.

ARTHUR LYONS

MISSING IN MIAMI

The yellow and black fish hung motionless in the green water and pinned me with a golden-eyed stare, as if he did not approve of morning drinkers. That might have been because he was dead. The joker across the table didn't have that excuse.

To hell with him, I thought, washing down three aspirins with a swallow of my Fog Cutter. This was no morning to be worrying about appearances; we were talking *survival* here. I wasn't crazy about him, anyway, prospective client or no.

I watched him and tried to determine just what it was about him I didn't like. Maybe it was the condescending way he sighted me down his long, aquiline nose, or the supercilious glint in his small eyes, or maybe it was his impeccable Ivy League not-a-strand-out-of-place haircut or his impeccable three-piece suit. Or maybe it was just because I was prejudiced against bankers.

"You usually meet clients in places like this?" he asked, looking around the room distastefully.

That made me feel better. "Sometimes. Depends on the circumstances."

The circumstances had been that I didn't like being called at home at 8:15 in the morning, especially after nights like last night. And especially-especially when the caller made it sound as if he were doing me a favor by waking me up.

"My name is Elliott Richardson, Mr. Asch," the voice had said. "Troy Wilcox gave me your number. He said you were a competent, discreet investigator." He didn't sound as if he really believed there was such a thing.

"That was nice of him."

"I wish to engage your services. Can you be in my office at eleven sharp? That's First Western Bank on Wilshire."

It was not a request, it was a summons. Troy Wilcox was one of my few friends in the banking business, but not a good enough friend that I was going to respond to any "Notice to Appear" from this yo-yo. I thought at first I'd make him come to my apartment but nixed that. My living room looked like the inside of a beaver dam, and I didn't want to give him the satisfaction of confirming his preconceptions.

"I'm afraid I can't make it then, Mr. Richardson," I told him. "I'll meet you at Harry's Hawaiian Bar at quarter to twelve."

"Harry's Hawaiian Bar? Where is that?" He sounded unsure of himself now.

"On Pacific, in Santa Monica."

"See here, can't we make it somewhere else—"

"Sorry, Mr. Richardson, but I'm tied up the rest of the day. If it's not there, I'm afraid it's going to have to wait until next week—"

"No, no, it can't wait," he said, then emitted a vexed sigh. "All right, 11:45."

Harry's was about as tacky as it sounded, which was why I'd chosen it. At one time it had been one of Santa Monica's nicest Polynesian restaurants, but that had been fifteen years ago, before Harry had sold out. After that it had gone through a series of hands, none of which had lifted a paint brush to retard its downhill slide, and now the cancerous-

looking white blotches on the bellies of the grass-skirted
dancers on the walls grew steadily bigger and the dried palm
frond shelter over the bar shed regularly into customers'
drinks, which was why I'd smartly chosen a cocktail table
beside one of the fish tanks, where the mortality rate for
tropical fish was seventeen times the national average.

Actually, besides taking Richardson out of his element,
which was what I'd intended to do, the surroundings were
quite appropriate, considering the tropical storm blowing at
gale force inside my skull. He stared as I took a sip from my
drink. "What's in that?"

"Fruit juices, a little grenadine. It's loaded with Vitamin C.
Want one?" I'd left out the 151-rum, but if he ordered one,
he'd find out about it without my telling him. Speaking of
151, it was finally beginning to do the job for which the drink
had been named, and my vision was starting to clear. "Now
what is your problem, Mr. Richardson?"

"My fiancée has disappeared," he said without hesitation.

"How long has she been missing?"

"Four weeks. I'm afraid something terrible has happened
to her."

That was a matter of opinion. I was sorely tempted to
disappear from his life, too, and the thought did not strike
me as particularly terrible. "Tell me about it," I said,
regretting the words instantly.

He took a breath and began. "A little over a month and a
half ago, Myra was notified that her father had been killed in
an automobile accident in Miami, and she went there to
settle his affairs. She was supposed to return on the third—
in fact, she called me the night before and gave me the flight
she would be arriving on—but when I met the plane, she
wasn't on it. I checked with the airline, and they said that
she had booked a seat but that she never showed up to claim
it. I figured she'd just missed the flight and went home to
wait for her to call, but I never heard from her. When I

phoned the Omni, where she'd been staying, they told me
she had checked out."

"And you never heard from her after that?"

"No. She left me the key to her apartment—she asked me
to water her plants—but nothing has been touched there
since she left. It's as if she has vanished into thin air."

"You've reported it to the police?"

"Of course," he said, as if I'd insulted his IQ. "Both here
and in Miami. They said there was no evidence that any
crime had been committed, so there was nothing they could
do."

He paused as a Filipino busboy scooped the dead fish out
of the tank with a little white net. I took out my notebook.
"What's her name?"

"Myra Webb."

"Address?"

"Two-three-four-six Overland, apartment three-oh-two,
Palms."

"Birthdate?"

"April 18"—he stopped to do some calculating in his
head—"1956."

"How long have you known her?"

"A little over a year."

"Occupation?"

"Escrow officer."

"At First Western?"

"Yes."

An intra-office love affair. Cozy. I tried to imagine them
doing it in the safe on a pile of soft hundreds. "When were
you two supposed to be married?"

He hesitated. "We hadn't really set a date yet. We weren't
even formally engaged, really. It was just an understanding
we had."

That ruled out flight from a case of prenuptial jitters. "You
two have a fight before she left or anything like that?"

"No," he said, his tone slightly indignant.

"What kind of person is she?"

"Kind, dependable, honest, stable . . ."

He was choosing all the traits that would make it seem highly unlikely that she would ever do anything as ridiculous as running away from him. "You know much about her past?"

"Only what she's told me."

"When you talked with her on the phone, how did she sound?"

"Fine. Her father's death had shaken her, naturally. Even though they didn't see each other that often, they were close, especially after Myra's mother was killed last year. They wrote and talked on the phone all the time."

The buzzing in my head was quieting now, replaced by the wavering plunkings of a steel guitar from Harry's sound system. "Killed? How?"

"Boating accident."

"She have any other family? Brothers? Sisters?"

He shook his head. "Myra's only sister died eight or nine years ago. In another freak accident, strangely enough." His gaze drifted off. "Apparently a beam from a construction site fell and crushed her. Myra didn't like to talk about it much."

I didn't blame her. It sounded as if her family had a big problem. Like a curse. I wondered if accidental death could be a genetic trait. I put away my notebook. "My fee is two hundred a day plus expenses, Mr. Richardson, and in cases like this, I require a thousand-dollar retainer."

He scowled at me. "Don't you think that's a little excessive?"

I shrugged. "It's all in your point of view. Some people think collecting fifteen percent on a thirty-year mortgage just for filling out a few forms in triplicate is excessive."

His eyes narrowed, and he leaned toward me. "Are you trying to insult me?"

"No," I replied calmly. "I'm just stating a fact. At least half of that thousand dollars is going to be spent immediately on a flight to Miami. I don't think it's excessive at all."

He waved a hand deprecatingly at my Fog Cutter, which was nearly gone. "What kind of expenses are you talking about? You can't expect me to finance your morning binges—"

I drained the drink, tossed a dollar tip on the table, and said, "I don't expect you to finance anything, Mr. Richardson. You've obviously gotten hold of the wrong man."

He caught up with me at the door. "Wait. Please."

I turned to face him.

"Look, I don't know where else to turn. Troy says you're good, and I trust Troy. Stop by the bank later, and I'll have a check for you."

That was probably as close as he would ever come to an apology. I thought about it. I would just as soon have had another Fog Cutter and gone back to bed. "I'll want to look around her place. You have the key with you?"

"Yes, but I can't get away from the bank until four—"

"I can handle it alone," I said, and held out a hand.

His face wrestled with the idea before finally saying uncle. He dug into his pocket and came up with a key, and I left, my mind already working on ways to pad his expense account.

Myra Webb's apartment was in a four-story, four-building complex connected by catwalks that overlooked the Santa Monica Freeway. The numerical sequence of the apartments had been cleverly worked out in code, and it was only by luck that I managed to crack it in under twenty minutes.

The place was hot and stuffy when I let myself in. The living room and adjoining kitchen were small, neat, and nondescript, furnished in the usual inexpensive Mediterranean. There were a lot of plants around, and their condition was not exactly a testament to Richardson's green thumb. He had been doing his job with the mail, however—there was a large stack of it on the table in the dining alcove—and I opened a window to let in some fresh freeway exhaust before sorting through it.

I wound up with five pieces worth following up. Two were her checking and savings account statements. The last transactions on either account had been made days before she had left for Florida, a withdrawal from her savings of $800 on January 15th, and a check written to Bon Voyage Travel on the sixteenth for $298. The third was a letter from the credit card recovery department of Barclay's Bank, saying that after numerous attempts to reach Myra by phone, they were informing her by letter that her VISA card had been recovered in Miami, and if she wished further information, she should contact a Sergeant Shyke at the Dade County Sheriff's Office there.

There was a Mobil Oil credit card statement for $77.75, and I went through the charge slips carefully. Two of the slips were from L.A. gas stations and four from stations around Miami—one as recent as two weeks ago. All of the slips had been signed "Myra Webb," but the signatures on the Miami slips were completely different from the ones from L.A. The automobile license numbers on all the Miami slips were the same—MIV334.

Last, there was a letter from an attorney named J. Leonard Greenfield at a Miami address, notifying Myra that there were a few minor details that had come up regarding her father's estate since her visit to his office and requesting that she get in touch with him as soon as possible. The letter was dated ten days earlier.

I left the mail on the table and went into the kitchen. The cupboards were full of bags of dried fruits and nuts, macrobiotic rice, unbleached whole wheat flour, and bottles of vitamin pills and mineral supplements, all carrying the labels of various health food stores. I stared at them, wondering which one of them would cure a hangover, then closed the cupboard doors and went down the hall toward the bedroom.

On the nightstand by the quilt-covered bed, there was a small, framed photograph of a tanned, silver-haired man with his arm draped around the shoulder of a twentyish-looking girl. The girl was a bit overweight and had one of those faces that was vaguely attractive until you started breaking it down into its components. Her shoulder-length brown hair was washed-out and stringy, her nose was too big, her brown eyes too far apart. The glue that held the parts together was the smile. It was the bright, radiant smile of a girl in a toothpaste commercial, and it threw shadows across the flaws in the rest of the face. I put the picture down and spied a scrapbook on the bottom shelf of the table. I sat down on the bed with the book on my lap and played "This Is Your Life."

The book was full of family snapshots, going back to Myra's childhood. As I suspected, the man in the bedside picture was Myra's father, and as I turned the pages, I watched the gray creep into his hair, like a Grecian Formula commercial being run backward. What was more interesting, however, was the changes in expression that took place in the pictures. In the front of the book, everybody looked happy, but then the characters began to drop out, and a strain showed behind the smiles of the remaining subjects. First, there was father, mother, sister, Myra, then just father, mother, Myra, then just father, Myra. Now Myra was the Last Little Indian. I wondered.

Sprinkled through the family pictures were snapshots of Myra with various young men, including half a dozen of her with Richardson. If the rest of the young men were boyfriends, Richardson seemed to be the only one with an apparent age difference. Maybe she had anticipated the death of her father and had gone out searching for a replacement before the fatal event. I pocketed several of the later pictures and put the book back.

There was nothing else in the bedroom I could see that would be much help, so I went back out to the living room and used the phone there to call the Dade County Sheriff's Office. After being transferred twice and being put on hold for five minutes, I finally got Shyke on the line, and once I explained who I was and what I was doing, his tone turned grudgingly cooperative.

Myra's VISA card had been left in a Miami department store by a Latino woman, possibly Cuban, who had tried to use it to purchase three hundred dollars' worth of clothes. The store clerk had become suspicious when the woman's signature didn't match the back of the card and had asked for corroborating identification, upon which the woman had materialized other cards with Myra's name on them. Even after determining that the card had not been reported stolen, the clerk was still suspicious and asked the woman for some ID with a photograph on it, at which time the woman told the clerk to forget the sale and tried to get the card back. The clerk, sensing he had a stolen card, tried to stall the woman and went into the back to call the police, but when he returned to the counter, the woman was gone.

I told Shyke about the Mobil statement and gave him the license number on the Miami slips, which he said he would have checked out by the time I arrived the next day. Following my unspoken line of thought, he also promised to have ready photographs of all Jane Does that had turned up in the Miami area during the past four weeks.

Before leaving, I watered the plants.

Richardson was trying his best banker's smile on a customer when I came in, and he acknowledged my presence over the woman's shoulder with an irritated nod. I sat in a nearby chair until the customer left, then slid into her still-warm seat. His smile immediately turned into a frown. "Well?"

"She's not there."

"I *know* she's not there," he snapped. "What did you find out?"

When I told him, he looked as if he wished I hadn't. The color washed out of his face, and he said worriedly, "My God, you don't think she's dead—"

"I don't think anything at this point."

He leaned toward me. "But she *has* to know her credit cards are missing. Why wouldn't she report it?"

I told him I had no idea and showed him the Mobil slips. He stared at them awhile, identified the L.A. charges as Myra's signature, but said the Miami signatures were definitely not. I gave him the bank account statements and asked him to check to see if there had been any activity on either account since Myra's departure to Florida. He made two calls, then slumped back in his chair. "Nothing."

His eyes had lost their cocksure contempt, at least temporarily, but that didn't make me feel particularly good. "If you want me to check this out further, I'll have to go to Miami."

"Of course," he said quickly. "Take the first available flight."

"I'll need that thousand-dollar retainer we discussed."

He hadn't forgotten, but he'd been hoping I had. He cleared his throat and scowled as he took a checkbook out of the desk and began writing. The check was conveniently from his bank, and I asked him if he could make sure I had no trouble cashing it. He grumbled but accompanied me to a teller, where the look on his face turned to one of pain as he watched her count out the amount in hundreds.

As I stepped away from the window, he said, "I'm not paying for any Florida vacations with that money, remember that. Keep your mind on what you're going down there for."

There he was, the same old lovable teddy bear I once knew, but with his grand in my pocket, I didn't somehow mind as much. I patted my breast pocket where my wallet was, gave him a knowing leer, and told him I would be in touch.

By the time I had gotten my bag and rented a car at the airport, it was close to midnight. Five miles outside town, the Miami skyline looked like stacks of glittering stars, but once I turned off the turnpike onto Biscayne Boulevard, the glitter was off.

Downtown Miami was a once-glamorous beauty queen missing her dentures. It wasn't that there wasn't a lot of money floating around the city these days; there was. It just wasn't the taxable kind.

Since Castro had emptied his prisons and sent America his "poor," and since cocaine had gained acceptance as the nation's preferred party drug, the Jewish New York snow-birds who had once flocked here to retire had flown inland, supplanted by another kind of "snowbird"—Colombian, Peruvian, and Cuban "businessmen" who came to ensure that the noses of their newly adopted country stayed well-packed. Spanish had replaced Yiddish as the city's second language, to the point that signs in many windows assured me as I passed by, "English Spoken Here."

The Omni was a modern, 20-story, black glass anomaly rising out of the dirty old brick of downtown. The bottom three floors were shopping mall, complete with a small amusement park on the ground floor for the kiddies. The merry-go-round was dark as I gave the valet my car and went toward the elevators, all of its horses put to bed for the night. That seemed like a good idea to me, but being the conscientious sleuth I am, I still had work to do.

My room was on the fourteenth floor, and having gotten situated, I put in a wake-up call for 3:30, poured myself a stiff vodka from the bottle I'd tucked away in my suitcase, and stretched out on the bed.

It seemed as if I'd just lain down when the telephone sent me bolting upright in bed. I thanked the operator sarcastically for her diligence, and after my eyes focused, I managed to locate the elevator.

Except for the sallow-faced clerk behind the front desk, the lobby was empty, which was what I had been hoping. I have always found graveyard shift employees more reasonable to deal with than their daytime counterparts; they are usually bored and therefore more willing to talk, less harried by customers and the prying eyes of supervisors, and often resentful of management for having stuck them on a shift only Dracula would enjoy. My guy turned out to be bored, talkative, *and* resentful, and after I explained the gravity of the situation, he was so concerned that for a mere fifty dollars, he was willing to punch Myra's name into his computer and come up with a printout of her charges. I took it back to my room and undressed this time before going to bed.

Over a room service continental breakfast, I went over the printout. Myra had stayed at the Omni a total of eight days and during that time had run up a $34.50 phone bill. Most of the calls had been to Richardson's number in L.A., but two numbers aroused my curiosity. Both had been less than two minutes long, and both were numbers in Key West. I called them.

Both were hotels, but neither had a Myra Webb registered. Neither receptionist sounded pleased when I asked if a Myra Webb had checked in during the past four weeks, but after I did a little soft shoe about being Dr. Asch, and it being an emergency, both reluctantly agreed to check. No go.

The merry-go-round was alive when I went downstairs to the garage, and I stopped for a moment to watch with envious eyes the gleeful faces of the children as they rode around on the backs of the painted horses. I was tempted to get on, just to see if it made me feel young again, even for a moment, but then waved a hand and went on. I doubted anything could ever make me feel young again.

The day was warm and muggy, and I turned on the car air-conditioning for the short drive over to Greenfield's office, which was in an older commercial building in the Art Deco district.

His office was on the eighth floor, a burl-wood affair with maroon velveteen furniture and a lot of windows. Despite the humidity the man still wore a dark three-piece suit, the shoulders of which were liberally dusted with dandruff. He was a short, middle-aged man with graying hair and eyes the color of mud. After exchanging pleasantries, he told me about Myra's last visit, shortly after her father's funeral.

Greenfield had been Nelson Webb's tax attorney, and it had been on his advice that Myra's father several years earlier had put all of his assets, including several bank accounts, a condo on Biscayne Boulevard, some undeveloped real estate, and assorted stocks and bonds, into a revocable living trust, with Myra as the sole trustee. He explained all this to Myra, who without hesitation instructed Greenfield, as lawyer for the trust, to liquidate everything and pay whatever inheritance taxes there were. The rest of the money was to be held in an account in Myra's name for six months, upon which time if Greenfield did not hear from her, he was to give away the money to whatever charities he chose.

"How much are we talking about?" I asked.

He tugged on his lower lip. "That's hard to say. There will be a lot of taxes. And the real estate market has been depressed lately. But I'd say a minimum of $190,000."

"That's a lot of good works. Didn't you find her instructions a little peculiar?"

"I found almost everything about the girl peculiar," he said flatly.

"How so?"

He paused and pulled down his vest. "I'm no psychologist, but I'd say she had tendencies toward paranoia. All the time she was here, she kept looking over her shoulder, as if someone were behind her. And several times she made passing remarks about how 'they' had 'gotten' her father and now were out to get her. I asked her what she meant, and who 'they' were, but she wouldn't elaborate. She just said she would take care of it. Then there was the matter of the gift account—"

"Gift account?"

He nodded. "According to federal law, a parent can bestow as a gift up to six thousand dollars a year, tax-free, to his or her offspring. Myra's father had been contributing to a gift account for Myra for six years. I told Myra about it, and she demanded the bank book, which I gave her. Shortly thereafter, I received a call from the manager of the bank, saying that Myra was there wanting to clear out the account—in cash."

"As in money-cash?"

He frowned disapprovingly. "Hundreds and fifties, to be specific. I got her on the phone and tried to talk her into having the money transferred to her own bank in California, or at least taking it out in a bank draft, but she insisted that she needed the cash and that was that."

"Thirty-six thousand bucks?"

"More than that, with the accumulated interest."

I didn't like the picture that was coming together. A young, vulnerable, and perhaps emotionally disturbed woman is last seen wandering around Miami, rip-off capital of the world, carrying some thirty-odd thousand dollars in cash, drops out of sight at the same time an imposter is caught trying to use her credit cards. It made me wonder if Myra's paranoid delusions were just that, or were more firmly founded in reality.

"What happens to the estate if something happens to Myra?"

He shrugged. "It goes to charity, I suppose. She has no living heirs."

"And she left you power of attorney to choose which ones?"

"That is correct."

Maybe it was just my innate distrust of attorneys, but I made a mental note to do some checking on Greenfield, just to make sure he didn't own any homes for wayward girls. I told him I would be in touch and drove over to the Sheriff's Office.

Shyke was a beefy, red-faced cop who sweated a lot, for which I couldn't blame him; it seemed like the thing to do on a day like this. We did a little small-talking about Florida humidity vs. California aridity, and then he got down to business. The plate number on the credit card receipts belonged to a 1981 Chevy registered to a Jeremy McBride of Coral Gables. Only four months ago, Mr. McBride reported that the plates had been stolen. Shyke had put out an alert to all Mobil dealers in the southern Florida area, but so far they had gotten no calls. When I told him about the cash the woman had drawn out of the bank, he shook his head ruefully and pulled out the Jane Doe pictures as if he had already consigned her to them. Five unidentified girls had found their way to the Miami morgue during the past four weeks, four murders and one OD, but none of them was Myra. I gave Shyke one of the photographs I'd brought, and he promised to spread it around.

It was a little before noon when I left the station house and started back to the hotel. Two blocks away I changed my mind and pulled into a gas station and bought a map. The only lead I had was thin to say the least, but it beat the hell out of sitting around the hotel waiting for Shyke to call me with bad news.

Highway One stretched on cement stilts across miles of blue-green ocean between the Keys, and although I had to admire the fortitude and skill of the men who had built it, I had to wonder why they had bothered. Those little clumps of coral covered with stunted lime trees and scrub bush seemed hardly worth the effort. But the farther I drove, the more grateful I was that they had. I rolled down the windows and let the sea breeze be my air-conditioning and watched the few puffs of white cloud float peacefully over the water, where the sun was playing its tricks. And then it was the end of the line.

At first, Key West looks like every other tourist town in America taken by Colonel Sanders and his troops, but then the Howard Johnsons and Holiday Inns begin to relinquish ground to history, and you find yourself in a time-stopped world of sun-washed wood-frame houses and ancient storefronts, some restored, some still in a state of decay. The streets of Old Town were crowded with pedestrians window-shopping or drinking in its many saloons, which had once been watering holes for many a pirate, and later the likes of Papa and Tennessee.

The Miramar was near the beach. It was an older, small hotel with gingerbread balconies and a large verandah out front surrounded by abundant sprays of pink and yellow blossoms. All it needed to make the picture perfect would be two white-haired gentlemen in white linen suits sitting in rocking chairs sipping mint juleps.

The white-haired man behind the desk wasn't sipping a mint julep, but he could have fit the part. His name was Butterworth and he owned the place, and when he found I didn't want to rent a room, he turned a bit sour, but after some convincing talk, he finally agreed to look at Myra's photograph. He studied it for a while, then handed it back.

"Missing person, you say?"

"That's right."

He scratched his chin thoughtfully. "I dunno. Looks like the woman, but the hair is different. The woman who stayed here was blonde."

I felt a pang of excitement. "How long ago did she leave?"

"About three weeks. She stayed a little over a week."

"What name did she check in under?"

He pulled out an ancient guest register from beneath the desk and flipped the pages back. "Here it is. Marguerite Sills."

"Did she leave a forwarding address?"

He shook his head. "I think she was trying to find an apartment. She kept checking the paper for rentals, I know that."

I thanked him and left. At the first pay phone, I stopped and called information for a new listing for a Marguerite Sills, but of course they didn't have one.

I drove to the office of the local newspaper and bought back issues of every paper for the past three weeks, and by 4:30 I'd checked out fifteen classified ads for rentals without any luck. At the rate I was going, I would have all of them checked out by next Wednesday. I wouldn't have worried about it—after all, the longer it took, the more money it was in my pocket—except that I could not shake this feeling of urgency I had about the case. The girl was running, that was for sure, but from what? Or from whom? Maybe it was just because I was in Hemingway's town, but I kept having visions of her lying on the bed of her newly rented apartment reconciled to her fate and waiting for her name-less killers to come through the door.

Then I remembered her wheat germ. I drove to the first pay phone and ripped out the page for "Health Food Stores," from the yellow pages. At my second stop, Ellen's House of Health, I hit. The perky little long-haired girl behind the counter looked at the picture while I told her I worked for an attorney in Miami and that it was imperative that we locate the girl in the photograph right away, that there had been a sudden death in the family, her father, and she had to be notified. I explained that she had just moved into this area and we didn't have her address, and the girl said suddenly: "She lives right around the corner, on Tulane."

I gave her a big smile. "She does come in here, then?"

The girl nodded enthusiastically. "She was in this morning, in fact."

"Do you know what address on Tulane?"

She shook her head. "No, but you can't miss it. It's a big white house with a sign out front, 'Rooms to Rent.'" As if she thought it needed explanation, she added, "I saw her walking into it one day."

She was right about the house; I had no trouble finding it. It was a freshly painted wood house with a gray gabled roof, and it could have been at home in a New England fishing village as easily as Key West. The owner was a doughy-faced, middle-aged woman named Evers, and she told me in a singsongy voice that Marguerite was not at home but that I might find her down at Mallory Pier. She went there every evening about this time, she explained, to watch the sunset.

Others besides "Marguerite" apparently had the same idea, for there was a mini Mardi Gras going on at Mallory Pier when I got there. Jugglers, fire eaters, acrobats and guitar players, lovers and friends, wine drinkers and pot smokers, all had congregated to bid adieu to the day in their own ways. I spotted her at the edge of the crowd, standing next to a long-haired man playing a conga drum. She was burned from the sun and her blonde hair was cut very short, and at first I was not sure it was her, but then she smiled. She was watching the red-orange tip of the sun sinking into the horizon, turning the ocean into a vast bowl of hot tomato soup, when I stepped up behind her. "Myra?"

She emitted a gasp and whirled to face me. Her eyes were wide as panic spread across her face, and her head darted quickly from side to side, as if searching for a place to run. Before she did, I said as soothingly as I could, "Don't be afraid. Please."

"Who are you?" she stammered. "What do you want?"

"My name is Asch. I'm a detective. Elliott Richardson hired me to find you. He's worried about you."

"Elliott?" She seemed only partly to comprehend.

I nodded. "He was afraid something bad had happened to you. So are a lot of other people, including the Miami police."

Behind her the sky was streaked with color as the last bit of sun disappeared into the sea, and the crowd erupted into cheers. "The police? But why?"

"Someone has been using your credit cards. The police think somebody might have done you in and taken them."

"Oh, no," she said, shaking her head. "I threw them away. They were the last of Myra Webb, and I had to get rid of them."

Before I had a chance to clear up that one, a large tanned hand attached itself firmly to my forearm. I turned to find that the hand belonged to a shirtless, well-muscled, bleached-hair beach specimen, whose cold blue eyes were trying to bore holes in my face. "Marguerite, this joker bothering you?"

"Get your hand off me, junior, and buzz off," I said. "This is a private matter." He had at least ten years on me and looked durable enough, and although I was not anxious to find out how durable, I still didn't like people putting their hands on me. Fortunately Myra stepped in before anything could get started, and said, "That's all right, Cliff. This man and I have something to talk about."

Cliff looked dubious. "You sure?"

"Yes."

Cliff reluctantly let go of my arm and walked away, scowling.

"Friend of yours?"

"Yes," she said. "I have a lot of new friends."

I needed a drink and told her so, and she took me into town to Sloppy Joe's, a dirty-floored, noisy bar whose

peeling plaster walls were covered with photographs of
Papa, bearded and clean-shaven, sitting, standing, fishing,
smiling, and not smiling. I got the point—Hemingway used
to hang out there. The place was crowded with young
rowdies and crusty looking commercial fishermen, but we
managed to find two empty stools at the bar and ordered two
beers.

"How did you find me?" she asked sheepishly.

"You left a trail of wheat germ behind you."

She gave me a confused look. "Huh?"

"Never mind. The thing that matters isn't how I found
you, but why I had to."

She began then, almost apologetically, and as she told me
her story, I began to feel sorry for her. "When my father
died," she said as she did a Watergate shredding job on her
cocktail napkin, "I knew something horrible was going to
happen to me. I felt as if some terrible, murderous force was
pursuing me. First there was my sister, then my mother,
then Dad, all dying strange, violent deaths. I couldn't handle
it. I panicked. I felt that whatever malevolent force got them
was going to get me, too, unless I did something. I knew I
had to make a complete break with my past, change my
identity and my life. It was the only way I could survive."

The accumulated trauma had shoved her into a childlike
world in which names took on a magical significance. By
changing her name she could prevent the complete Fall of
the House of Usher. "Why did you pick this place?"

She shrugged. "The land ran out here. I probably should
have gone north; maybe that way you wouldn't have found
me. But in a way I'm glad I didn't. I like it here. I have the
sun and a new life and new friends. For the first time in
years, I'm happy." Her eyes grew suddenly fearful, and she
said imploringly, "You're not going to tell Elliott where I am?
I can't go back to that life. If I do, I'll die. I *know* it."

"Nobody says you have to go back to that life. But you
should call him and explain things—"

The fear stayed in her eyes. Her head wagged back and forth. "No. Please. You don't understand. Elliott will make me come back. He can be very . . . persuasive."

At first I couldn't see her and Richardson together, but it was beginning to gel for me. She was scared and unsure of herself, perfect prey for a man like Richardson, who would play on that and convince her that she need only lean on him and everything would be all right, although it never would be. I thought about it. I could see the girl was serious; the terror in her voice was too real to be fake. I found myself nonplussed. On the one hand, it was my job to intrude on other people's lives; that was what a detective did. On the other, I didn't want to be responsible for causing the woman an emotional breakdown; she had had enough pain already. "I'll make you a deal," I said finally. "You get things straightened out with the cops and the credit card company, and get your affairs cleaned up, and I promise not to tell Richardson where you are."

"Oh, thank you—"

"And you're going to have to write Richardson a note, explaining things. He's my client, and I owe him that much. So do you."

She agreed and scribbled out a note on a piece of paper she procured from the bartender, thanked me again, and disappeared into the twilight.

I ordered something a little stronger than beer, and while I sipped it, I stared at a picture of Papa and wondered what he would have done. Probably the same as I—*nada*. After all, this was a clean, well-lighted place. Well-lighted, anyway.

The Filipino busboy scooped the two dead fish out of the tank gingerly, dropped them into a bowser bag, and disappeared into the kitchen. I didn't like to think what he was going to do with them back there.

Richardson finished reading the note and scowled at me. "I want to know where she is."

I took out my wallet, extracted seventeen dollars and my expense sheet, and put them down in front of him. "You'll find everything listed there."

He stared at the money. "What is this bullshit?"

"It's not bullshit, it's your change. From your thousand-dollar retainer. My expenses came to a little over $983. Since I didn't complete the job to your satisfaction, I'm not charging you for my time."

He leaned toward me, his face angry. "I'm not going to screw around with you, Asch. I want to know where she is."

I smiled at him and took another sip of my Fog Cutter. I wasn't sure, but I might have been enjoying this more than I would have the money.

His lips thinned, showing some teeth. "You were hired to do a job. You are breaking a fiduciary trust. I'll have your license—"

I gave him an appraising look. "I think my original diagnosis was correct, Richardson. You're definitely anal-retentive."

His chair scraped loudly on the floor as he stood up. "I'll sue you for every dime you've got—"

"You'll die broke."

"You'll be hearing from my attorney. I'm going to make you talk. Then I'm going to make sure you never work in this town again."

I looked up, snapped my fingers, and pointed at him. "Got it! Louis B. Mayer!"

His face grew red, and he turned abruptly and went out the door. I went back to my Fog Cutter, feeling extremely good. A steel guitar plucked out a soggy version of "Aloha Hoy," and I hummed along and thought about going out to the pier and watching the sun set. There probably wouldn't be any fire eaters, but then, you couldn't have everything.

SARA PARETSKY

AT THE OLD SWIMMING
HOLE

I

THE GYM WAS DANK—chlorine and sweat combined in a hot, sticky mass. Shouts from the trainers, from the swimmers, from the spectators, bounced from the high metal ceilings and back and forth from the benches lining the pool on two sides. The cacophony set up an unpleasant buzzing in my head.

I was not enjoying myself. My shirt was soaked through with sweat. Anyway, I was too old to sit cheering on a bleacher for two hours. But Alicia had been insistent—I had to be there in person for her to get points on her sponsor card.

Alicia Alonso Dauphine and I went to high school together. Her parents had bestowed a prima ballerina's name on her, but Alicia showed no aptitude for fine arts. From her earliest years, all she wanted was to muck around with engines. At eighteen, off she went to the University of Illinois to study aeronautics.

Despite her lack of interest in dance, Alicia was very athletic. Next to airplanes, the only thing she really cared about was competitive swimming. I used to cheer her when she was NCAA swimming champ, always with a bit of irritation about being locked in a dank, noisy gym for hours at a time—swimming is not a great spectator sport. But after all, what are friends for?

When Alicia joined Berman Aircraft as an associate engineer, we drifted our separate ways. We met occasionally at weddings, confirmations, bar mitzvahs (my, how our friends were aging! Childlessness seemed to suspend us in time, but each new ceremony in their lives marked a new milestone toward old age for the women we had played with in high school).

Then last week I'd gotten a call from Alicia. Berman was mounting a team for a citywide corporate competition—money would be raised through sponsors for the American Cancer Society. Both Alicia's mother and mine had died of cancer—would I sponsor her for so many meters? Doubling my contribution if she won? It was only after I'd made the pledge that I realized she expected me there in person. One of her sponsors had to show up to testify that she'd done it, and all the others were busy with their homes and children, and come on, V.I., what do you do all day long? I need you.

How can you know you're being manipulated and still let it happen? I hunched an impatient shoulder and turned back to the starting blocks.

From where I sat, Alicia was just another bathing-suited body with a cap. Her distinctive cheekbones were softened and flattened by the dim fluorescence. Not a wisp of her thick black hair trailed around her face. She was wearing a bright red tank suit—no extra straps or flounces to slow her down in the water.

The swimmers had been wandering around the side of the pool, swinging their arms to stretch out the muscles, not talking much while the timers argued some inaudible point with the referee. Now a police whistle shrilled faintly in the din and the competitors snapped to attention, moving toward the starting blocks at the far end of the pool.

We were about to watch the fifty-meter freestyle. I looked at the hand-scribbled card Alicia had given me before the meet. After the fifty-meter, she was in a 4×50 relay. Then I could leave.

The swimmers were mounting the blocks when someone began complaining again. The woman from the Ajax insurance team seemed to be having a problem with the lane marker on the inside of her lane. The referee reshuffled the swimmers, leaving the offending lane empty. The swimmers finally mounted the blocks again. Timers got into position.

Standing to see the start of the race, I was no longer certain which of the women was Alicia. Two of the other six contenders also wore red tank suits; with their features smoothed by caps and dimmed lighting, they all became anonymous. One red suit was in lane two, one in lane three, one in lane six.

The referee raised the starting gun. Swimmers got set. Arms swung back for the dive. Then the gun, and seven bodies flung themselves into the water. Perfect dive in lane six—had to be Alicia, surfacing, pulling away from all but one other swimmer, a fast little woman from the brokerage house of Feldstein, Holtz and Woods.

Problems for the red-suited woman in lane two. I hadn't seen her dive, but she was having trouble righting herself, couldn't seem to make headway in the lane. Now everyone was noticing her. Whistles were blowing; the man on the loudspeaker tried ineffectually to call for silence.

I pushed my way through the crowds on the benches and vaulted over the barrier dividing the spectators from the water. Useless over the din to order someone into the pool for her. Useless to point out the growing circle of red. I kicked off running shoes and dove from the side. Swimming underwater to the second lane. Not Alicia. Surely not. Seeing the water turn red around me. Find the woman.

Surface. Drag her to the edge where, finally, a few gal-
vanized hands pulled her out.

I scrambled from the pool and picked out someone in a
striped referee's shirt. "Get a fire department ambulance as
fast as you can." He stared at me with a stupid gape to his
jaw. "Dial 911, damn it. Do it now!" I pushed him toward the
door, hard, and he suddenly broke into a trot.

I knelt beside the woman. She was breathing, but shallow-
ly. I felt her gently. Hard to find the source of bleeding with
the wet suit, but I thought it came from the upper back.
Demanding help from one of the bystanders, I carefully
turned her to her side. Blood was oozing now, not pouring,
from a wound below her left shoulder. Pack it with towels,
elevate her feet, keep the crowd back. Wait. Wait. Watch the
shallow breathing turn to choking. Mouth-to-mouth does no
good. Who knows cardiopulmonary resuscitation? A muscu-
lar young man in skimpy bikini shorts comes forward and
works at her chest. By the time the paramedics hustle in with
stretcher and equipment, the shallow, choking breath has
stopped. They take her to the hospital, but we all know it's
no good.

As the stretcher-bearers trotted away, the rest of the room
came back into focus. Alicia was standing at my side, black
hair hanging damply to her shoulders, watching me with
fierce concentration. Everyone else seemed to be shrieking in
unison; the sound re-echoing from the rafters was more
unbearable than ever.

I stood up, put my mouth close to Alicia's ear, and asked
her to take me to whoever was in charge. She pointed to a
man in an Izod T-shirt standing on the other side of the hole
left by the dead swimmer's body.

I went to him immediately. "I'm V. I. Warshawski. I'm a
private detective. That woman was murdered—shot through
the back. Whoever shot her probably left during the confu-

sion. But you'd better get the cops here now. And tell everyone over your megaphone that no one leaves until the police have seen them."

He looked contemptuously at my dripping jeans and shirt. "Do you have anything to back up this preposterous statement?"

I held out my hands. "Blood," I said briefly, then grabbed the microphone from him. "May I have your attention, please." My voice bounced around the hollow room. "My name is V. I. Warshawski; I am a detective. There has been a serious accident in the pool. Until the police have been here and talked to us, none of us must leave this area. I am asking the six timers who were at the far end of the pool to come here now."

There was silence for a minute, then renewed clamor. A handful of people picked their way along the edge of the pool toward me. The man in the Izod shirt was fulminating but lacked the guts to try to grab the mike.

When the timers came up to me, I said, "You six are the only ones who definitely could not have killed the woman. I want you to stand at the exits." I tapped each in turn and sent them to a post—two to the doors on the second floor at the top of the bleachers, two to the ground-floor exits, and one each to the doors leading to the men's and women's dressing rooms.

"Don't let anyone, regardless of *anything* he or she says, leave. If they have to use the bathroom, tough—hold it until the cops get here. Anyone tries to leave, keep them here. If they want to fight, let them go but get as complete a description as you can."

They trotted off to their stations. I gave Izod back his mike, made my way to a pay phone in the corner, and dialed the Eleventh Street homicide number.

II

SERGEANT MCGONNIGAL was not fighting sarcasm as hard as he might have. "You sent the guy to guard the upstairs exit and he waltzed away, probably taking the gun with him. He must be on his knees in some church right now thanking God for sending a pushy private investigator to this race."

I bit my lips. He couldn't be angrier with me than I was with myself. I sneezed and shivered in my damp, clammy clothes. "You're right, Sergeant. I wish you'd been at the meet instead of me. You'd probably have had ten uniformed officers with you who could've taken charge as soon as the starting gun was fired and avoided this mess. Do any of the timers know who the man was?"

We were in an office that the school athletic department had given the police for their investigation-scene headquarters. McGonnigal had been questioning all the timers, figuring their closeness to the pool gave them the best angle on what had happened. One was missing, the man I'd sent to the upper balcony exit.

The sergeant grudgingly told me he'd been over that ground with the other timers. None of them knew who the missing man was. Each of the companies in the meet had supplied volunteers to do the timing and other odd jobs. Everyone just assumed this man was from someone else's firm. No one had noticed him that closely; their attention was focused on the action in the pool. My brief glance at him gave the police their best description: medium height, light, short brown hair, wearing a pale green T-shirt and faded white denim shorts. Yes, baggy enough for a gun to fit in a pocket unnoticed.

"You know, Sergeant, I asked for the six timers at the far

end of the pool because they were facing the swimmers, so none of them could have shot the dead woman in the back. This guy came forward. That means there's a timer missing—either the person actually down at the far end was in collusion, or you're missing a body."

McGonnigal made an angry gesture—not at me. Himself for not having thought of it before. He detailed two uniformed cops to round up all the volunteers and find out who the errant timer was.

"Any more information on the dead woman?"

McGonnigal picked up a pad from the paper-littered desk in front of him. "Her name was Louise Carmody. You know that. She was twenty-four. She worked for the Ft. Dearborn Bank and Trust as a junior lending officer. You know that. Her boss is very shocked—you probably could guess that. And she has no enemies. No dead person ever does."

"Was she working on anything sensitive?"

He gave me a withering glance. "What twenty-four-year-old junior loan officer works on anything sensitive?"

"Lots," I said firmly. "No senior person ever does the grubby work. A junior officer crunches numbers or gathers basic data for crunching. Was she working on any project that someone might not want her to get data for?"

McGonnigal shrugged wearily but made a note on a second pad—the closest he would come to recognizing that I might have a good suggestion.

I sneezed again. "Do you need me for anything else? I'd like to get home and dry off."

"No, go. I'd just as soon you weren't around when Lieutenant Mallory arrives, anyway."

Bobby Mallory was McGonnigal's boss. He was also an old friend of my father, who had been a beat sergeant until his death fifteen years earlier. Bobby did not like women on the crime scene in any capacity—victim, perpetrator, or investigator—and he especially did not like his old friend Tony's daughter on the scene. I appreciated McGonnigal's unwillingness to witness any acrimony between his boss and me, and was getting up to leave when the uniformed cops came back.

The sixth timer had been found in a supply closet behind the men's lockers. He was concussed and groggy from a head wound and couldn't remember how he got to where he was. Couldn't remember anything past lunchtime. I waited long enough to hear that and slid from the room.

Alicia was waiting for me at the far end of the hall. She had changed from her suit into jeans and a pullover and was squatting on her heels, staring fiercely at nothing. When she saw me coming, she stood up and pushed her black hair out of her eyes.

"You look a mess, V.I."

"Thanks. I'm glad to get help and support from my friends after they've dragged me into a murder investigation."

"Oh, don't get angry—I didn't mean it that way. I'm sorry I dragged you into a murder investigation. No, I'm not, actually. I'm glad you were on hand. Can we talk?"

"After I put some dry clothes on and stop looking a mess."

She offered me her jacket. Since I'm five-eight to her five-four, it wasn't much of a cover, but I draped it gratefully over my shoulders to protect myself from the chilly October evening.

At my apartment Alicia followed me into the bathroom while I turned on the hot water. "Do you know who the dead woman was? The police wouldn't tell us."

"Yes," I responded irritably. "And if you'll give me twenty minutes to warm up, I'll tell you. Bathing is not a group sport in this apartment."

She trailed back out of the bathroom, her face set in tense lines. When I joined her in the living room some twenty minutes later, a towel around my damp hair, she was sitting in front of the television set changing channels.

"No news yet," she said briefly. "Who was the dead girl?"

"Louise Carmody. Junior loan officer at the Ft. Dearborn. You know her?"

Alicia shook her head. "Do the police know why she was shot?"

"They're just starting to investigate. What do you know about it?"

"Nothing. Are they going to put her name on the news?"

"Probably, if the family's been notified. Why is this important?"

"No reason. It just seems so ghoulish, reporters hovering around her dead body and everything."

"Could I have the truth, please?"

She sprang to her feet and glared at me. "It is the truth."

"Screw that. You don't know her name, you spin the TV dials to see the reports, and now you think it's ghoulish for the reporters to hover around? . . . Tell you what I think, Alicia. I think you know who did the shooting. They shuffled the swimmers, nobody knew who was in which lane. You started out in lane two, and you'd be dead if the woman from Ajax hadn't complained. Who wants to kill you?"

Her black eyes glittered in her white face. "No one. Why don't you have a little empathy, Vic? I might have been killed. There was a madman out there who shot a woman. Why don't you give me some sympathy?"

"I jumped into a pool to pull that woman out. I sat around in wet clothes for two hours talking to the cops. I'm beat. You want sympathy, go someplace else. The little I have is reserved for myself tonight.

"I'd really like to know why I had to be at the pool, if it wasn't to ward off a potential attacker. And if you'd told me the real reason, Louise Carmody might still be alive."

"Damn you, Vic, stop doubting every word I say. I told you why I needed you there—someone had to sign the card. Millie works during the day. So does Fredda. Katie has a new baby. Elene is becoming a grandmother for the first time. Get off my goddamn back."

"If you're not going to tell me the truth, and if you're going to scream at me about it, I'd just as soon you left."

She stood silent for a minute. "Sorry, Vic. I'll get a better grip on myself."

"Great. You do that. I'm fixing some supper—want any?"

She shook her head. When I returned with a plate of pasta and olives, Joan Druggen was just announcing the top local story. Alicia sat with her hands clenched as they stated the dead woman's name. After that, she didn't say much. Just asked if she could crash for the night—she lived in Warrenville, a good hour's drive from town, near Berman's aeronautic engineering labs.

I gave her pillows and a blanket for the couch and went to bed. I was pretty angry: I figured she wanted to sleep over because she was scared, and it infuriated me that she wouldn't talk about it.

When the phone woke me at 2:30, my throat was raw, the start of a cold brought on by sitting around in wet clothes for so long. A heavy voice asked for Alicia.

"I don't know who you're talking about," I said hoarsely.

"Be your age, Warshawski. She brought you to the gym. She isn't at her own place. She's gotta be with you. You don't want to wake her up, give her a message. She was lucky tonight. We want the money by noon, or she won't be so lucky a second time."

He hung up. I held the receiver a second longer and heard another click. The living room extension. I pulled on a dressing gown and padded down the hallway. The apartment door shut just as I got to the living room. I ran to the top of the stairs; Alicia's footsteps were echoing up and down the stairwell.

"Alicia! Alicia—you can't go out there alone. Come back here!"

The slamming of the entryway door was my only answer.

III

I DIDN'T SLEEP WELL, my cold mixing with worry and anger over Alicia. At eight I hoisted my aching body out of bed and sat sneezing over some steaming fruit juice while I tried to focus my brain on possible action. Alicia owed somebody money. That somebody was pissed off enough to kill because he didn't have it. Bankers do not kill wayward loan customers. Loan sharks do, but what could Alicia have done to rack up so much indebtedness? Berman probably paid her seventy or eighty thousand a year for the special kinds of designs she did on aircraft wings. And she was the kind of client a bank usually values. So what did she need money for that only a shark would provide?

The clock was ticking. I called her office. She'd phoned in sick; the secretary didn't know where she was calling from but had assumed home. On a dim chance I tried her phone. No answer. Alicia had one brother, Tom, an insurance agent on the far south side. After a few tries I located his office in Flossmoor. He hadn't heard from Alicia for weeks. And no, he didn't know who she might owe money to.

Reluctantly Tom gave me their father's phone number in Florida. Mr. Dauphine hadn't heard from his daughter, either.

"If she calls you, or if she shows up, *please* let me know. She's in trouble up here, and the only way I can help her is by knowing where she is." I gave him the number without much expectation of hearing from him again.

I did know someone who might be able to give me a line on her debts. A year or so earlier, I'd done a major favor for Don Pasquale, a local mob leader. If she owed him money, he might listen to my intercession. If not, he might be able to tell me whom she had borrowed from.

Torfino's, an Elmwood Park restaurant where the don had a part-time office, put me through to his chief assistant, Ernesto. A well-remembered gravel voice told me I sounded awful.

"Thank you, Ernesto," I snuffled. "Did you hear about the death of Louise Carmody at the University of Illinois gym last night? She was probably shot by mistake, poor thing. The intended victim was a woman named Alicia Dauphine. We grew up together, so I feel a little solicitous on her behalf. She owes a lot of money to someone: I wondered if you know who."

"Name isn't familiar, Warshawski. I'll check around and call you back."

My cold made me feel as though I was at the bottom of a fish tank. I couldn't think fast enough or hard enough to imagine where Alicia might have gone to ground. Perhaps at her house, believing if she didn't answer the phone no one would think she was home? It wasn't a very clever idea, but it was the best I could do in my muffled, snuffled state.

The old farmhouse in Warrenville that Alicia had modernized lay behind the local high school. The boys were out practicing football. They were wearing light jerseys. I had on my winter coat—even though the day was warm, my cold made me shiver and want to be bundled up. Although we were close enough that I could see their mouthpieces, they didn't notice me as I walked around the house looking for signs of life.

Alicia's car was in the garage, but the house looked cold and unoccupied. As I made my way to the back, a black-and-white cat darted out from the bushes and began weaving itself around my ankles, mewing piteously. Alicia had three cats. This one wanted something to eat.

Alicia had installed a sophisticated burglar alarm system—

she had an office in her home and often worked on preliminary designs there. An expert had gotten through the system into the pantry—some kind of epoxy had been sprayed on the wires to freeze them. Then, somehow disabling the phone link, the intruder had cut through the wires.

My stomach muscles tightened, and I wished futilely for the Smith & Wesson locked in my safe at home. My cold really had addled my brains for me not to take it on such an errand. Still, where burglars lead shall P.I.s hesitate? I opened the window, slid a leg over, and landed on the pantry floor. My feline friend followed more gracefully. She promptly abandoned me to start sniffing at the pantry walls.

Cautiously opening the door I slid into the kitchen. It was deserted, the refrigerator and clock motors humming gently, a dry dishcloth draped over the sink. In the living room another cat joined me and followed me into the electronic wonderland of Alicia's study. She had used built-in book-cases to house her computers and other gadgets. The printers were tucked along a side wall, and wires ran everywhere. Whoever had broken in was not interested in merchandise—the street value of her study contents would have brought in a nice return, but they stood unharmed.

By now I was dreading the trek upstairs. The second cat, a tabby, trotted briskly ahead of me, tail waving like a flag. Alicia's bedroom door was shut. I kicked it open with my right leg and pressed myself against the wall. Nothing. Dropping to my knees I looked in. The bed, tidily covered with an old-fashioned white spread, was empty. So was the bathroom. So was the guest room and an old sun porch glassed in and converted to a solarium.

The person who broke in had not come to steal—everything was preternaturally tidy. So he (she?) had come to attack Alicia. The hair stood up on the nape of my neck. Where was he? Not in the house. Hiding outside?

I started down the stairs again when I heard a noise, a heavy scraping. I froze, trying to locate the source. A movement caught my eye at the line of vision. The hatch to the crawl space had been shoved open; an arm swung down. For a split second only I stared at the arm and the gun in its grip, then leaped down the stairs two at a time.

A heavy thud—the man jumping onto the upper landing. The crack as the gun fired. A jolt in my left shoulder, and I gasped with shock and fell the last few steps to the bottom. Righted myself. Reached for the deadlock on the front door. Heard an outraged squawk, loud swearing, and a crash that sounded like a man falling downstairs. Then I had the door open and was staggering outside while an angry bundle of fur poured past me. One of the cats, a heroine, tripping my assailant and saving my life.

IV

I NEVER REALLY LOST CONSCIOUSNESS. The football players saw me stagger down the sidewalk and came trooping over. In their concern for me they failed to tackle the gunman, but they got me to a hospital, where a young intern eagerly set about removing the slug from my shoulder; the winter coat had protected me from major damage. Between my cold and the gunshot, I was just as happy to let him incarcerate me for a few days.

They tucked me into bed, and I fell into a heavy, uneasy sleep. I had jumped into the black waters of Lake Michigan in search of Alicia, trying to reach her ahead of a shark. She was lurking just out of reach. She didn't know that her oxygen tank ran out at noon.

When I woke finally, soaked with sweat, it was dark outside. The room was lit faintly by a fluorescent light over the sink. A lean man in a brown wool business suit was sitting next to the bed. When he saw me looking at him, he reached into his coat.

If he was going to shoot me, there wasn't a thing I could do about it—I was too limp from my heavy sleep to move. Instead of a gun, though, he pulled out an ID case.

"Miss Warshawski? Peter Carlton, Federal Bureau of Investigation. I know you're not feeling well, but I need to talk to you about Alicia Dauphine."

"So the shark ate her," I said.

"What?" he demanded sharply. "What does that mean?"

"Nothing. Where is she?"

"We don't know. That's what we want to talk to you about. She went home with you after the swimming meet yesterday. Correct?"

"Gosh, Mr. Carlton. I love watching my tax dollars at work. If you've been following her, you must have a better fix on her whereabouts than I do. I last saw her around 2:30 this morning. If it's still today, that is."

"What did she talk to you about?"

My mind was starting to unfog. "Why is the Bureau interested in Miss Dauphine?"

He didn't want to tell me. All he wanted was every word Alicia had said to me. When I wouldn't budge, he started in on why I was in her house and what I had noticed there.

Finally I said, "Mr. Carlton, if you can't tell me why you're interested in Miss Dauphine, there's no way I can respond to your questions. I don't believe the Bureau—or the police—or anyone, come to that—has any right to pry into the affairs of citizens in the hopes of turning up some scandal. You tell me why you're interested, and I'll tell you if I know anything relevant to that interest."

With an ill grace he said, "We believe she has been selling Defense Department secrets to the Russians."

"No," I said flatly. "She wouldn't."

"Some wing designs she was working on have disappeared. She's disappeared. And a Soviet functionary in St. Charles has disappeared."

"Sounds pretty circumstantial to me. The wing designs might be in her home. They could easily be on a disk someplace—she did all her drafting on computer."

They'd been through her computer files at home and at work and found nothing. Her boss did not have copies of the latest design, only of the early stuff. I thought about the heavy voice on the phone demanding money, but loyalty to Alicia made me keep it to myself—give her a chance to tell her story first.

I did give him everything Alicia had said, her nervousness and her sudden departure. That I was worried about her and went to see if she was in her house. And was shot by an intruder hiding in the crawl space. Who might have taken her designs. Although nothing looked pilfered.

He didn't believe me. I don't know if he thought I knew something I wasn't telling, or if he thought I had joined Alicia in selling secrets to the Russians. But he kept at me for so long that I finally pushed my call button. When the nurse arrived, I explained that I was worn out and could she please show my visitor out? He left but promised me that he would return.

Cursing my weakness, I fell asleep again. When I next woke it was morning, and both my cold and my shoulder were much improved. When the doctors came by on their morning visit, I got their agreement to a discharge. Before I bathed and left, the Warrenville police sent out a man who took a detailed statement.

I called my answering service from a phone in the lobby. Ernesto had been in touch. I reached him at Torfino's.

"Saw about your accident in the papers, Warshawski. How you feeling? . . . About Dauphine. Apparently she's signed a note for $750,000 to Art Smollensk. Can't do anything to help you out. The don sends his best wishes for your recovery."

Art Smollensk, gambling king. When I worked for the public defender, I'd had to defend some of his small-time employees—people at the level of smashing someone's fingers in his car door. The ones who did hits and arson usually could afford their own attorneys.

Alicia as a gambler made no sense to me—but we hadn't been close for over a decade. There were lots of things I didn't know about her.

At home for a change of clothes I stopped in the basement, where I store useless mementos in a locked stall. After fifteen minutes of shifting boxes around, I was sweating and my left shoulder was throbbing and oozing stickily, but I'd located my high school yearbook. I took it upstairs with me and thumbed through it, trying to gain inspiration on where Alicia might have gone to earth.

None came. I was about to leave again when the phone rang. It was Alicia, talking against a background of noise. "Thank God you're safe, Vic. I saw about the shooting in the paper. Please don't worry about me. I'm okay. Stay away and don't worry."

She hung up before I could ask her anything. I concentrated, not on what she'd said, but what had been in the background. Metal doors banging open and shut. Lots of loud, wild talking. Not an airport—the talking was too loud for that, and there weren't any intercom announcements in the background. I knew what it was. If I'd just let my mind relax, it would come to me.

Idly flipping through the yearbook, I looked for faces Alicia might trust. I found my own staring from a group photo of the girls' basketball team. I'd been a guard—Victoria the protectress from way back. On the next page, Alicia smiled fiercely, holding a swimming trophy. Her coach, who also taught Latin, had desperately wanted Alicia to train for the Olympics, but Alicia had had her heart set on the U of I and engineering.

Suddenly I knew what the clanking was, where Alicia was. No other sound like that exists anywhere on earth.

V

ALICIA AND I GREW UP under the shadow of the steel mills in South Chicago. Nowhere else has the deterioration of American industry shown up more clearly. Wisconsin Steel is padlocked shut. The South Works are a fragment of their former monstrous grandeur. Unemployment is over thirty percent, and the number of jobless youths lounging in the bars and on the streets had grown from the days when I hurried past them to the safety of my mother's house.

The high school was more derelict than I remembered. Many windows were boarded over. The asphalt playground was cracked and covered with litter, and the bleachers around the football field were badly weathered.

The guard at the doorway demanded my business. I showed her my P.I. license and said I needed to talk to the women's gym teacher on confidential business. After some dickering—hostile on her side, snuffly on mine—she gave me a pass. I didn't need directions down the scuffed corridors, past the battered lockers, past the smell of rancid oil coming from the cafeteria, to the noise and life of the gym.

Teenage girls in blue shirts and white shorts—the school colors—were shrieking, jumping, wailing in pursuit of volleyballs. I watched the pandemonium until the buzzer ended the period, then walked up to the instructor.

She was panting and sweating and gave me an incurious glance, looking only briefly at the pass I held out for her. "Yes?"

"You have a new swimming coach, don't you?"

"Just a volunteer. Are you from the union? She isn't drawing a paycheck. But Miss Finley, the coach, is desperately shorthanded—she teaches Latin, you know—and this woman is a big help."

"I'm not from the union. I'm her trainer. I need to talk to her—find out why she's dropped out and whether she plans to compete in any of her meets this fall."

The teacher gave me the hard look of someone used to sizing up fabricated excuses. I didn't think she believed me, but she told me I could go into the pool area and talk to the swim coach.

The pool dated to the time when this high school served an affluent neighborhood. It was twenty-five yards long, built with skylights along the outer wall. You reached it through the changing rooms, separate ones with showers for girls and boys. It didn't have an outside hallway entrance.

Alicia was perched alone on the high dive. A few students, boys and girls, were splashing about in the pool, but no organized training was in progress. Alicia was staring at nothing.

I cupped my hands and called up to her, "Do you want me to climb up, or are you going to come down?"

At that she turned and recognized me. "Vic!" Her cry was enough to stop the splashing in the pool. "How— Are you alone?"

"I'm alone. Come down. I took a slug in the shoulder—I'm not climbing up after you."

She shot off the board in a perfect arc, barely rippling the surface of the water. The kids watched with envy. I was pretty jealous, myself—nothing I do is done with that much grace.

She surfaced near me but looked at the students. "I want you guys swimming laps," she said sharply. "What do you think this is—summer camp?"

They left us reluctantly and began swimming.

"How did you find me?"

"It was easy. I was looking through the yearbook, trying to think of someone you would trust. Miss Finley was the simple answer—I remembered how you practically lived in her house for two years. You liked to read *Jane Eyre* together, and she adored you.

"You are in deep trouble. Smollensk is after you, and so is the FBI. You can't hide here forever. You'd better talk to the Bureau guys. They won't love you, but at least they're not going to shoot you."

"The FBI? Whatever for?"

"Your designs, sweetie pie. Your designs and the Russians. The FBI are the people who look into that kind of thing."

"Vic. I don't know what you're talking about." The words were said with such slow deliberateness that I was almost persuaded.

"The $750,000 you owe Art Smollensk."

She shook her head, then said, "Oh. Yes. That."

"Yes, that. I guess it seems like more money to me than it does to you. Or had you forgotten Louise Carmody getting shot? . . . Anyway, a known Russian spy left Fermilab yesterday or the day before, and you're gone, and some of your wing designs are gone, and the FBI thinks you've sold them overseas and maybe gone East yourself. I didn't tell them about Art, but they'll probably get there before too long."

"How sure are they that the designs are gone?"

"Your boss can't find them. Maybe you have a duplicate set at home nobody knows about."

She shook her head again. "I don't leave that kind of thing at home. I had them last Saturday, working, but I took the diskettes back . . ." Her voice trailed off as a look of horror washed across her face. "Oh, no. This is worse than I thought." She hoisted herself out of the pool. "I've got to go. Got to get away before someone else figures out I'm here."

"Alicia, for Christ's sake. What has happened?"

She stopped and looked at me, tears swimming in her black eyes. "If I could tell anyone, it would be you, Vic." Then she was jogging into the girls' changing room, leaving the students in the pool swimming laps.

I stuck with her. "Where are you going? The Feds have a hook on any place you have friends or relations. Smollensk does, too."

That stopped her. "Tom, too?"

"Tom first, last, and foremost. He's the only relative you have in Chicago." She was starting to shiver in the bare corridor. I grabbed her and shook her. "Tell me the truth, Alicia. I can't fly blind. I already took a bullet in the shoulder."

Suddenly she was sobbing on my chest. "Oh, Vic. It's been so awful. You can't know . . . you can't understand . . . you won't believe . . ." She was hiccuping.

I led her into the shower room and found a towel. Rubbing her down, I got the story in choking bits and pieces.

Tom was the gambler. He'd gotten into it in a small way in high school and college. After he went into business for himself, the habit grew. He'd mortgaged his insurance agency assets, taken out a second mortgage on the house, but couldn't stop.

"He came to me two weeks ago. Told me he was going to start filing false claims with his companies, collect the money." She gave a twisted smile. "He didn't have to put that kind of pressure on—I can't help helping him."

"But Alicia, why? And how does Art Smollensk have your name?"

"Is that the man Tom owes money to? I think he uses my name—Alonso, my middle name—I know he does; I just don't like to think about it. Someone came around threatening me three years ago. I told Tom never to use my name again, and he didn't for a long time, but now I guess he was desperate—$750,000, you know. . . .

"As to why I help him . . . You never had any brothers or sisters, so maybe you can't understand. When Mom died, I was thirteen, he was six. I looked after him. Got him out of trouble. All kinds of stuff. It gets to be a habit, I guess. Or an obligation. That's why I've never married, you know, never had any children of my own. I don't want any more responsibilities like this one."

"And the designs?"

She looked horrified again. "He came over for dinner on Saturday. I'd been working all day on the things, and he came into the study when I was logging off. I didn't tell him it was Defense Department work, but it's not too hard to figure out what I do is defense-related—after all, that's all Berman does; we don't make commercial aircraft. I haven't had a chance to look at the designs since—I worked out all day Sunday getting ready for that damned meet Monday. Tom must have taken my diskettes and swapped the labels with some others—I've got tons of them lying around."

She gave a twisted smile. "It was a gamble: a gamble that there'd be something valuable on them and a gamble I wouldn't discover the switch before he got rid of them. But he's a gambler."

"I see. . . . Look, Alicia. You can only be responsible for Tom so far. Even if you could bail him out this time—and I don't see how you possibly can—there'll be a next time. And you may not survive this one to help him again. Let's call the FBI."

She squeezed her eyes shut. "You don't understand, Vic. You can't possibly understand."

While I was trying to reason her into phoning the Bureau, Miss Finley, swim coach-cum-romantic-Latin-teacher, came briskly into the locker room. "Allie! One of the girls came to get me. Are you all—" She did a double-take. "Victoria! Good to see you. Have you come to help Allie? I told her she could count on you."

"Have you told her what's going on?" I demanded of Alicia.

Yes, Miss Finley knew most of the story. Agreed that it was very worrying but said Allie could not possibly turn in her own brother. She had given Allie a gym mat and some bedding to sleep on—she could just stay at the gym until the furor died down and they could think of something else to do.

I sat helplessly as Miss Finley led Alicia off to get some dry clothes. At last, when they didn't rejoin me, I sought them out, poking through half-remembered halls and doors until I found the staff coaching office. Alicia was alone, looking about fifteen in an old cheerleader's uniform Miss Finley had dug up for her.

"Miss Finley teaching?" I asked sharply.

Alicia looked guilty but defiant. "Yes. Two-thirty class. Look. The critical thing is to get those diskettes back. I called Tom, explained it to him. Told him I'd try to help him raise the money but that we couldn't let the Russians have those things. He agreed, so he's bringing them out here."

The room rocked slightly around me. "No. I know you don't have much of a sense of humor, but this is a joke, isn't it?"

She didn't understand. Wouldn't understand that if the Russian had already left the country, Tom no longer had the material. That if Tom was coming here, she was the scapegoat. At last, despairing, I said, "Where is he meeting you? Here?"

"I told him I'd be at the pool."

"Will you do one thing my way? Will you go to Miss Finley's class and conjugate verbs for forty-five minutes and let me meet him at the pool? Please?"

At last, her jaw set stubbornly, she agreed. She still wouldn't let me call the Bureau, though. "Not until I've talked to Tom myself. It may all be a mistake, you know."

We both knew it wasn't, but I saw her into the Latin class without making the phone call I knew it was my duty to make and returned to the pool. Driving out the two students still splashing around in the water, I put signs on the locker room doors saying the water was contaminated and there would be no swimming until further notice.

I turned out the lights and settled in a corner of the room remote from the outside windows to wait. And go over and over in my mind the story. I believed it. Was I fooling myself? Was that why she wouldn't call the Feds?

At last Tom came in through the men's locker room entrance. "Allie? Allie?" His voice bounced off the high rafters and echoed around me. I was well back in the shadows, my Smith & Wesson in hand; he didn't see me.

After half a minute or so another man joined him. I didn't recognize the stranger, but his baggy clothes marked him as part of Smollensk's group, not the Bureau. He talked softly to Tom for a minute. Then they went into the girl's locker room together.

Whey they returned, I had moved part way up the side of the pool, ready to follow them if they went back into the main part of the high school looking for Alicia.

"Tom!" I called. "It's V. I. Warshawski. I know the whole story. Give me the diskettes."

"Warshawski!" he yelled. "What the hell are you doing here?"

I sensed rather than saw the movement his friend made. I shot at him and dived into the water. His bullet zipped as it hit the tiles where I'd been standing. My wet clothes and my sore shoulder made it hard to move. Another bullet hit the water by my head, and I went under again, fumbling with my heavy jacket, getting it free, surfacing, hearing Alicia's sharp, "Tom, why are you shooting at Vic? Stop it now. Stop it and give me back the diskettes."

Another flurry of shots, this time away from me, giving me a chance to get to the side of the pool, to climb out. Alicia lay on the floor near the door to the girls' locker room. Tom stood silently by. The gunman was jamming more bullets into his gun.

As fast as I could in my sodden clothes I lumbered to the hitman, grabbing his arm, squeezing, feeling blood start to seep from my shoulder, stepping on his instep, putting all the force of my body into my leg. Tom, though, Tom was taking the gun from him. Tom was going to shoot me.

"Drop that gun, Tom Dauphine." It was Miss Finley. Years of teaching in a tough school gave creditable authority to her; Tom dropped the gun.

VI

ALICIA LIVED LONG ENOUGH to tell the truth to the FBI. It was small comfort to me. Small consolation to see Tom's statement. He hoped he could get Smollensk to kill his sister before she said anything. If that happened, he had a good gamble on her dying a traitor in their eyes—after all, her designs were gone, and her name was in Smollensk's files. Maybe the truth never would have come out. Worth a gamble to a betting man.

The Feds arrived about five minutes after the shooting stopped. They'd been watching Tom, just not closely enough. They were sore that they'd let Alicia get shot. So they dumped some charges on me—obstructing federal authorities, not telling them where Alicia was, not calling as soon as I had the truth from her, God knows what else. I spent several days in jail. It seemed like a suitable penance, just not enough of one.

BILL PRONZINI

ACE IN THE HOLE

I was twenty minutes late to the poker game that Friday night, but the way Eberhardt and the other three looked at me when I came in, you'd have thought I was two hours late and had sprouted tentacles besides. The four of them were grouped around the table in Eberhardt's living room—Eb, Barney Rivera, Jack Logan, and Joe DeFalco—and I could feel their eyes on me as I shrugged out of my overcoat and took the one empty chair. I put twenty dollars on the table and said, "All right, who's banking?" I said, "Well? Come on, you guys, are we going to play poker or what?" I said, "For Christ's sake, why do you keep *staring* at me like that?"

"You're on the spot, pal," DeFalco said, and grinned all over his blocky face. He was a reporter for the *Chronicle*, but he didn't look like a reporter; nor, for that matter, did he look Italian. He looked like Pat O'Brien playing Father Jerry in *Angels with Dirty Faces*. People told him things they wouldn't tell anybody else.

"Meaning what?"

"Meaning Eb and Barney have a hot bet on you. Your exalted reputation as a detective is on the line."

"What the hell are you talking about?"

Eberhardt said, "I bet Barney twenty bucks you can make sense out of the Gallatin thing within twenty-four hours."

"What Gallatin thing?"

"The shooting this noon. Jack's baby. Don't tell me you didn't hear about it?"

"As a matter of fact, I didn't."

"You see, Eb?" Barney Rivera said. He was a tubby little Chicano, Barney, with a mop of unruly black hair, big doe eyes, a fondness for peppermints, and a way with women that was as uncanny as it was unlikely. He didn't look like what *he* was, either: chief claims adjuster for the San Francisco branch of Great Western Insurance. "Your partner just won't read the newspapers or listen to news programs. When it comes to current events, he lives with his head in a hole like an ostrich."

I told him which hole he could put his ostrich in. Everybody laughed, including Barney. He's not a bad guy; he just likes to use the needle. But he's got a sense of humor, and he can take it as well as dish it out.

Jack Logan hadn't said anything, so I turned to him. He was in his mid-fifties, Eberhardt's and my age—a quiet, hard-working career cop who had been promoted to lieutenant when Eberhardt retired a couple of years ago. Now that I was looking at him up close, I saw that he seemed a little worn around the edges tonight.

"What's this all about, Jack?"

He sighed. "Frank Gallatin . . . you know who he is, don't you?"

"Westate Trucking?"

"Right. This morning we thought we finally had him nailed on racketeering and extortion charges, maybe even a mob connection. This afternoon we thought we had him nailed on something even better—a one-eight-seven. Tonight we don't have him on either score."

One-eight-seven is police slang for willful homicide, as

defined in Section 187 of the California Penal Code. I said, "Why not?"

"Because even though we know damned well he shot an accountant named Lamar Trent a little past noon," Logan said, "we can't prove it. We can't find the gun he used. Nor can we find an incriminating file we know—or at least are pretty sure—Trent had in his possession earlier. Without the file, now that Trent is dead, the D.A. can't indict Gallatin on the racketeering and extortion charges. And without the gun, Gallatin's cockamamie version of the shooting stands up by default."

"How come you're so positive he killed this Trent?"

"I was there when he did it. So was Ben Klein. Not fifty feet away, outside Trent's locked office door. We piled in on Gallatin inside of fifteen seconds; there's no way he could have got the gun out of the office in that length of time, just no way. Only it wasn't anywhere *in* the office when we searched the place. And I mean we did everything but pry up the floorboards and strip the plaster off the walls."

"Just your kind of case, paisan," Eberhardt said happily. "Locked doors, disappearing guns—screwball stuff."

I gave him a look. There were times, like right now, when I was sorry I'd taken him into my agency as a full partner. "Thanks a lot."

"Well, you've worked on this kind of thing before. You're good at it."

"Not good," Barney the Needle said, "just lucky. But this one's a pip. If the rest of us can't figure it, neither can he."

"Hey," I said, "I came here for poker, not abuse."

"So you're not even interested, huh?" DeFalco asked. He was still grinning. But behind the grin and his Father Jerry facade, his journalistic zeal was showing; *his* interest in all of this was strictly professional.

"Did I say I wasn't interested?"

"Ah," he said. "I thought so."

Rivera said, "Wait until you hear the rest of the story," and rubbed his pudgy hands together in exaggerated anticipation.

"I'm sure I'll hang on every word."

Eberhardt was firing up one of his smelly pipes. "So am I," he said between puffs. "Jack, lay it out for him."

I said, "All right, but can we play cards while I'm listening?"

Nobody objected to that. So we played a few hands of five-card stud, none of which I won, while Logan told the story. It was a pip, all right. And in spite of myself, just as Eberhardt had predicted, my own professionalism had me hooked from the start.

This morning, one of the SFPD's battery of informants had come through with the tip that Lamar Trent was Gallatin's private accountant—a fact that Gallatin had managed to keep an ironbound secret until now. The word was that Gallatin and Trent had had a falling out, either over money or some of the nastier aspects of Gallatin's operation, and that Trent had grown so afraid of his employer he might be willing to sell him out in exchange for police protection and immunity. And what he had to sell was a complete and documented file on Westate Trucking's illegal enterprises, which it was rumored he kept in his office safe.

So as soon as they got the tip, around noon, Logan and Ben Klein had gone over to the Wainright Building, a relic of better days on lower Market, for a talk with Trent. When they came into the lobby, they found both of the ancient and sometimes unreliable elevators in use; instead of waiting they took the stairs up, since Trent's office was only one flight up. They were moving along the empty second-floor hallway when they heard the shot.

"It came from inside Trent's office," Jack said, "there isn't any doubt of that. Then there was some kind of commotion, followed by a yell and a thud like a body hitting the floor. We

were already at the door by then. It was locked, but it wasn't
much of a lock; Ben kicked it open first try.

"First thing we saw when we barreled inside was a man
we later IDed as Trent lying face down across his desk. Shot
once in the middle of his face, blood all over the remains of
his brown bag lunch. Gallatin was down on the floor,
holding his head and looking groggy. The window behind
him was open—looks out onto a fire escape and down into
an alley that intersects with Market. It's a corner office; the
other window, the one at right angles that overlooks Market,
was jammed shut."

"Let me guess," I said. "Gallatin claims somebody came
up or down the fire escape, shot Trent through the open
window, knocked him to the floor when he tried to interfere,
and then went back up or down."

"That's about it. He says he went there to see Trent on a
routine business matter. They were talking while Trent was
eating his lunch; the window was open because Trent was a
fresh-air nut. Then this phantom with a gun showed up out
of nowhere on the fire escape. Gallatin's story is that he
didn't get a good look at him, it all happened too fast—the
usual crap. But the odds of it having gone down that way are
at least a couple of thousand to one.

"In the first place, the Wainright Building has six floors;
two of the corner offices on the four floors above Trent's were
occupied at the time. None of the people in those two offices
saw anybody go up or down the fire escape past their
windows. Nobody except Klein, that is, on *his* way to the
roof. He didn't find a trace of anyone up there; and no one
could have got *off* the roof except by way of the fire escape
because the closest building is only four stories high—too far
down to jump—and the door to the inside stairwell was
locked tight.

"It's not any more likely that this phantom assailant came
up from the alley or went down into it afterward. A

teamster was unloading his truck down there, not fifty yards away, and he didn't see or hear anybody on the fire escape; and he sure as hell would have because the lower section is weighted and hasn't been oiled in twenty years, if ever: it makes plenty of noise when you swing on it. I know that for a fact because Klein played Tarzan after he came down from the roof. We also checked the teamster out, just to make sure he has no connection with Gallatin. He hasn't; he's a model citizen.

"And if that isn't enough, we had a doctor examine Gallatin. His claim—Gallatin's—is that the assailant whacked him on the side of the head to knock him down, but there's not a mark on him."

"What about a nitrate test to determine if he fired a gun?" I asked.

"Negative. He must have used gloves or something and got rid of them the same way he got rid of the gun."

"Didn't the people in the offices near Trent's see or hear anything?"

"No, because the only two offices close by were empty at the time. The elevators are directly across the hall from Trent's office, and the stairs are next to them, so there aren't any offices on that side. The one adjacent to Trent's belongs to a CPA, who was out to an early lunch; the one next to that is occupied by a mail-order housewares outfit that was closed for the day. Nearest occupied office was halfway to the rear of the building and off another corridor, and the woman holding it down is half deaf."

"You search the two empty offices?"

"Damn right we searched them," Logan said. "Got a pass key from the janitor and combed them as fine as we combed Trent's. All the other offices on that floor, too, just to be safe. Nothing. Not that we expected to find anything; like I told you, Klein and I were in on Gallatin within fifteen seconds after he shot Trent. He just didn't have time to get out of that office and hide the gun somewhere else."

"There's no chance of some clever hiding place in Trent's office that you might have overlooked?"

"None—I'll swear to that. And that's the hell of it. He couldn't have made that damn gun disappear, yet he did. Just as if he'd thrown it down a hole somewhere."

"Maybe he ate it," Barney said.

"Ha ha. Very funny."

"No, I'm serious. I read about a case like that once. Guy used a zip gun, knocked it down into its components after the shooting, and then swallowed the pieces. He was an ex-carnival sideshow performer—one of those dudes with a cast-iron stomach."

"Well, Gallatin's not an ex-carnival sideshow performer, and I'd like to see anybody eat a Beretta in fifteen seconds or fifteen *hours.*"

I asked him, "How do you know it's a Beretta?"

Logan smiled grimly. "Gallatin just happens to have one registered in his name. Same caliber as the bullet that killed Trent."

"Which is?"

"Twenty-five."

"One of those small, flat pocket jobs?"

"Right. Not much of a piece, but deadly enough."

"Any way he could have got rid of it through the open window?"

"No. If he'd chucked it into the alley, we'd have found it. And the teamster unloading his truck would have heard it hit; even a little gun makes plenty of noise when you drop it twenty feet onto pavement."

"How about if Gallatin chucked it straight *across* the alley?" I said. "Through an open window in the facing building, maybe?"

"Nice try, but no dice there, either. The first two floors of that building belong to a men's haberdashery; windows are kept locked at all times, and there were sales personnel and customers on both floors. Third and fourth floors are offices, most of them occupied and all with their windows shut. It was pretty cold and windy today, remember. I had the empty offices checked anyway: no sign of the Beretta."

He made an exasperated noise and shook his head. "Even as weak as Gallatin's story is, we can't charge him without hard evidence—without the gun. It's his ace in the hole, and he bloody well knows it."

I folded another lousy hand and ruminated a little. At length I said, "You know, Jack, there's one big fat inconsistency in this thing."

"There's more than one," he said.

"No, I mean the shot you heard, the commotion and the yell and the thud. It has a stagey ring to it."

"How do you mean?"

"As if he put it all on just for your benefit."

Jack scowled. "He couldn't have known it was Ben and me out in the hallway."

I said musingly, "Maybe he could. Had he ever seen either of you before today? Had any dealings with either of you?"

"No."

"Was it just you and Ben? Or was anyone else with you?"

"Couple of uniformed officers, as backups. They stayed down in the lobby."

"Well, he could've spotted them, couldn't he, through the window that overlooks Market Street? The four of you coming into the building together?"

"I guess he could have," Logan admitted. "But hell, if he *did* know police officers were on the scene, it doesn't make sense he'd have shot Trent. Gallatin is a lot of things but crazy isn't one of them."

Eberhardt, who was raking in a small pot with a pair of queens, said, "Could be he didn't intend to shoot Trent.

Maybe there was a struggle, the gun went off, and Gallatin decided to improvise to cover up."

"Some fast improvisation," I said.

He shrugged. "It's possible."

"I suppose so. But it still doesn't add up right. Why was the door locked?"

Rivera said, "Gallatin wanted privacy when he confronted Trent. He might not have gone there to kill him, but he did go there to get that file; otherwise, why bring the gun with him?"

Logan nodded. "We figure he picked up the same information we got about Trent's willingness to sell him out. He just didn't expect us to get it and come after Trent as fast as we did."

"I still don't like that door being locked," I said. "Or that window conveniently being open."

Barney gave me a sly look; he had the needle out again. "So what's your theory, then? You must have one by now."

"No. Not yet."

"Not even a little one?"

"I'm as stymied as you are."

Eberhardt said, "Give him time, Barney. He can't come up with an answer in fifteen minutes; he's not a goddamn genius." He sounded disappointed that I wasn't.

"I'm beginning to wish I'd stayed home," I said. "Eb, is there any beer?"

"Fridge is full. Help yourself. Maybe it'll help you think."

I went and got a bottle of Schlitz, and when I came back we settled down to some semi-serious poker. Nobody said much about the Gallatin business for the next two and a half hours, but we might as well have been talking about it all along: the events as Jack Logan had described them kept running around inside my head, and I couldn't concentrate on the flow of cards. It all seemed so damned screwy and

impossible. And yet, if you looked at it in just the right
way . . .

Five-card stud was what we played for the most part—
strict traditionalists, that was us; anybody who even suggested a wild-card game would have been tossed out on his
ear—and DeFalco was dealing a new hand. My up card was
the ace of hearts. I lifted a corner on my hole card: ace of
clubs. Wired aces. The best start of a hand I'd had all night.

Joe nodded at me and said, "Your bet," and I said, "Open
for ten," and pushed a dime into the middle of the table.
Then I looked at my down card again, my ace in the hole.

Eberhardt called my dime; he had a king showing. Jack
and Barney folded. Joe called with an eight up, and then
dealt me a deuce of something and Eb and himself cards that
I didn't even notice.

Ace in the hole . . .

I sat there. Then somebody—Barney—poked me with an
elbow and said, "Hey, wake up. We're waiting."

"Huh?"

"For you to bet. What are *you* waiting for?"

"Nothing. I was just thinking."

Eberhardt perked up. "About the Gallatin thing?"

"Yeah. The Gallatin thing."

"You're onto something, right? I know that look. Come
on, paisan—spill it."

"Give me a minute, will you?"

I got up and went into the kitchen and opened another
bottle of Schlitz. When I came back with it, the poker game
had been temporarily suspended and they were all watching
me again, waiting. Time for the Big Dick to perform, I
thought sourly. And maybe do a comical pratfall like
Clarabelle the Clown. Bah.

I sat down again. "All right," I said, "I've got an idea.
Maybe it's way off base, I don't know, but you asked for it. It

fits all the facts, anyhow. Just don't anybody make any smart cracks if it fizzles."

Eb said, "Go, boy. Go."

I ignored him. To Logan I said, "The key isn't what Gallatin did with the murder weapon, Jack. It's that shot you and Ben heard."

"What about it?"

"Well, suppose it was a phony. Suppose Gallatin staged it and everything else to make you think that was when Trent was killed, when in reality he'd been dead from two to five minutes—shot *before* the two of you were even in the building."

Frown lines made a puckered V above Jack's nose. "You mean Gallatin fired a second shot out the window?"

"No. He didn't have the gun then. I mean a phony all the way—it *wasn't* a gunshot you heard."

DeFalco said, "How do you fake a gunshot?" He had his notebook out and was scribbling in it.

I didn't answer him directly. Still talking to Logan, I said, "You mentioned that Trent was eating a brown bag lunch when he was killed or just before it. You meant that literally, right?" He nodded. "Okay, then. Where was the paper bag?"

"Wadded up in the wastebasket—" He broke off abruptly, and his frown changed shape.

"Sure," I said. "An old kids' trick. You blow up a paper sack, hold the opening pinched together to keep the air in, and then burst the sack between your hands. From a distance, from behind a closed door, it would sound just like a small-caliber gun going off."

There was silence for a few seconds while they all digested that. Then Rivera said, "Wait a minute. I'll grant you the possibility of a trick like that being worked. But why would Gallatin get so fancy? He's not some amateur playing games. If he killed Trent before Jack and Ben came into the building, why did he hang around? Why didn't he just beat it out of there?"

"Circumstances. And some bad judgment."

"All right, what's your scenario?"

"Try it like this. He arrives at Trent's office while Trent is eating his lunch; he waves his gun around, gets Trent to open his safe and hand over the incriminating file, and then shoots him for whatever reason. Afterward he pokes his head out the office door; the hallway's deserted, nobody seems to have heard the shot. So far, so good; he figures he's in the clear. Now . . ." I paused. "Jack, is there a window at the end of the hallway, overlooking Market?"

"Yeah, there is."

"I thought there might be. Back to the scenario: Gallatin pockets the Beretta, goes out with the file tucked under his arm, and pushes the button for the elevator. While he's waiting for it, he happens to glance through the window; *that's* when he sees you and Ben and the uniformed officers entering the building. Gives him quite a jolt. He's got to figure you're there to see Trent, the man he's just killed. And he's got both the murder weapon and the file in his possession. If he hangs onto them and tries to take them out of the building, he runs the risk of capture—too big a risk. For all he knows, cops are swarming all over the place. He's got to get rid of them, and fast. That's his first priority."

"But where, for God's sake? Not in the hallway; we searched it, just like we searched the offices and everything else on that floor."

"The gun and file weren't *on* that floor when you searched it. Not anymore."

"Where the hell were they, then? Where are they now?"

"I'll get to that in a minute," I said, and watched the four of them grumble and squirm. A little payback for putting me on the spot the way they had. "Let me lay out the rest of it first. Gallatin dumps the gun and the file in a matter of seconds. . . . *Now* what does he do? The smart thing is to play it cool, take the elevator down to the lobby and try to walk out unobserved; but he doesn't see it that way. He's afraid he'll be recognized and detained; that it'll look like he's trying to run away from the scene of the murder. Maybe he hears you and Ben coming up the stairs just then; in any case, he gets a bright idea, and bad judgment takes over. Why not stay right where he is, right *on* the scene, and divert suspicion from himself by making it look as if somebody else shot Trent? After all, he's already dumped both the gun and the file; as long as you don't find either one, he's in the clear. And he doesn't believe you're going to find them.

"So he ducks back into Trent's office, locks the door to give himself a little extra time, opens the window, and then goes into his act. He hasn't had time to think it through or to check who might be down in the alley; the result is that the whole thing comes off weak and stagey. Still, as you said before, without the murder weapon . . ."

"Will you quit dragging it out? What did he do with the gun?"

I let them stew another few seconds while I drank some of my beer. Then I said, "You supplied the answer yourself, Jack: you said he made it disappear as if he'd thrown it down a hole somewhere. Well, that's just what he *did* do. The file, too."

"Hole? What are you talking about?"

"I was in the Wainright Building once, about six months ago. At that time those cranky old elevators didn't always stop flush with the level of each floor, going up or down. If they've been fixed since then, my whole theory goes down a different kind of hole. But if they haven't been fixed, if they still sometimes stop a couple of inches above or below floor level . . ."

Logan sat up straight and stiff, as if somebody had just

goosed him. "Well, I'll be damned. They *don't* stop flush, no."

Eberhardt said, "The elevator shaft!"

"Why not?" I said. "One of those flat, .25 caliber Beretta pocket jobs is about an inch and a half wide. Even a thick file of papers probably wouldn't be any wider. It would only take a few seconds, once the elevator doors opened, for Gallatin to spot the opening between the car floor and the shaft, wedge both the gun and the file through it, and then push one of the buttons inside to close the doors again and start the car."

DeFalco was scribbling furiously now. He said without looking up, "So Gallatin *literally* had an ace in the hole all along. I love it."

"Well, I don't," Barney the Needle said. He sounded pissy, but he wasn't; he was still playing Devil's Advocate, a role he enjoys almost as much as that of Grand Seducer. "I don't believe a word of it."

"No? Why not?"

"It's got too many holes in it."

Eberhardt glared at him. "Is that supposed to be a pun?"

"I don't make puns," Barney said, straight-faced. "On the whole, I mean."

Logan was on his feet. "We'll see about this," he said, and hurried off to use the phone. Three minutes later he was on his way to the Wainright Building downtown.

The rest of us were still hanging around Eberhardt's living room, drinking beer and playing desultory four-handed poker, when Logan telephoned a few minutes before midnight. Gallatin's Beretta had been at the bottom of one of the elevator shafts, all right. Along with the papers from Trent's file and a pair of custom-made doeskin gloves with the initials F.G. inside each one. They had Frankie boy but good.

Murderers, especially the ones who think they're clever, are all damned fools.

So Barney paid off to Eberhardt, with a great show of grumbling reluctance. Eb said, grinning, "I told you, didn't I? I told you the paisano here was a whiz when it comes to this kind of screwball stuff. Three hours, that's all it took him. *Three*, Barney, not twenty-four."

"Luck," Barney the Needle said. "Pure blind luck. He's the luckiest private eye on the face of this earth."

Sure I am. Eberhardt collected on his twenty-buck bet, and won gloating rights in the bargain. Barney won twenty-nine dollars on the poker table, which left him nine bucks up for the evening. Jack Logan won five dollars early on, got to put the blocks to a nasty bastard like Frank Gallatin, and had a large burden lifted from his shoulders. Joe DeFalco won three dollars and got a story that he didn't dare print as straight news—it would have embarrassed Jack and made the SFPD look bad; but he'd find a way to turn it into a feature or something. And what did I get? I got a headache from too much beer, an empty wallet—I won exactly two hands all night and ended up thirty-seven dollars poorer—and the privilege of plying my trade and overworking my brain for no compensation whatsoever.

Mr. Lucky, that's me . . .

DICK STODGHILL

WRONGFUL DEATH

"**S**o this is where the shamus will hang his hat? I'll bet he wears one, doesn't he? An Indiana Jones fedora."

Roth smiled condescendingly from the doorway of the windowless cubbyhole. Blades scowled up at him. "Why're you on his case, Lou? You haven't even met the guy. Give him a chance, huh?"

"To do what? The same thing we've been doing for years without a private eye on the payroll?"

"Come on, Lou. We spent more than his salary last year hiring agencies on insurance cases alone. You know that."

"Correct. Then charged the expenses to the clients. Tell me we'll do that with the shamus's salary. Come on, Ron, tell me we'll do that."

Blades leaned back in his chair, sighing. "Look, Lou, quit calling him the shamus, will you? Believe me, hiring him is cost-efficient. We studied that out, and you figure the time the young turks on the staff spend doing what he'll be doing, it's cost-efficient. And the guy's good. So give him a chance, okay?"

"If he's so good, why's he closing up shop and going to work for us?"

"If you'd been at the meeting when—"

"If I'd been at the meeting, we wouldn't have hired him."

"Maybe, Lou, but I think you'd have been as enthused as the rest of us. Hell, you know how tough it is to make it on your own in anything today. So he wasn't cutting it; that doesn't mean he isn't good. Five years a cop, another five with Pinkerton's, twenty operating his own agency. He's good, Lou, he really is."

Roth's reply was a contemptuous snort.

"Look, Lou, he'll be here anytime now, so give him a break, okay?"

"What's this prizewinner's name again?"

"Paige. Henry Paige."

Paige turned at the doorway and took a final look around the office. For the first time he realized it was shabby. He had always thought of it as comfortable, but now he saw it as the dwindling list of clients must have seen it.

Closing the door behind him, he waved a hand at the receptionist he had shared with a dentist and a collection agency, then walked down four flights of stairs rather than risk a last ride in the ancient elevator. In the years the building had been his headquarters—a home, really—he had been trapped in the elevator eleven times. He didn't want the twelfth to be his final memory of the place.

Outside on Main Street he turned left, then saw a break in traffic and trotted to the other side. A foolish move, he decided once he was safely across. The police in Akron sometimes handed out tickets for jaywalking. Getting his fourth would be a poor way of starting a new job.

The thought left him feeling queasy. After so long a time on his own, could he handle working for someone else again? Especially for a law firm, where an investigator, no matter how skilled, would be looked on by some as an inferior?

He'd soon find out. The offices of Layne, Roth, Blades &

Hanley were half a block away in one of the two tall buildings connected by the Orangerie Mall. Without looking back, Paige set his shoulders and went inside.

"Think that's enough to keep you busy awhile?" Ron Blades plopped a stack of file folders on the desk, smiling at Paige. "The others will be giving you more. You set up your own schedule, Henry, except when somebody brings in a top-priority case. I'm tied up on one coming to trial in three days, but if you have questions, anybody'll be glad to help."

Not anybody, Paige thought to himself. Not Lou Roth, for one. Roth hadn't even attempted to hide his contempt when they were introduced. There probably were others among the dozen lawyers and a like number of clerks and secretaries who felt the same way.

"The one going to trial," he said, "there's nothing on it you want checked out?"

Blades shook his head. "Cut and dried." He turned away, then changed his mind and sat down across from Paige. "A wrongful death suit. You know, somebody shouldn't have died. A couple of brothers were tanked up and tangled with a building at fifty miles per. The elder, the passenger, never knew what hit him. Or vice versa, maybe. The driver, he came out of it alive but not much more than a vegetable. The parents have been spoon feeding him for three years now. They're suing for the wrongful death of their other son."

"Suing the driver's insurance company, you mean?"

"In effect, sure. Actually the son who was driving is the defendant, and the company isn't named in the suit. You can bet, though, that Will Hamblin—he's on it for the parents— will ask the prospective jurors if they own stock in Michiana Life and Casualty. They'll know who *really* is defendant, believe me."

"Sounds weird. Think a jury'll buy it?"

"Who knows what a jury's going to buy? Hamblin's one

helluva persuasive guy, remember. He won't come right out and say it, but his thrust will be that taking care of the kid who survived is more than the parents can afford. In effect he'll be telling the jury it's up to the son's insurer to foot the bill. Hamblin will be subtle in making the point, of course. He'll talk about the other son who died as if that's what it's all about, but the jury'll know better before he's through."

"And you're satisfied everything's the way it appears on the surface?"

"Seems clear enough to me. From the police report and the first witnesses on the scene, there's no question the survivor was driving. We've taken depositions from the plaintiff's witnesses, including the bartender at a tavern where the boys were drinking earlier. That's the only strange thing— they left less than an hour before the smashup, and he says they only had a couple of beers apiece."

"So who says they were tanked up?"

"The police report says the smell of alcohol was strong in the car. But the autopsy report confirmed what the bartender said about Frank, the one killed. He'd been drinking, but not all that much. The driver, Angelo Chiappetta, we don't know about."

Paige raised his eyebrows. "He wasn't given a blood-alcohol test?"

"Hell, Henry, it was a battle just to keep him alive. That was the last thing they were worried about at the time. Look, let me get you copies of the important stuff in the file, and you judge for yourself, okay?"

Paige spent an hour with the documents. In reading, he recalled the downtown accident three summers earlier. There seemed little doubt that Angelo Chiappetta had been under the influence of something. The car had descended a steep hill on Center Street at high speed at a point where it dead-ended at Main. Without any apparent attempt on the driver's part to slow down, they had crashed into a store-front.

The bartender, Hersh Lundy, had said the brothers left his tavern at 8:50, having consumed two beers apiece. The accident occurred at 9:30, just forty minutes later.

Earlier, a third brother, Kyle, had been in the tavern. He went out alone fifteen minutes ahead of Angelo and Frank. Just before the pair left, Frank looked at his watch and said, "We'd better go. I said I'd be there at nine."

When he had finished reading, Paige sat a moment looking around the small, impersonal room that was his new office. The trim chair he was sitting on wasn't as comfortable as the big, stuffed one he had left behind. The metal desk was tinny and without substance, nothing at all like the massive wooden one at the old place. The only personal item was a small photograph of his late wife.

He shrugged in reluctant acceptance, then pushed himself out of the chair and walked down the hall to Blades' office. When Blades looked up, Paige said, "Ron, where was it the boys had to be at nine o'clock?"

"Nobody knows. Trying to talk to Angelo Chiappetta is a waste of time. He's really out of it. You think something's fishy?"

"I don't know. Not having all the answers, I guess that always bothers me. Unless any of that other stuff is urgent, I think you ought to let me check it out a little."

"Go to it, Henry. That's what you're here for, you know. We want to rely on your judgment and experience."

Paige nodded, then turned and walked away, again doubting if everyone looked on his new role the way Blades did. He smiled wryly, thinking of Lou Roth relying on his judgment.

After riding the down elevator, he crossed the skywalk to Cascade Plaza, thinking back as usual to the time when the area below, now a parking garage, had been a busy street and a Quaker Oats factory. The cereal shot out of guns they had called it, and when he was a boy in the late years of the

Great Depression, you could hear the cannons firing under the downtown streets. Sometimes he wished he could still hear them.

After settling on a stool at the Holiday Inn lounge, Paige ordered a Manhattan with extra bitters, then leaned back and thought over the material he had read. Frank Chiappetta, who died in the crash, had been a twenty-nine-year-old rubber worker out of a job. Angelo, two years his junior, was also laid off from a rubber shop. The youngest brother, Kyle, twenty-two, had been discharged from the Army a week before the accident. There were three girls in the family, as well—married daughters in Atlanta and Denver and the eldest of the Chiappetta children, Esther, who had never married and lived at home with her parents.

Anthony and Teresa Chiappetta had purchased the family home on Bellows Street shortly after their marriage in 1948. Anthony operated a Banbury mixer at Firestone but had taken early retirement when the company quit building tires in Akron.

Nothing unusual about any of them, Paige decided, yet something about the case bothered him. He was pleased, though, that it did. He had been worried that most of the work he would be involved with might lack even the hint of challenge. At a robust fifty-eight he wasn't ready to settle into a comfortable routine. Comfortable might mean boring.

The young policeman was polite in responding to Paige in the terse, stilted manner of most policemen. "No question about it, sir, the man who survived was driving. He was pinned by the steering wheel. Had to be extricated by the rescue unit. The other man was dead when we arrived."

He paused in opening the door of his white Chevrolet cruiser, grinning sheepishly. "I won't forget that one. It was my first fatal, and messy. I went around the corner in the alley and lost my dinner."

Paige nodded sympathetically. "It happens to the best of us, son. They say they'd been drinking, but I can't find anything showing the driver was given a blood-alcohol test."

"I don't know about that, sir. The smell of whiskey was strong in the car, I remember that."

"Was there a broken bottle in it?"

"I don't recall one. If there was, it would have been in our report. Bob Casey, my partner at the time, writes the most detailed reports of anybody in the department."

Paige thanked him and turned away, trying to remember just when it was that young policemen had started calling him sir. Sometime far in the past, he decided.

The tavern was narrow and dimly lit, a neighborhood bar for workingmen in an area where a lot of men were no longer working. Two customers spaced far apart drank beer in quiet solitude.

Hersh Lundy, about fifty with tired eyes and a mouth that drooped at each end, talked while wiping the top of the bar mechanically. "Sure I noticed the time the Chiappetta boys left. Take a gander around the place, friend. Look to you like I'm worked to death here? Believe me, when you stand back of a bar fourteen hours a day and aren't making any money, you take a look at the clock when you find you're the only one left in the place."

"I understand. And all the boys had to drink were a couple of beers?"

"Right. They liked their beer, sure, but they was out of work like nearly everybody else at the time. No way could they spend the night drinking unless somebody else was buying. Even then they wasn't the kind for it, know what I mean? Don't get me wrong, the boys had their fun. But it wasn't often they overdone it, and then just beer."

"Neither drank the hard stuff?"

"Frank never touched it that I saw. Angelo, he'd have a

shot now and then, but that was it. Believe me, friend, I did
not get rich off the Chiappetta boys."

"The young one, Kyle. He was with them that night?"

"Not long. Fifteen, twenty minutes, maybe."

"He didn't hang out with the other boys much?"

"Like I keep telling people, he just got back from the
Army. Besides, he was practically another generation, know
what I mean? And after being away, he had nothing in
common with people anymore. On top of that, he's what
you'd call a loner. Looks out for number one."

"I get the idea you don't much care for him."

"Hell, that's no secret. Kyle, he knows it. A real piece of
work, that one."

"How do you mean?"

"For one thing, he was just back a week at that time and
already was putting the moves on Frank's wife."

"His own brother's wife?"

Lundy laughed laconically. "Kyle, he's not gonna let a little
thing like that bother him. Hell, he's been shacked up with
Joyce in the house Frank rented over on Brown Street since
right after Frank was killed. Matter of fact, he'd been in here
with her earlier that day. Frank knew it, too."

"Sounds like a nice kid. Any idea where the boys were
going when they left here?"

"None. It couldn't of been much; they didn't have time.
But it wasn't something they looked forward to with joy,
know what I mean? More of a chore to get over with."

"What do you mean they didn't have time?"

"Because at 9:30 they had a family meeting. The boys had
been kidding around about it. You know, wondering what
the old man wanted, stuff like that."

"A family meeting? Was that a regular thing?"

"Naw, just special occasions. That's why they was kidding
around. The old man, Tony, he's second generation and still
has the old-country ways. The kids, they don't go much for
that stuff. You know how it works."

"So when the boys left here, they weren't headed for a party, anything like that?"

Lundy laughed again. "A party? Hell, no, they wasn't headed for a party. Like I said, more like a chore."

Paige finished the beer in front of him, then stood up. "Kyle, does he still come in?"

"Now and then. Enough to suit me, even though God knows I could use the business."

In the morning Paige left his year-old Chrysler Fifth Avenue, the one indulgence he allowed himself, in the spot reserved for him in the parking garage behind the office. No more running downstairs to feed coins to a meter, he told himself. No more slipping into someone else's private space in an alley late in the afternoon, then hoping they wouldn't come back.

Rather than going upstairs, Paige walked south on Main to where Center Street ended at the foot of a steep hill. The building Angelo Chiappetta's car had hit at high speed showed no ill effects. It was faced in tile, two-tone tan and brown, and by looking closely, Paige could see where repairs had been made just to the left of arched windows and a doorway. Had they been twenty feet south, the car would have gone into an alley, but it wouldn't have made much difference in the end.

Paige walked into the outer office of the law firm at quarter to ten. Lou Roth interrupted talking to the blonde receptionist and glanced at the clock behind her, then smiled frostily. "Just getting to work, are we?"

"I don't know about you," Paige said on his way by, "but I've been at it since nine."

For an instant he considered elaborating, then decided against it. Starting out by accounting for his time and movements to Roth or anyone else would be a bad idea. If his work habits didn't please them, so be it. And if his comings and goings were to be kept track of, the arrangement wouldn't work out.

Blades was alone in his office again, the door ajar. Paige said, "If I had taken this case for a client, Ron, I'd go out and talk to everybody in the Chiappetta family. Now I don't suppose I can do that, right?"

"You can talk to Angelo. He's our client, remember? It won't do you any good, of course. Don't talk to the parents, though, unless we get their lawyer's okay. You're on salary now, an employee of the firm, even though you still have your own license."

"Considering his condition, how do I talk to Angelo without talking to the parents?"

"Good question. Maybe you can set it up with the sister. If not, I'll get Will Hamblin to arrange it."

"So I can talk to the sister? How about Kyle, the other brother?"

"Fine. Neither's a party to the suit, or even on the list of witnesses Hamblin says he's going to call. That doesn't mean he won't add them, but whether he does or not, they're still fair game for talking to."

"If you're there at seven, I'll make sure you see him," Esther Chiappetta said in the brisk manner of a veteran nurse. Paige had found her working in a dentist's office in the First National Tower, just across Mill Street from the Orangerie Mall.

"I'd like to talk to you for a few minutes, too."

"Of course," she said. Her no-nonsense way of speaking went with her angular features, mannish haircut, disregard for makeup. "But this evening. I'm working now."

"Fine. See you at seven."

A strange one, Paige thought on his way out. He stopped for coffee in the restaurant downstairs, thinking Esther was the kind of woman frightened by her own femininity. She didn't want a man thinking of her as a female of the species, but probably felt his age rendered him safe.

When his cup was empty a second time, Paige crossed the street again to the garage. He drove south and then east to Brown, a heavily traveled residential street with small shopping areas spaced well apart. The house shared by Kyle and Joyce Chiappetta, who also shared the same last name but not a marriage, was in a neighborhood suffering long-term neglect.

Like most of those around it, the house was a large but unpretentious one with a front porch so dilapidated that Paige wondered if his weight on the steps might not bring it crashing down around him. It was nearly noon, but the sleepy-eyed woman who opened the door was wearing a bathrobe over an ankle-length nightgown. Her brown hair, streaks of premature gray showing, was tousled. She carried a cup of coffee.

"Yes?"

"Joyce Chiappetta?"

"Yes."

"I'm Henry Paige from the law firm representing Angelo Chiappetta. Could I talk to you a minute?"

She shrugged disinterestedly but opened the screen door between them. Paige followed her to an untidy living room, then sat on the chair she waved him to. When she was on a couch facing him, he said, "Is Kyle here?"

"He's takin' a shower."

"Does he work?"

"Sometimes. Work ain't easy to find, you know."

"How much insurance did you collect when your husband was killed?"

She stopped sipping coffee to stare at him. "I don't see how that's none of your business."

Paige smiled. "It's a question you probably will be asked at the trial."

"You mean I gotta go to that trial?" The idea startled her. She mulled it over a moment. "Okay, then, it's no secret I got twenty thousand bucks. Which ain't much, you know. Not for losin' the breadwinner."

"At least you had another waiting."

"What kinda crack's that supposed to be?"

"No crack. I just meant you were lucky to have Kyle around. Our records don't show, are you married?"

"You know we ain't. Wha'd'ya want here, mister?"

"To talk to Kyle. How about telling him I'm waiting?"

She shrugged again, then got up and walked to the foot of the stairs at the end of the room. "Hey, Kyle, there's some guy down here wants to talk to you."

"What about?" a man called back.

"That trial from the wreck when Frank was killed."

There was no reply, but a minute later a slim, olive-skinned man came down the stairs buttoning a white shirt. He studied Paige a moment with distrustful eyes. "Yeah?"

"I'm from the firm representing your brother."

"That's a laugh. The old man's not suing Ange. Hell, you know that."

Paige nodded. "The night of the accident, where were your brothers going at nine o'clock?"

"Don't ask me. I didn't know they was goin' anywhere. We was all supposed to be over at the old man's at 9:30."

"What for?"

"How should I know?"

"Didn't you show?"

"Sure, but Ange and Frank never. The old man was teed off about it till he heard what happened, then he never got around to sayin' why he wanted everybody there in the first place. Not to me, anyhow."

"How come the family gathering was so late in the evening?"

"Ange was down in Columbus about a job and wasn't

supposed to be back till then. It didn't work out, though. The job, I mean, so he come back early."

"What time did you get to your parents' house?"

"Before nine. I was just outta the Army and livin' there at the time. Why?"

"Just wondered. You didn't see Frank or Angelo again after you left the bar?"

"That's right."

"So you don't know what the meeting was about or why your brothers were downtown at the time it was supposed to get started?"

"How many times you want me to say it, fella?"

Paige stared at him, not trying to hide his distaste. "I hear you didn't mind a little nibble of your brother's wife while he was still alive. Did you know how much insurance Frank carried?"

Kyle balled his right fist, eyes narrowing. "Look, wise guy, you'd better get outta here 'fore you get hurt. I don't like to hit an old guy, but—"

Paige stood up, grinning. "Be my guest. If you think you're up to finishing the job."

Kyle glared over at Joyce. "Get him outta here, will you?" Then he turned and went back upstairs.

Angelo Chiappetta sat in a wheelchair, looking at Paige but not really seeing him. Or not comprehending that it was another man sitting beside him. After a minute or two his eyes drifted back to the television set, attracted by the flickering light, aware of it but not really seeing it or passing the vision along to a comprehending mind.

Esther Chiappetta stood watching from just inside the doorway. Paige looked at her, then got up shaking his head.

"I told you it would be useless," she said.

"There's no hope for improvement?"

She shook her head.

"Can I ask you a few questions?"

"Certainly. Let's go back to the living room. My parents are sitting in the kitchen."

"If you'd rather go out somewhere—"

"No, we aren't disturbing them. They like to sit out there."

"Have they managed to hold up okay under this?"

"Better than they would have if Frank and Angelo hadn't been drunk. My parents are very religious, you know. They don't approve of drinking at all. In their opinion, what happened was punishment for what my brothers had done."

Paige shook his head again. "From what I hear, they hadn't done much at all. A couple of beers—"

"Oh, it was more than that."

"How do you know?"

She looked away from him. "It was obvious, wasn't it? Come, let's go to the living room."

"Do you share your parents' opinion? Are you very religious, too?"

"Yes, I'm religious. But no, I don't necessarily share their opinion."

Paige waited until they were seated on facing chairs in an immaculate room, where a crucifix hung over the mantel of a gas fireplace. Then he said, "Do you know where your brothers were going at nine o'clock the night of the accident?"

"How would I know? I'd been working late."

"You had? What time did you get home?"

"Nine-thirty."

"Just in time for the meeting. What was it about?"

"I'm surprised you even know about it. It was routine family business, that's all."

"Such as?"

"Nothing of importance. Especially after what happened. All it was, my parents were going to change their wills so Frank would inherit this house. He was having the roughest time of it during the recession and the factories shutting down, and he was the only one married and with obligations. Of those of us here in town, that is. The other girls are married, and their husbands have good jobs."

"You mean that's all the meeting was for? Who was to get the house before?"

"I was. But I didn't need it, and Papa felt it would do Frank more good because I have a profession." She paused, compressing her lips. "Of course Papa didn't know what that wife of Frank's was like—a little harlot. He does now, since she and Kyle . . ."

Paige nodded. "Money, what about that?"

"It was to be equally divided among Angelo, Kyle, the other girls, and myself. There wasn't much, of course, and a lot less now because of Angelo."

"So that was it? I guess that's all I need to know. By the way, though, I've got a tooth that needs to come out. How do you handle it?"

"What do you mean?"

"Novocaine or what?"

"Sometimes. Usually sodium pentothal."

"That stuff that really puts you under?"

"Yes."

"It's dangerous, isn't it?"

"Not in the proper dosage."

"That's what I want, then. It's funny, but something about a dentist . . ."

She smiled patronizingly. "I know. A lot of you he-men types are that way."

Paige stood up and walked to the door. "Being cut out of the will, that must have hurt."

"Not at all, I understood perfectly. If it hadn't been for that slut Joyce, I wouldn't . . ."

"You wouldn't have done anything about it?"

"Done anything about it? What do you mean by that?"

"You know what I mean, Esther."

"No, I'm afraid I don't."

"Look, haven't you figured it out yet? Why do you think

I'm here? We're on to you; we know what happened. So why
not go ahead and make it easy on yourself and fill in the
details? First you called Frank and told him your car was
broken down, right? But you didn't have any idea Angelo
would come back early from Columbus, did you? You
thought Frank would be alone so you could work your little
scheme."

"Are you crazy or—"

"Of course you didn't plan on it turning out the way it did.
Just a little something to discredit Frank was all it was
supposed to be. Come on, Esther, we have it figured, so get
it off your chest, get it over with. It won't go as hard for you
as you've been imagining all this time."

She sat down abruptly. "Let me think a minute." She put
her hand to her head, then looked up at Paige. "Why did
you have to come around, anyway?"

Blades was still bent over papers in his office when Paige
tapped lightly on the open door. He looked up and said,
"Yes, Henry? Something new?"

"Something new. I don't think you'll be going to trial after
all, Ron. What we have here is an accidental murder."

"An accidental murder? Henry, there is no such thing.
Legally it's either—"

"I know, I know. What I meant is a murder unintentionally
committed. The sister . . . well, it's a complicated story, but
she's a little on the goofy side. She came up with this
cockamamie scheme because her parents were going to
change their wills and—"

"Are you saying she killed her brother?"

"Without meaning to, yes. Esther's got some kind of
complex when it comes to men. They scare her, or the
relationship between men and women scares her. What it
comes down to is she has a real hangup about women who
like men. Kind of a combination of fear and religion,
something like that. Really mixed up in her thinking.

"She had it in for her brother Frank's wife. Joyce isn't exactly a charmer, I'll have to admit that. Anyway, under the new wills, Frank would have inherited the family home. So Esther cooked up this far-out scheme to discredit Frank in her parents' eyes. Not because of him, because of Joyce. The parents think drinking's a sin. You know the type, a little overboard on judging people. They were going to have this family powwow about the new wills at 9:30 because Angelo was out of town and wasn't going to be back before then.

"So in the middle of the afternoon Esther calls Frank and asks him to pick her up at her office because she was working late and her car wasn't running right. Then when he got there, she had this nutty plan in mind. When he knocked on the door, she was going to have it unlocked and would call to him to come in. She'd be waiting right inside with a glass of whiskey in one hand, a hypodermic needle in the other, and her purse hung over that arm. She was going to pretend to stumble and fall against Frank, spilling the whiskey on him and giving him a short dose of sodium pentothal at the same time. Then before he could figure what was happening, she'd drop the needle in her purse."

"Jeez, Henry, that sounds crazy."

"I told you so. She was an amateur, remember, and not completely right in the head to boot, so she made it way too complicated. Anyhow, the shot would be just enough to make Frank good and woozy. She's a dentist's nurse, gives people the stuff all the time, so she knew how much to use. Then she was going to accuse him of being drunk and tell him her car was okay again and insist on driving him to their parents' house. Then, she figured, the parents would be so outraged when they smelled the booze and saw the condition Frank was in, they wouldn't change their wills after all."

"That's the nutsiest idea I ever heard."

"To you and me maybe, but to Esther it didn't sound too

bad. Trouble was, Angelo had gotten back ahead of schedule, and it was him who came in the door first."

"You know, this would be almost funny, except—"

"Yeah, I know. But to give her credit, Esther was nonplussed when she realized what had happened. After a short
argument with Frank, she rushed the two of them out, still
thinking of Frank coming to pick her up so he'd be driving.
What she didn't know was that they had come in Angelo's
car.

"Of course we can only guess what happened when the
brothers left. Frank had to see there was something the
matter with Angelo, but he was having his own problems; it
hadn't been too good a day for him. Maybe the screwy
episode was the last straw and he was too burned up to pay
as much attention as he should. There's a little time
unaccounted for, so apparently Angelo had trouble getting
back to the car. Then, like I said, Frank mustn't have been
thinking too good himself because when they started out,
Angelo was back of the wheel. I figure they went up Mill to
High, then south toward home. For some reason we'll never
know, Angelo took a right on Center and then on down the
hill at full speed."

Blades leaned back, gnawing his lower lip and staring at
the ceiling. When he straightened up again, he looked at
Paige and said, "This changes everything, of course. What a
hell of a mixed-up story."

Paige nodded. "Like I said, goofy. Do you get a lot of 'em
like this, Ron?"

"So now what do you think of our investigator?" Blades
asked, grinning.

Lou Roth grimaced. "What do I think of him? I'll tell you
what I think of him. He's been here two days and already
he's cost us a nice fee for a trial that's out the window. That's
what I think of him."